ELECTRIC FRIENDS
YOUNG
WRITERS'
ANTHOLOGY
2016

First edition

www.electricreads.com

ISBN (print): 978-1-911289-10-4
ISBN (e-book, kindle): 978-1-911289-11-1

Thanks to Stephen, Chandrashekhar, Vanessa, Dragan, Rajendra, and Lizzie for their help in preparing the anthology for publication.

10 9 8 7 6 5 4 3 2 1

YOUNG WRITERS' ANTHOLOGY 2016

ELECTRIC READS

CONTENTS

LUCY SPOONER
THE CHANGELING AND THE RINGMASTER

Lucy Spooner is a twenty-four-year-old writer, baker, cosplayer, and am-dram performer. She lives with her husband James, a growing collection of superhero memorabilia, and a little blue car named Ernie. Lucy spends her days working for a digital marketing agency, and her evenings cooking up a storm in her tiny kitchen, watching movies, rehearsing for shows, and playing Dungeons & Dragons every fortnight. She has been writing various fictional pieces on and off for over a decade.

"Ladies and gentlemen, boys and girls, for one hundred years our humble performance has been entertaining crowds up and down the continent, and now, tonight, we have the honour - nay, the privilege! - of appearing for you here."

A great cheer went up from the crowds gathered around the arena. Many of the people watching the show were stood on the grass under the brightly coloured canopy, with those that could afford it sat on raised wooden seats. In the centre of the ring, dressed flamboyantly in shades of red and gold, the ringmaster beamed out at them all, gesticulating as he described the delights to come in a dramatic, booming baritone.

"We've got beasts and creatures the likes of which you've never seen," he said, creeping closer to some children in the front row with his hands spread wide, like a monster reaching out from under the bed. "We've got magic and mystery, danger, fantastic feats of strength and agility that you will all remember for years to come…"

And so he went on. The crowd were enthralled, hanging on his every word, but backstage the performers were all too busy to listen to him setting the scene. A troupe of tumblers were busy practising their tricks, while the barbarian practised lifting heavier and still heavier weights over his head, roaring with the exertion. Beside him lay a pile of chairs and tables, assorted heavy weaponry, and a small cart filled with rocks. Out in the temporary stables, three elven riders, with bright feathered costumes and exotic makeup, were tending to their horses. Nearby, a tiger stalked around its cage, emitting a low growl at whatever happened to catch its eye.

Inside the cage next to the tiger's was a small, huddled figure, covered in layers of blankets, trying to block out the threatening noise. One of the stagehands, a large man named Bruno, wandered up and banged a wooden stick loudly against the bars. Slowly, the figure rose to its knees, and from under the blankets peered a pair of large, black eyes, set in a pale grey face.

"I'm not going out there tonight," the figure said.

"Oh, really?" Bruno chuckled, and clenched his fist around the nearest bar until his knuckles turned white. "So you're just going to let everyone down? You're going to ruin our show? You're going to count all the money we'll lose?"

"No." Shakily, the figure stood up, and the blankets fell to the floor of the cage to reveal the emaciated figure of a teenage changeling, dressed in a ragged brown tunic. "I'm going to stay here. I'm not doing my 'act' tonight. It hurts too much."

Bruno shook his head, still chuckling to himself. He withdrew a set of keys from inside his coat and unlocked the door of the cage, stepping inside. The changeling immediately moved away, backing herself up against the opposite side of the cage. At her sides, her hands flexed and the fingers twisted as she readied herself. Bruno saw what she was doing, and grinned.

"No tricks, *freak*," he said. "You realise that everybody out here will turn against you if you do anything to hurt me? They know me - I've grown up with this circus. We're a family. You, on the other hand, are still a stranger, and the only reason the ringmaster keeps you around is because you're our star attraction right now. None of us like you, but we'll tolerate you for the sake of the ticket sales." He advanced on her, raising his stick in the air. "Now tell me. What do you think will hurt more? You going out in the ring tonight, and making hundreds of people happy with your little transformations - or me, with my stick? Maybe even the ringmaster, with his whip?"

The changeling swallowed. She should have known it was pointless to try and wriggle out of performing for the crowds that night, but she'd at least wanted to try. After weeks of travelling in conditions not even fit for an animal, barely eating, barely sleeping, she knew her magic was weak. She didn't have the energy for anything more than a few nasty sparks, and then what? She'd be forced out there anyway. Sighing, she hung her head.

"Fine," she mumbled. "When am I going on?"

Satisfied, Bruno clapped her on the shoulder, making her flinch. "You'll be on after the tumbling act - our grand finale. Bethrynna will help you dress. And no screaming - the crowds don't like it when we show our pain. Keep a straight face for them, no matter which one you're using."

The changeling waited behind the curtain, peeking through a gap in the fabric to watch the tumblers' performance. In spite of herself, and how much she hated being part of it, she did somewhat enjoy observing the other acts, and the tumbling was her favourite. She liked the way that the five of them were as one, sometimes working together, sometimes each doing their own movements, but always synchronised. It was like dancing, but more spectacular, and she could tell by the awestruck faces of the crowd that the show was making them happy. She would have to make sure they were left feeling just as happy, not disappointed with the grand finale.

She stepped back from the curtain and adjusted her costume. It was a strange, loose outfit, consisting primarily of a deep purple robe in floaty fabric, and a silver cloak that shimmered in the torchlight. The cloak had a wide hood, which she would use to keep her face partially hidden until the time came for her to transform.

To the sound of rapturous applause and raucous cheering, the tumblers finished their final trick and came bounding out of the ring into the backstage area, grinning at each other and congratulating themselves on a job well done. The changeling stood apart, waiting nervously for her cue, and trying to keep herself calm in the face of inevitable pain.

In the ring, the ringmaster cracked his whip once and immediately the torches dimmed, eliciting gasps of surprise from the audience. With a wave of his hand, a light mist filled the arena while he set the scene for the changeling's entrance.

"Ladies and gentleman, we have reached the climax of our evening. To leave you mystified and mesmerised while we journey on to pastures new, we will now present to you ... our final act. She has travelled far from a distant land" - here, a murmur of speculation rippled across the crowd - "and is here tonight for your delight and delectation. She will show you power beyond belief; she will show you magic and mystery; she will show you... your true faces. Ladies and gentlemen, boys and girls, she can be anyone she wishes to be, but we like to call her... The Shifter..."

Eerie, tinkling music began to play, and the changeling stepped out from behind the curtain. Shrouded in mist, she made her way to the edge of the arena and began to circle the crowd, peering into their faces, hating the way that they shrank back from her when they saw what was under the hood. The audience was mostly human, and she doubted any of them had ever seen a changeling in its natural form before. Once she had completed a full lap of the ring, she walked slowly into the centre to stand beside the ringmaster, who beamed at her with yellowing teeth.

"Shifter," he cried, his voice booming out over the crowd, "have you chosen a face?"

On cue, the changeling threw back her hood and revealed her own face in full. Pale grey skin that shone slightly in the dim torchlight and made her seem almost insubstantial; hair the lightest shade of blue, cropped closely against her skull; huge black eyes with no visible whites, in a strange, angular face. "I have indeed," she replied. Her voice was pitched low, but still loud enough to be heard by the people at the back.

"And who is it to be?" the ringmaster continued, gesturing to the crowd. Slowly, deliberately, the changeling turned on the spot, her eyes searching, until finally she landed on her target. She raised her arm and pointed with one long finger.

"I have chosen... him."

A gasp went up from the crowd, as she'd known it would. The ringmaster immediately headed over and pulled the chosen man into the light; he looked apprehensive, but excited, as he was led into the ring. In a seemingly friendly gesture that was specifically designed to keep 'volunteers' from running away, the ringmaster put his arm around the man's shoulders and welcomed him cheerily, encouraging him to tell the crowd a little about himself – again, a practised move, to allow the changeling to hear his voice. Finally, the man was positioned opposite her, and once he saw her up close, he visibly blanched.

"Good evening, sir," she said softly. "Have we met before?"

Silently, the man shook his head - then his eyes widened as he watched the changeling's face transform into his own. Bones shifted and crackled under the skin, which now took on a rugged and freckled complexion; her eyes became rounder and lightened to chocolate brown, fringed with short, pale lashes; her hair lengthened down to just under her ears, now larger and slightly disfigured, and turned from palest blue into a blend of brown and grey strands. She hid the pain the changes caused her with some difficulty, but the man didn't notice anything aside from his own face appearing on a body that was also beginning to resemble his own in height and stature. The chest and shoulders widened, and the changeling grew a couple of inches taller, the looseness of her clothing easily accommodating the shift in size. When it was over, he was staring at himself.

The changeling opened her mouth, and his own voice came out of it, gruff and thickly accented. "What do you think, sir? Am I convincing?" She addressed the audience with her second question, and they responded with enthusiastic cheers and claps.

After that, the ringmaster and the cheering encouraged six more transformations. The changeling wandered through the crowd, feet hidden by the costume so it seemed as if she were floating, choosing her subjects at random and allowing people to see the changes take place up close. They were enthralled, especially the children, but while many of them would lean in slightly to get a closer look, none of them approached her, and most would actively try and move away from her as she walked among them.

Finally, under the guise of a suggestion, the ringmaster allowed her to revert back to her natural form. Accompanied by a crash of cymbals, flashing lights and billowing smoke, she 'disappeared' from the ring to a backdrop of cheers, whistles, and applause.

It was only when she was safely backstage, hidden from the eyes of the crowd, that she collapsed to the ground with an agonised cry and gave in to the pain crippling her body, clutching her head in her hands. Transforming that many times as quickly as she had, bones shifting and muscles stretching over and over - it was torture. While the other performers went back out into the ring to take their bows, she remained on the floor in tears, curled in a ball, trying not to lose consciousness. That was fine by everyone else; she only had to perform, and if she wasn't seen otherwise, it only helped to heighten the mystery surrounding her onstage persona.

She didn't know how much time had passed, but suddenly Bethrynna, one of the elven riders, was helping her to her feet. Bethrynna was kind, and because she was usually out in the stables tending the horses, she sometimes gave the changeling fresh straw to lie on and the occasional carrot to top up her meagre rations. Just then, she put her delicate gloved hand to the changeling's forehead and murmured a few words in her own language.

A soft, gentle warmth crept through her bones, easing the pain somewhat and making it easier to stand on her own two feet. She took a deep breath, still feeling a twinge in her chest, but it was nowhere near as painful as it had been. Gratefully, she looked up at the beautiful elf's face, and smiled. "Thank you."

"Don't thank me yet." Bethrynna's face was grim but apologetic, and she kept a firm grip on the changeling's arm as she led her away from the stables and towards the ringmaster's caravan. "He wants you again tonight."

The changeling froze. "No. Not again. Please. I can't transform any more tonight. I can't do *that*." She dug her heels into the soft grass and tried to break free of the elf's hold, but to no avail. She was still weak. Tears threatened to spill down her cheeks again, and she shook her head in defiance.

Bethrynna's grip on her arm tightened slightly. "I am sorry, young one. He said he wants you, and if it is not to be you then it would be me, or one of my sisters. He may ask for that anyway, but he knows at least you are more... pliable than us." She chose her words carefully.

"No... no." The changeling was crying now. "Don't make me, not you. I thought... I mean... you give me food..."

"Only because if you die, the ringmaster will be in a foul mood for weeks, and we will all suffer as a result." Roughly, the elf pushed her up the caravan steps, and she almost slammed into the brightly painted door. "In you go. I'm not leaving until you do."

The changeling stared at her, her black eyes shining. After a pause, she choked back a sob and turned away to knock on the door. Four times, so the ringmaster would know it was her.

"Come in," he called, sounding pleased with himself.

She pushed the door open, and stepped into the caravan. It was large, much bigger than anyone else's, and decorated in deep shades of burgundy, gold, purple, and green. The main room was a mixture of lounge, kitchen, and dressing room, and behind a thick brocade curtain on the wall opposite was the bedroom. The ringmaster sat in his armchair, sipping something in a tankard and clinking coins together from the pile on the table beside him. "Come in," he said again, "sit down, make yourself comfortable."

Slowly, the changeling made her way closer, and perched on a fat footstool next to the ringmaster's chair. He looked down on her almost benevolently, sipping from his tankard. "Good evening, my finale," he said. That was what he called her, when they were alone and she looked like herself - that was all she was to him at times like this. "I wanted to have a little chat, if I may, before we get down to business." He waved his hand and the door clicked shut. He only knew a few spells, usually just enough to increase the atmosphere during shows, but there were other times when knowing a little magic came in handy.

"What do you want to talk about?" the changeling asked, forcing herself to look up at him and not stare at the floor. Hidden in the sleeves of her robe, her hands were shaking.

"Well, a little bird told me that you refused to go on tonight. Again." He raised an inquisitive eyebrow, and took another sip from his tankard. "That's the fifth time this month, my finale. I must ask - what's the matter? Don't you like making all these people happy? Seeing their smiling faces, their shock and awe, all because of you? Doesn't that make *you* happy?"

The changeling narrowed her eyes. "Maybe it would, if it didn't hurt so much."

"Ah, yes, that was what Bruno said. You told him it *hurts too much.*" The ringmaster stood from his chair - not without some difficulty - and crossed the room to an ornate set of drawers. With his back to her, she couldn't see what he was picking up, but she knew it probably wouldn't be another cup so she could join him in drinking. Then she heard a sharp snap, and she knew what was coming. Something stirred within her – perhaps it was the memory of all the pain she had experienced for the sake of entertainment, or the feel of the ringmaster's unwashed hands on her skin; perhaps it was her magic, weak at the moment but always there, silently egging her on. Whatever it was, she knew when she felt it that she would not allow him to hurt her again.

He still had his back to her, and she looked around quickly for something with which to defend herself. On the table, balancing precariously next to the overflowing bag of coins, was a plate with the remnants of some bread and fruit, a lump of cheese, and a knife. *A knife.* Holding her sleeve to stop the fabric swishing, she reached out and grabbed the knife's handle, stowing it away amid the folds of her cloak. When the ringmaster turned back around, it appeared that she hadn't moved at all.

"You see, here is what I don't understand, my finale," he went on. "I have given you food, water, shelter, and night after night of unbound admiration, and how do you repay me? By refusing to do the only thing I ask of you. The *only* thing. Just because it hurts you?" He advanced on her, holding not his whip but a mean-looking riding crop. "It hurts *me* when you don't do what I ask. It hurts every single person who shares that ring with you, because their show is not complete. It hurts the audience, paying customers, when they miss out on what they wanted to see. Suddenly, they want their money back. We get a bad reputation, we lose money, we fail. So I think, for their sakes and mine, you can endure a little bit of pain each night. Don't you?" He snapped the riding crop against his hand, then raised it high in the air to bring it lashing down.

It was the last straw. The changeling saw her chance, and she took it - she lunged forward, and the hidden knife shot out and connected with the solid mass of the ringmaster's chest, making him gasp in shock. It was on the right side, not the left, but it was still enough for him to let the riding crop fall onto the rug and for him to collapse back into his chair. She got up off the floor, where she'd landed on her knees, and stood over him.

"Let me make something clear," she hissed. "You are not doing me a favour, keeping me here. The shelter you have given me is a cage barely fit for an animal. The food you give me is barely enough for one meal a day. And the show? Yes, they applaud me, and yes, they're amazed, but they are all afraid of me. Each night I am surrounded by the faces of people who fear to look at me - they want to see the transformations, yes, but when I'm near them, and they see I'm actually a person? It makes them confused, and scared, and drives them to hate. I've seen it happen before." Leaning over the ringmaster, she grabbed hold of the knife handle and twisted it, making him cry out in pain. She laughed, hollow as an empty coffin.

"Imagine that pain, sir, all over your body. In your very bones, night after night, as you're forced through too many transformations until you almost pass out. And why? So a fat ringmaster with a taste for young flesh can make his money off you." She twisted the knife again, harder this time. "You are a sick man. You kidnapped me from my home, you treat me worse than your precious tiger, and at least three times a week you want me in your bed looking like someone else. You're disgusting." She turned away from him, leaving the knife in his chest, and picked up the bag of coins, watching as a few loose discs of gold bounced and rolled across the floor.

The ringmaster moaned in pain, trying to sit up. "You can't take that," he gasped, reaching out for the bag. "You can't take my money!"

"Why not? I earned most of it." The changeling headed for the door and opened it slowly, checking that the coast was clear. "I'm your grand finale, remember?"

Hatred and rage burned in the ringmaster's eyes. "You can't run forever," he said through clenched teeth. "I'll find you. I'll take my circus across the world to find you. Nobody takes my money and lives!"

Stepping over the caravan threshold, she smiled, and despite all she'd said about the pain of transforming over and over, she took a moment to change herself in front of him until she was his exact likeness. It hurt like hell after everything else, but it was worth it to see the look on his face.

"Sorry, but you won't even know who you're looking for."

~o~

My inspiration for *The Changeling and the Ringmaster* originally came from a Dungeons & Dragons campaign; in creating a new character, I chose a changeling sorcerer, who hid her true face with a mask and hooded cloak. As the campaign progressed, I began to wonder about my character's past - being a changeling of around forty years old, had she led many different lives? How had she ended up in the realm we were currently playing in? Was there ever a time when she did show her face? With these questions in mind, I started working on a range of short stories detailing some of her exploits, the idea being that each story would work on its own as a one-shot tale, or as part of a larger collection.

The Changeling and the Ringmaster was the first of these stories that I wrote. I really wanted to dig deep into the reason the changeling kept her true face hidden, which led me onto thinking that perhaps someone exploited her power in the past. I chose a circus setting as previous encounters with non-playable characters within our campaign had led me to believe that not many people in the realm knew what changelings were, or what they were capable of; it seemed obvious to me that one might use such abilities to shock and amaze a paying audience in a sort of 'freak show' environment.

The story was something I'd never really tried before, but attempting something with fantasy, mystery, and magic was quite an interesting prospect. I wanted to look at two themes, the first being bodily autonomy - with no control or power, the changeling is treated like an animal, exploited for her abilities, forced through horrible pain every night for the sake of entertainment - and the second being fear. The audience is afraid of the changeling, but only when they see her transformations up close and they realise what she must be going through; it unnerves them to see it that way, to see her as an actual person and not the 'grand finale' of the show. This fear becomes another part of the reason why the changeling hides her face after her escape - not only is she worried about being recognised, but the audience's reaction to her true face leads her to believe that the reactions of everyone else she meets will be similar, and their fear of her will turn into mistrust.

Creating this initial piece has led me to flesh out the changeling's character much more easily, and I have written three other individual stories about her since, as well as several which recount the events of our campaign. I plan to hopefully create a few more pieces so I can have a small series for this character, then move on to other writing projects that have been on the backburner for quite a while. I am determined to write a complete novel within the next two years.

AOIFE INMAN
A PAWN IN SPRING

Born to a family of generational avid booklovers, Aoife Inman's fate was sealed from an early age. Reading quickly transitioned to writing and creating, with her work heavily influenced by her time reading History at the University of Manchester. Currently in her final year of undergraduate study, Aoife writes regularly, contributing both short fiction and journalistic-lifestyle articles to a variety of international online publications as well as running her own blog.

Prague. 1968.

It was August and uncomfortably hot. The unshakable itch of fear made the days drag long into the nights, and they woke, palms heavy with sweat. Only to realise that in waking there was no escape.

It was a Wednesday. Eva rose early, eyes clouded with dreams. The bakery on the corner opened its doors a little after eight and soft white *houska* and rounds of *konzumní* filled the counter. Although the weather was mild the old baker Jan with his crooked, stooped stance stood with defiance at the shop front, where the blast of the bread oven met the stagnant humidity of the summer air. He saw her cross the road and pushed a filled bag across the counter.

"No *vanocka* today *beruška*." He smiled a gummy grin. Eva smiled back at the old man kindly and took the bag, placing the money on the counter.

"That's quite all right *pane.*" The smell of the bakery was soft and doughy and every inch of the old man's arms and hands were covered in a white dusting of flour. Even his graying beard held speckles of it. She knew him well. His grandchildren would sometimes come and sit on the floor of her apartment with plates of toasted bread and jam after school, their buttery fingers leaving oil slicks on the equations and calculations of their workbooks.

Outside she dipped her hand into Jan's bag of daily offerings. He had made fresh *koláče.* She smiled. Already she had felt her waistband tighten in the last few weeks from Jan's sweet offerings. The *koláče* were warm and soft from the heat of the oven. The glazed pastry was spattered with poppy seeds and the sweet divot in the centre was filled with a soft cheese and swirls of strawberry jam that were sharp and sugary. Eva placed one in her mouth letting the syrupy sweetness melt around her tongue and teeth. She inhaled the bread quickly and rolled the paper bag tightly around the remaining contents, making her way back to the apartment.

Inside the confines of the kitchen, Eva poured a deep mug of coffee. She had let it brew too long and it was thick like tar, dark and bitter. She sniffed the tub of cream they kept inside the refrigerator. There was a hint of bitterness to its scent that made her wrinkle her nose but the contents was milky white so she spooned it into the mug, scraping out the edges of the empty jar. She arranged herself in the old worn armchair by the window. A light breeze swept in and brushed the curtains with its fingertips. The street outside was quiet, content. It was not just the heat that kept its inhabitants behind locked and bolted doors with eyes sleepy, limbs and tongues heavy. There was a tension within the auspicious calm, tight as an overwound clock. Undeniable and ever-present it had become overgrown since the tanks rolled onto the city streets. All at once summer had stopped. The heat that had made morals looser and smiles wider now formed towering walls, boxing in the city.

She sighed, sinking deeper into the chair. Sweat stuck the backs of her arms to the red leather. Raising a hand she reached for a book on the shelves above her head, sliding a slim volume from its snug nest. *Tender is the Night.* Like most of the apartments' collection its pages were barely turned and clearly never devoured with great enjoyment by its owner. Eva saw the library of works Jakub had collected in their home as terribly wasted. Jakub believed their mere existence within the vicinity gave him an edge of sophistication. Eva didn't have the heart to tell him that reading the works he had amassed was the only way of securing this intellectual prowess he so craved. Yet in Jakub's self-gratifying pursuit of sophistication Eva had found comfort. These un-thumbed volumes with their soft cream pages, crisp as linen, reminded her of home. Endless Octobers spent in leaky libraries listening to the drum of the rain outside. Lines of type arranged like soldiers' shoulders, hunched. Awaiting, with anticipation, hands to pore over them, to caress their content and fall in love with the creations they held within. Certainly she had found comfort in whiling away afternoons and days cooped up in their small sequence of rooms by escaping through these worlds of type. As a child she had found more comfort and affection in the written word than any of the numerous nannies and schoolmistresses she had been passed between like baggage. As for her mother, a weak constitution and an overwhelming love of the bottle meant she provided little maternal warmth. Memories of her consisted for Eva of awkward encounters between strangers. A thin frail wisp of a woman who pecked her cheek and smiled emptily at the child before her. Eva remembered she was beautiful but little else. Features pinched, skin stretched thin over bones that folded over one another in quick succession as she walked. Eva felt from an early age her own company must be dire and boring in comparison to the thrill of dinners with politicians, the stimulation of debate far from the chore of motherhood. She set out to make herself pleasing, interesting, yearning all the while for a space in her mother's cold, clenched heart. In this respect at least Eva could relate to her mother at the present time. She craved stimulation from sources of adrenaline not the mediocrity and mundane repetitiveness of womanly duties. She therefore no longer felt reproachful of her mother's absence, but rather a sense of loss regarding her childhood. It seemed beyond infancy she had been subject to little childlike frivolity and instead became a little woman, stern-faced and reflective. She had acquired the burdens of adult disappointment far sooner than her peers and perhaps, she pondered, this had led to her absence of secure friendships as she matured. She felt as though the other girls at school had almost been a burden to her. Their flirtations and fantasies bored her and she had acquired no concept of polite patience when it came to the dullness of others. Instead she was left to entertain herself during hours of solitary reflection in which her imaginary worlds became infinitely more appealing than the real one she was forced to return to. And so in school, as in adulthood, her comfort came from folded pages and worlds of text and print.

With this thought she snapped the cover shut and placed it back on the shelf, her melancholy thoughts had soured the romanticism of Fitzgerald and she had no desire to ruin the beauty of his work with memories of her pitiful past.

It was past ten before the sleepy town wiped clean the clear film on its shutters, as if the buildings themselves were consumed in a fitful sleep. No doubt dreaming of a Prague scrubbed clean of the spreading Soviet stain. Now upon waking they were thrust once more into the cycle of realisation.

Eva dreamed no such dreams. Those pretty fantasies were for frightened children and veterans who alone occupied a world halfway between reality and insanity. She saw no reason to disturb their peaceful disillusionment nor to join them in their disappointing fanaticism.

Outside a little boy began to play with a ball. He threw it up into the air, bouncing it on the flat of a wooden bat over and over so that a hollow thud rang out in the narrow street. He was tall for his age, with the gallant air of a man and, Eva observed, the arrogance of a child. Eva thought to wake Jakub and call down to the boy and offer him a game, but she didn't. She was content to watch him play. A few weeks ago the mere echo of a ball on the cobbles would have sent children flooding out into the streets, chasing the sound of a game. Now the streets were mellow, dank with grief and dirt and age. Tiny footsteps walked slower now, with caution. Experience weighed heavy on little shoulders. When the tanks rolled in, the city and its people aged a hundred years. They had been swept up in the flood of Moscow's rage like sinners upon Noah's earth. To say they had been fearless would be mistaken. To say they had been giddy on hope would be more fitting. And now a vibrant, deathly red seeped beneath their doors, through cracks in plaster and in through open windows. It adorned their politics and flags, ran heavy through their veins like lead. This war was far crueler than the battles of storybooks, of swords and knights and castles. It was secret rooms and secret doors, monsters who looked like men and a fear, a fear so constant is became everything you breathed. It swallowed up the nights and days so one grew old without acknowledging that time had even passed at all.

In the street soldiers had gathered outside Jan's shop. They were young, only a little older than the boy, but with men-sized guns slung over their shoulders. Jan had retreated to the safety of his kitchen, to roll out yards of dough, twisting in lemon rind and currents, to knead out the bitterness of war from the rolls he baked.

The soldiers were laughing. One, a well-built but sickly-pale individual with the faint shadow of a beard shaded across his cheeks, began handing out cigarettes to the others. They were bored. All the fight had been drained from the city and their job was dull. Perhaps that was why he lifted his gun. Perhaps boredom made him shake it at the boy, to see the look of fear that ran across his little face. He took a pot shot at his heels to make him run. The soldier laughed at the fun of the game but his gaunt eyes were tired and cold as he raised the rifle again. The boy was scared, he cried out as he fell. He spun for a second before landing on the cobbles. Time ticked slower and slower, its rhythm drunken and swaying like an addict fallen off the wagon once more. Its tick became a waltz then a tango, speeding through rapidly changing tempos, alongside her racing heart, nose pressed to the glass of the window. He had broken his glasses. They lay shattered on the ground, metal frames mangled, twisted like his bird-like legs. The broken glass mingled with the blood that pooled around the fallen boy. His hair, matted and damp, would soon dry stiff in the midday sun.

The soldiers had long since walked away but as time passed and the sun rose higher the boy lay still. His arms were spread-eagled at awkward angles, knees turned inward, one shoe on, one half off, laces dangling. His face was downturned in the road. Eva wondered where his mother was, why she hadn't come. Where were the anguished screams, the grief that would fill the doorways and seep under floorboards?

She imagined she could smooth his soft blonde hair back from his forehead, clean the dirt streaks from his cheeks. She would cradle his broken body in her looped arms, piece him back into place and close his glassy eyes with one finger. But fearful reality held her still, kept her rooted. She couldn't turn away and the street swam before her eyes. She pressed her forehead against the cold glass and let her breath go, unaware she had been holding it in. Hot, thick air whistled down her throat and she turned away from the window. Tears collected in her lashes but she blinked them clear, her vision swayed.

Jakub was awake now. The shots had woken him and a deep crease was etched between his brows as though sleep had brought no relief. He moved quietly through the apartment rooms, to clear away the breakfast things. He moved Eva from the window, caught a glimpse of the scene below. From up here the broken glass was little more than an artist's clever optical illusion and the streaks of blood, bright vermillion oils, glistening with the sheen of fresh brush strokes against white canvas. Shop owners scrubbed at dark stains on their shop exteriors, as if to wash away any part they played in the scene that lay before them. He held her close, her body stiff with shock and age. In that embrace she felt a warmth she felt incapable of reciprocating, a tenderness she herself had never been taught. Though she could not emulate the affection in his circled arms she allowed herself to be held. He did not treat her like a broken women, rather, she imagined, like he would a brother, as if to press their suffering together might make it easier to bear. He smoothed her hair from her eyes and touched the tip of her nose with his forefinger before moving away.

In the kitchen Jakub had lit a cigarette and was sitting back, sprawled in an armchair, the cigarette end glowing bright between his lips. His half-curled smile, the lazy smirk, was gone, replaced with a hard-set line of concentration. There was no animosity between them but equally neither felt the need to speak at that present moment. He raised his eyes from the empty fire grate to meet her gaze and held it for a moment. In that gaze was inquisition; are you ok? Yes, fine, well not now, but we will be? A question, tinged with doubt.

Yes we will.

All the while he avoided her eyes. Like dancers they circled the hot room in a disjointed waltz. He saw the heavy weight of grief that played upon her face. The wear and tear of years showed though. With little lines that had begun to play across the underside of her eyes and furrows that indented between her brows. Aging appeared to her a funny thing. As if time itself could not bear to let her go and scratched at her with sharp caresses. Reminders. With a sigh her eyelids closed. She tried to shake the images of broken glass and broken boys. She shivered as if to purge the memory with movement.

No screams echoed in the solemn streets. At home a mother cooked over a boiling stove with five children who ran about her feet. Later she would wonder where the eldest was, she would send out her daughter to the street to scold him, but there would be no sign of him. That night she would not cry but in her husband's arms she would lie, torn in anguish. There is no grief more powerful than that without a body to pour it over.

Night came quickly and as the sky darkened Jakub watched as doors bolted shut, windows slammed and the inhabitants retreated like animals into burrows. He could barely remember a time when the nights were alive. As a child perhaps, but those memories were interspersed with skies red with fire, the acrid smell of burning rubber, fabric, flesh. His nose curled at the memory and he shook his head.

He reached for the schnapps bottle with one lazy hand, a nightcap, almost the only sure-fire way he knew of to ensure he slept soundly. Glass in hand he trailed over to the door of the bedroom. Eva lay, tightly wrapped in a tiny ball. That was the way she always slept, an origami butterfly in the vast expanse of sheets. She looked so vulnerable and fragile now with dreams that flitted across her open face with scowls and smiles. Even Jakub himself had only ever caught a glimpse of her unguarded, mostly in moments like this. He walked over and shut the bedroom window; the harsh cold finally ceased its incessant offensive against the room and the silence struck an uncomfortable chord with him. He pulled across the drapes. He was tired and the city was drowsy. Perhaps his childlike loneliness made him crawl sleepily into bed that night when he would usually have paced for several more hours, or perhaps the several glasses of schnapps were to blame for his sudden drowsiness. But either way he slept soundly for the first time in months, deep and untroubled, spread-eagled like a bird, his empty glass balanced on the edge of the nightstand.

~o~

A Pawn in Spring started almost three years ago in my first year of undergraduate study. It was born out of a love for history, I was fascinated by individual stories, the photographs, the diaries, tiny pieces that so often get lost in large historical studies, consigned to larger bodies of "data" or "evidence". *A Pawn in Spring* is quite literally the translation of that. The stories of individuals; everyday accounts of the aftermath Prague Spring 1968 that have become lost as data; "pawns" in the event itself and our historical analysis of it.

Two and a half years later, what had started as a rough skeleton of a story was fleshed out between lectures and deadlines when time would allow. And as I matured through university so did my characters and their stories. Slowly through archive photographs of post-war Prague, snippets of first-hand accounts and numerous descriptions of Czech bakeries I began to construct much more than simply a story but a reconstructed world, every piece lovingly handcrafted in lines of type, from the consistency of the perfect *koláče* to the architecture of Eva and Jan's apartment.

For as long as I can remember I have loved reading. As I grew up through school that love transitioned and grew into a love of writing as well. I sent off my first "novel" to a publishing house at the age of 12. Entirely handwritten, it was the one and only draft, accompanied by a note on Charlie & Lola letter paper. It is safe to say that was not the start of my writing career, but it is a moment I look back on fondly, in admiration of my brash optimism. Since then I've grown, acquired a laptop and now a Word-processed CV accompanies my writing. However, my 12 -year old drive to write remains intact, if slightly matured.

JACK WILLIAM RENDELL
CAUSING A FENCE

Jack William Rendell writes comic fantasy and nature poetry. He lives with his fiancée Alice near Aberystwyth, where his work has featured in small magazines and multiple times in the University's MA anthology. Jack aspires to have a modest career as a published writer and to eat copious amounts of cake.

The man came into her bedroom, high-vis jacket reflecting in the make-up mirror. He ran his hand over the fence and frowned.

'Not too many splinters,' he said, breathing in the smell of the wood. 'This one I had last week that was all over the place. I was pullin' spikes out all night.'

'Yes, but why exactly is it here?' said Lauren. 'You are trained for this, aren't you?'

The man gestured to the ID card hanging round his neck. It was faded to the point of being indecipherable. 'See there? Derek Thingymajig, fully quantified.'

She wasn't entirely sure about this. His eyes were crossed just enough to be disconcerting and his eyebrows met in the middle. She itched to reach for the tweezers. The directory, however, had said that his company, FRED (Fence Removal and Eradication Department) were very competent, so she tried to put it out of her mind.

'Know what I mean?' said Derek.

Lauren blinked. He had one of those voices like random background noise, so she hadn't registered that he was still speaking. 'Pardon?'

'I said they're caused by bein' uncivil. Rude, like, if you get my meaning.'

'I don't really care what it's caused by,' said Lauren, biting her lip, 'I just want it gone, please, Derek.'

'It's Dave,' he said, walking around the bed and squeezing past the end of the fence. 'It's about normal size for a ROF,' he said, measuring it with one eye closed and arms outstretched.

'Rof? What's a Rof?'

Derek slash Dave grinned. 'Sorry love.' He winked in the precise way she really hated. 'It's a technical term, see? Randomly Occurring Fence. Course, they're not really random per se. Nor are they (by proper definition) actual fences, come to think of it. But that's beside the point.'

The sound of next door's lawnmower was giving Lauren a headache. She took a deep breath. 'Well, you know Dave, fences don't usually appear out of nowhere. The slats are going straight through my bed for Christ's sake.' She swept round the make-up dresser and pulled the rug over the stain on the carpet in what she hoped was a surreptitious manner.

'Name's, Donald, actually,' said Dave, 'but yes, I suppose to the common lay-lady like yourself it's not the usual concurrence.'

'Yes, but can you actually get rid of it?' Lauren scrunched her toes up in the carpet as Derek slash Dave slash Donald pondered the question. He looked at her, then at the fence, then glanced at her bra hanging on the back of the chair, and then back at her face. 'I don't know really. It'll need specialist equiptment.'

Lauren knew there was no 't' in equipment, but supposed it didn't matter in the grand scheme of things. 'How long am I looking at Da- er, Donald? I need somewhere to sleep. Plus, I've got my boyfriend to deal with.'

'Boyfriend eh?' said Donald, running his hand along the top of the fence, 'that's interesting that is. By the way, I'm Damien.' Lauren watched Damien take a pencil from behind his ear and draw a smiley face on one end of the fence. She was beginning to think that this FRED lot weren't all they were cracked up to be.

'Any chance of a cuppa?' asked Derek slash Dave slash Donald slash Damien, 'I'm right starched.' He was drawing sunglasses on the face now. Lauren put one hand on the door frame, the other on her hip.

'Right. No tea until you give me some sort of assurance you're going to do the job!' There was a moment of silence. A bird tweeted outside in an intermission between the blasts of the lawnmower.

'Don't get your knickers in a twist, love. If anyone can get this fence eradicated, then Dan is your man.'

'But you're only drawing—wait, *Dan*? How many names have you got, exactly?'

Derek slash Dave slash Donald slash Damien slash Dan looked at her like an embarrassed sheep. His pencil dropped to the floor. 'Well, to tell you the truth, love, I don't really remember it. Got whacked on the head with this wrought iron thing last week and my name's, like, totally gone. I know it starts with "D" though. So that marrows it down a bit – doesn't it, love?'

Lauren twisted her hand in the knot of her hair. 'If you call me "love" *one* more time I'll shove that bloody fence up your arsehole!'

'Don't be rude!' cried the man-whose-name-began-with-D, 'Please! Don't be rude— It'll cause a—' He looked down at his chest. A long piece of wood was protruding from it, spurting blood all over the bedspread. '—fence,' he finished weakly. He fell to the floor, gurgling blood all over the carpet.

Causing offence is causing a fence, thought Lauren. *Sort of makes sense.* She checked her hair in the mirror while she waited for the bleeding to stop. Then she put the dead body in the airing cupboard with the other one, and went to put the kettle on.

~o~

'Causing A Fence' is a perfect example of why I like writing comic fantasy. It's the only genre that allows a writer to base their entire plot around a fairly juvenile pun and expect the reader to go along with it. Of course, too much reliance on the absurd and the whole thing can easily fall apart. The important distinction lies between making the reader feel that anything *could* happen, but avoiding stories where everything *does* happen. It was tempting to have insults thrown with ferocious gusto across battlefields and innocent bystanders mercilessly skewered by the fences that appear as a result, but that would have certainly been too far.

It was much better to have the madness grounded (albeit only partially) in reality. I spent as much time on details such as the sound of the neighbour's lawnmower as I did on the concept of Randomly Occurring Fences. The peeved but presentably composed Lauren counterbalances the annoyance and criminal malapropism of Derek slash Dave (et cetera), and the dialogue they produced while bouncing off each other was the main thing that made this such fun to write.

Of course, there are always deeper way to read one's own writing. Is it a coincidence that this story happened to fall out of my head in 2016, a year that has produced some of the most fervent political electricity seen in years, creating much Brexity tension and (if you will forgive me re-invoking my own pun) causing offence in various ways? Probably. It may be that the complete opposite is true, and this twisted story is just some whimsical escapism from everyday life.

At the end of the day, fantasy is just that, but as the late Sir Terry Pratchett said: 'Fantasy is an exercise bicycle for the mind. It might not take you anywhere, but it tones up the muscles that can.' Where will my work go from here? Who knows! All the puns and strange thoughts in my head will stay there for the foreseeable future, so I may as well use them to tone those writing muscles. Now I think I'll sign off, before I say something truly a fence-ive. (Sorry)

IONA MacCALL
THE WOLF OF MOSCOW

Iona MacCALL is a twenty-two-year-old student English teacher from Fraserburgh in Aberdeenshire. She graduated from the University of Aberdeen with an MA in English with Creative Writing and immediately began training to become a secondary school English teacher. Although immensely busy with her teaching workload, Iona continues to find time to write and has written two novels which she has shared with her friends and family. She hopes someday to have her novels published and read worldwide.

"Sit or stand?"

A target board is hung around my neck.

"Stand," I say. I've been sitting long enough.

The piece of card covers my torso. The men's eyes focus on my chest. Imagining what lies underneath I'm sure; imagining their pulsing, thudding mark.

I notice how loud my breathing is when they secure the blindfold. It seems to resonate between my ears and echo in my head.

"Ready, men."

I hear boots shuffle and clothes crinkle. It's as if they're preparing themselves for a race. First off the mark wins.

"Take aim."

I'm only a small area, don't take up much room. The space feels immense in darkness, as if I'm standing in an open void, teetering on the edge. I wonder if they've ever missed.

There's a warm June breeze. A series of clicks – bullets loading into place – makes me jump. I almost laugh at myself. Its nerves I suppose.

"Fire!"

I flinch. He's right. I do feel as though I'm burning.

The trio of men stand to give their verdict. I can already anticipate what the outcome will be.

"Death by firing squad."

Through the screaming in my head I hear one of the men mention a date.

June eighteenth.

The leaves outside are already turning shades of green.

A thick pile of black and white photographs are spread across the table in one quick sweep. I shift forward in the hard, wooden chair and feel my back contract and squeeze. I've been sitting for hours, maybe days, and can almost feel my spine knot itself in protest.

"Do you recognise any of these men, Mrs. Komaroff?"

I scan the glossy images. These are the images of the men I've been claiming to know nothing about. I maintain a blank expression and raise my eyebrows. If I know, I incriminate myself. If I don't, then I'm innocent.

"I'm afraid not. I do not know any of these men."

The policeman, I forget his name, drops his head and sighs. I notice his knuckles whiten around the edge of the table.

His index finger lands on a photograph of a middle-aged man.

"This is Ermolai Kozar." He pauses and looks at me.

I give nothing away.

From underneath the picture he slides another. Its all-too-familiar; the thick piles of straw left for the horses, the dusty wooden planks Vasili never cleaned and the tied up naked man on the floor.

"This is how we found Mr. Kozar. He was bound in this way, left in a large sack and hidden beneath a pile of hay in your husband's stable, Mrs. Komaroff."

I turn away from the wide, vacant eyes staring up at me from the photograph. It's as if it is a different man from the picture Mr. Kozar's wife has given the authorities. A gaping mouth rather than happy smile.

I try to avoid the other men too but the table is a sea of family photographs and humiliating deaths. It's a loop of men embracing children one minute, strangled to death the next. Shades of pale white skin marred with pansy-bruised throats. Fair blonde hair matted and discoloured in sticky blood.

"Why does he truss them like chickens?" the policeman asks. It's a question he's asked me before. He's willing me to answer, willing me to give him something. My eyes stop on one picture- a hefty man with his arms pulled out of their sockets and tied to his ankles. He is like a chicken, ready to be cooked.

I meet the policeman's gaze. "I honestly do not know."

"But you know what the press calls him I assume?"

I say nothing.

"The Wolf of Moscow?"

"How absurd."

A gentle knock on the door sounds and he moves away from me. He knows I'm lying; I can see it in his eyes.

I hear a voice mutter something from outside.

"Yes, I'll tell her." The policeman closes the door then moves to the table and begins stacking the photographs. He collectively knocks them against the metal surface.

"A troika trial is being held for you, Mrs. Komaroff."

"On what grounds?"

Picture after picture of chickens are filed into a folder.

"On the grounds that you aided your husband in the murder of thirty-three men."

I open my mouth to answer but he cuts me off.

"There's no point arguing, Mrs. Komaroff. Your husband has admitted to all charges against him and has named you as being aware of his crimes."

Vasili's grinning face flashes across my eyes.

"I want to call my son," I say.

As I expect, the policeman returns the silence I so readily gave him.

I'm not surprised when they come to the door. I'm not surprised when they tackle Vasili and wrestle him into handcuffs.

I am surprised when they handcuff me too and take me away.

I read and re-read the final words over and over until I sear them into my mind. I run my fingers across Maksim's slanted hand-writing, pausing on three little words.

"Are you coming?" Vasili's voice calls from the bedroom.

I turn the tap on and pretend to spit. "Just finishing brushing my teeth." I quickly fold the precious letter and stow it away; hidden in an old perfume bottle and away from Vasili's interest. I store them all here. Maksim sends me letters often, keeps me up to date on the years and years I have missed.

I enter the bedroom, padding across the trampled, old carpet with my bare feet. He sits propped up on two pillows, fingers interlaced across his stomach. He smiles at me, big, yellowing teeth underneath his bristly moustache.

"I see you were in the paper again today" I say as I shrug off my tatty dressing gown. Standing in nothing but my nightgown I feel exposed and vulnerable.

"Did you see they've finally given me a name?"

I nod. "The Wolf of Moscow."

He grins, excitement shining in his eyes. "I dumped number twenty-four today." My toenails dig into the trodden carpet.

He pats my side of the bed and I've nothing to do but lift the duvet and slide in next to him. With the lights out, in the darkness, he growls from beside me.

The cold October breeze nips my skin. I hear Vasili speak but I barely understand the words. I pick out a few— money seems important —but I can't focus on his voice. I focus only on the bleeding man in my stable. He has been stripped of his clothes and I can see he has a woman's name, Lilya, tattooed on his back. I notice the way his shoulders jut out at the wrong angle, wrenched from the comfort of their sockets and dragged behind him. A thick line of twine binds wrists to ankles as the man balances on his protruding stomach.

"How could you do this?" I hiss.

"This is what I do" Vasili replies. "We need the money." His eyes are wide and bright, shining with something wild and unknowable. He is alive amidst death.

"You'll be killed for this." I leave the words hanging, hoping they will strike him down. One of his horses brays from behind me.

"Only if I get caught," Vasili replies. He flaps open a large sack and begins inching it over the man. "And I don't plan to be caught."

Streaks of black coat the wooden floorboards, streaming from the gash across the man's head. Vasili bags his chicken and seals it tight, patting the area where the head would be.

"I'm not sending them down the river anymore. I want people to find them."

I gape at him. "What do you mean 'anymore'? Vasili, how many have you killed?"

He smiles and brushes my cheek with his thumb. I see flecks of blood dried into the grooves of his skin.

"I just want you to have nice things" he says, lowering his hand from my face and letting it rest on the silver chain round my neck.

As he heaves his bagged meat from the stable, I wrench the necklace from my throat and let it drop to the floor. It disappears between the gaps in the wood. My mother's voice rings in my ears.

I press Maksim's latest letter to my chest. It helps knowing he is settled and happy; even if he is settled and happy without me. I suppose the pain comes hand in hand with being a mother. I put him first; keep him safe at my own expense.

Vasili has been happier the past few days. I've noticed the change in how he speaks to me when he comes home from the market. He hasn't been this way for years; not since Maksim left. He seems to be doing well for himself – I've seen him bring back several men to the stables for business. He says a lot of people need horses.

He smiles at me, his wide, too-much-teeth grin, and I crinkle my eyes in response. I hide my pursed lips behind the mug at my mouth; mask my uncertainty behind the rising steam. I can't help but look at him differently. It's instinctive, natural now, as if I should have been seeing him this way the whole time.

His hand dips into his coat pocket and for a second I almost take a step back. He produces a small box with writing embossed on the lid.

"A gift for my beautiful wife" he says.

He presses his lips to my cheek, his whiskers scratching my skin. A wolf in sheep's clothing.

I examine the silver chain in the box and touch the cool metal. He must be doing well if he can afford to buy me jewellery. The dutiful, unafraid wife that I know to be fastens the cord around my neck.

I wave at Maksim as my sister takes him away.

The bruises around Maksim's throat will forever be in my mind. The sound of him gasping for air will haunt me always. Vasili's voice, his threats and promises, telling me what will happen if I go to the authorities still resonate in my head. His hands around our son's throat.

I watch my son, my only son, leave me. My eight year old son sent away for his own sake.

I can see my mother, her piercing eyes and wrinkled mouth, shaking her head disapprovingly at me. She knew better than I. She knew what kind of man my husband was.

Vasili is struggling to find buyers for his horses. He worries that, if things don't pick up soon, we'll lose the stables.

He seems tense, almost angry.

❖

"From this day forward, for better or worse…"

❖

I laugh loudly, clinging to his arm. It feels better for people to know I'm with him. I feel special with him. I'm someone important when I'm with him. He grins down at me and it's a smile that I cannot resist; wide and reassuring.

I won't let Mother's words spoil my evening. I block her pleas from my mind, shut out the image of her begging me to reconsider.

"This isn't what I wanted for you, Sofia. Don't stray from the path I set for you because of him," she had said. "Don't throw your future away on this man."

I rest my head on his shoulder.

"He's a no-good sort. I can see it in his eyes."

I squeeze his arm.

❖

A blinding smile. A pair of shining eyes.

"I'm Vasili" he says.

I smile, my heart pacing, thudding.

"Sofia."

⁓o⁓

I wrote this piece as part of my dissertation. I centred my dissertation on alternative fairy tales and *The Wolf of Moscow* was my attempt at redefining the classic story of Little Red Riding Hood. I did some research on any serial killers who were labelled as a wolf by the press and came across the true story of Vasili and his wife. It was fascinating reading about the couple and the murders and I was even more intrigued by the fact that no one knew if Vasili's wife had an involvement in the killings. She was executed regardless and so I wanted to give a voice to a woman who may or may not have been innocent.

I am immensely proud of the reverse narrative of the piece. By starting at the point of Sofia's execution and going backwards in time to the point where she met Vasili I wanted to highlight how one seemingly perfect moment can lead to tragic circumstances. I also wanted to evoke sympathy for Sofia and as we travel through her past and see that she was in fact not involved in the murders, only too scared to disobey her husband, we see a strength and resilience that is admirable. The story is set in Russia in the 1920s and so she would have been fully dependent on her husband and because of this she cannot free herself from him. When Vasili tells the police that she was involved and implicates her in the crimes it is an extremely tragic moment because nothing she could possibly say in defence would ever change her fate.

I link into the original fairy tale not only with the references to Vasili's murderous alias but through subtle touches and references. The moment which reads 'with the lights out, in the darkness, he growls from beside me' was a homage to the original version of Little Red Riding Hood titled 'The Story of Grandmother.' It is a very dark and twisted tale and I wanted to include that in my adaptation. Sofia's mother warning her to stay away from Vasili was also a reference to the original where Red Riding Hood's mother tells her to stay on the path and never talk to strangers. I wanted to highlight Sofia's naivety and innocence at the beginning of her journey and juxtapose it with how distanced she is from herself by the end of her life.

My love for this piece knows no bounds and I think that it is clever, fast-paced and entertaining. It's also very affecting and poignant, almost relatable in a sense to anyone who has experienced a bad relationship. I'm happy to say this piece was very well received by the exam board along with my three other pieces and I firmly believe *The Wolf of Moscow* helped me achieve my final A-grade.

SHAKELA BEGUM
AORA'S MOUNTAIN

Shakela is a twenty-year-old student from London, who is currently reading Creative Writing at the University of Greenwich. The Creative Content editor of her university magazine, she has been published in three anthologies. In her own time, she enjoys writing stories and screenplays, and documenting her adventures on her blog, WndrLDN. In the future, she wants to publish a novel or collection of short stories, as well as pursue other creative endeavors.

The wind swirled past the cave entrance, carrying the whispers of a faraway land, and echoed against the stone walls. Located at the far wall, Aora's library of leather-bound books were stacked up to the ceiling, insulating the room. An open book lay on the floor. The fraying pages turned in the breeze, until they settled.

Aora placed her fingers on the first words that she saw and read, "For in that sleep of death what dreams may come." She sat on a bearskin rug, cradling a warm bundle wrapped in a smeared cloth, repeating the words to it. Close by a stub of a candle was dying, creating feral shadows that flitted across the stone. The shivering flame drew its last breath, before a draft of air snatched its life away. Aora rocked back and forth, trembling with the bundle in her arms, the warmth fading from it. She swayed like a pendulum as she stood up, and then moved towards the mouth of the cave.

Aora walked into the forest, humming. The fur coat around her shoulders kept the cold out, and on her feet she wore burlap shoes, held together by a series of knots and string. At her chest, she carried the bundle. Twigs cracked and crisp leaves crumbled under her footsteps. Nature crowded around her: white-barked trees and columns of grass, sprinkles of flowers and scuttling insects. Filtered shafts of golden light decorated the forest floor in dots. A disfigured shadow stretched across the ground and walked in parallel with Aora, among a mess of twisted tree limbs.

At a spot of light, she bent down. Using her fingers, she shoveled dirt until she had dug out a pit several inches deep. She placed the bundle inside the hole and unfolded the cloth, revealing a clump of fur. Then she untied the leather pouch at her waist, extracting a nut from it. She wiped away the sweat from her forehead, leaving a streak of brown.

'Sleep now. May you dream wonderful dreams,' she said, resting the nut on the squirrel's chest. The dirt from her hands clung to the fur on its white underbelly. Whispered prayers floated past her lips, as she worked to refill the hole. She looked around at her surroundings. A flash of lilac from some nearby flowers was the only colour that cut through the monotonous browns and greens of the forest floor. The scent of the flowers dissolved on her tongue, and Aora could taste damp soil and a honey-like sweetness. She pulled a clump out and scattered the lilac petals above the mound of dirt.

Before she left, Aora circled around the area. She dropped her prayers, like the petals, on the other mounds of dirt that were beginning to show tufts of green on top.

Aora left the squirrel's grave and continued walking into the forest. She rubbed the trunks of each tree she passed, in greeting. There was a track mapped into the ground, splitting off into different directions. Shrubs and patches of grass bordered each side of it, leaving the centre of the path a copper brown. Up ahead there was a trickling of water. Aora zigzagged her way through the trees, until they cleared away. At the bank of the stream she balanced her weight on two stones and dipped her hands into the water. She formed a cup with them and drank. The cool touch of the water at her lips sent a shiver through her body.

For a while she sat at the edge of the stream, letting the evening chill rest on her skin. She watched the water slap playfully at the stones in their descent through the forest. How far off was the river? How vast was the ocean? She busied her mouth by chewing on a few nuts from her leather pouch, the rations at the bottom of it dwindling. The nuts finished, she jumped to her feet. As she made her way back to the cave, rubbing her palms together, she occupied her thoughts with the crackling of a fire.

Aora settled down beside the mouth of the cave, where the trees stood several metres away, and the sky peeked over the top of them. The last rays of sunlight basked the tree tops in gold, then faded away to nothing. Aora strained her neck to look up further, at the mountain that towered above the cave. If she were to climb it, maybe she could touch the clouds, or at night, pluck a star from the sky and hold it in the palm of her hand.

She searched the inside of her coat, looking for the buns that she found when foraging the day before. One of the villagers must have thrown them away. She tore into one of the hunks of bread, swallowing it like a lion would a deer. She didn't care that it was stale, so when some of the burnt bits fell away, she would catch them with her thumb and suck until they dissolved on her tongue. She saved the remaining bun for later.

A small pile of dry leaves and twigs lay limp next to the cave, reminding Aora of her own failed attempts at kindling a fire. She tucked her legs up to her chest and encircled her coat around them. When she closed her eyes she became a ball of fur, existing at one end of the universe. Images of what the world looked like in her books flitted past her eyelids. They spoke about large groups of people living together and families and children playing with one another. They spoke about purpose, because everyone seems to have a role to play. She pictured going along with the characters on their journeys. She wanted to see the ocean and be lulled by the sounds of its waves. The descriptions from her books were foreign and far from her, yet ones that she longed to see. Aora opened her eyes. The puffs of smoke rising far beyond the trees looked much closer. Maybe if she reached out towards them, they would lift her away, blanket her in their smoky fog. But she didn't. They floated up into the air and disappeared.

A little way off, there was a disturbance in the undergrowth. Footsteps approached the cave. In a crouch, Aora poured her weight onto her feet. She made out the silhouette of a human and sat back down.

'Animals conceal their presence better,' she said. The figure stopped. 'You are a new visitor?'

'Is true, then?' said the figure. The yawning stars twinkled in the waking night sky, casting an iridescent glow. This was a rather small person. Perhaps a child. The compact human stood there, waiting for something to happen.

'It is late. You should not be here,' Aora said.

The child spoke out softly. 'I fear what they do if I go back.' The silence of the darkness diffused in the air. Her trespasser took the liberty of sitting cross-legged on the ground. 'Villagers say you a god.'

'I am?'

'Is what they say.'

Aora sighed. The child followed her gaze, facing upward: the sky was a canvas scattered with clusters of stars and handfuls of cotton clouds smeared midnight shades of blue.

'I have had a few visitors before. Never as young as you.' Aora shuffled closer to the child, handing over the last bun. 'What is your name?'

'Robyn. You have name?'

'What is the use of one when there is no one to call me by it?'

'No name.'

'I am Aora.'

They sat in silence. Their breath formed puffs of vapour in the cool air. Robyn bit into the bread with a crunch and licked up the crumbs with each subsequent bite. Aora reached out to the child and lifted a pointed chin. She looked properly, for the first time, at the young face. It was a pretty one. An androgynous face. The child looked no older than a twelve-year-old boy.

'What is it you wanted to know?' Aora asked.

Robyn swallowed. 'Others see you. Why they come?'

'Perhaps the same reason you have come. Which is?'

'I-I...'

Aora stood up. She shook her feet, trying to get the numbness out of them and the blood flowing again. Without a word she headed back into the cave.

In the insulated darkness of her home, she blindly placed her palms over the spines of her books. She tried to wiggle one out of its place - they seemed to have stuck together, almost like a link of chains. After a few tries it came loose. It flew out into her hand like a baby tooth. Aora laughed. She passed her hands over the front and back of the book, checking and nurturing it.

She jogged out of the cave, and plopped the book onto Robyn's lap. He looked up, confusion clouding his expression.

'That there is a book. The other villagers come in search of this. Open it.' Aora watched him fumbling with the pages. He was discovering something extraordinary. It would probably be the first and last time that he would get to see one. The village wouldn't have such a thing as absurd as a written language. Robyn turned to an illustration of a sibling pair surrounded by trees and a ring in the sky. Their eyes were fixed on something in the distance, in the world of the page.

'What this?'

'A picture. It goes with the story, see?' Aora pointed at the neat body of text next to the trembling children. 'It is a story called Hansel and Gretel. With a book, you read the story rather than knowing the whole thing and reciting it to others.' Her hands moved in circular motions, as she searched for the right words to use. 'You read for enjoyment and entertainment and knowledge. In there I have a whole wall of them. Far too many for me to ever carry!' She smiled.

'What I do with this?' His grip on the book tightened. His nostrils flared. It was difficult to decipher his expression: was the child angry, sad or confused? A strange warmth entered her cheeks, as Aora placed a hand over his in comfort. Somehow, it seemed appropriate.

'If you stay here long enough I will tell you the story, okay?'

The child turned page after page, scanning each illustration he came across, devouring them with his eyes.

A snarl came from the behind the forest trees. Aora's head snapped up. Two circles flashed in the darkness. Robyn seemed to shrink into himself, next to her. Just a cowering child, not ready to face the real dangers of the world. Aora shifted to her feet, and looked straight ahead with a fixed stare. 'Do not show that you are afraid.'

Aora moved to shield Robyn. A rusty snout poked out through the shrubbery, followed by a set of paws as white as snow. A pair of golden eyes interrogated the child. Aora relaxed. The wolf, almost the height of herself, came towards her.

'Yu.' She buried her face into the wolf's thick fur. The hug filled up her heart like a balloon. When was the last time she had seen her? And where did she go? Her mind raced with the places illustrated in her books and the rich details of their descriptions.

Robyn staggered to his feet. 'Get away! Get away!' He launched the book at the wolf. A couple of pages floated to the ground, plucked out of place like feathers of a bird.

'Don't hurt her!'

Yu bared her teeth at him, a rumble forming deep within her. Then, deciding it was not worth it, she ran back into the cover of the trees.

Aora locked eyes with Robyn. A lump was forming in her throat. The boy's chapped lips parted. She turned back to the trees, and dived into the forest in pursuit of Yu. This time she would go with her. She would not be left alone once more.

Behind her, Robyn followed, struggling to navigate through the darkness of the night. After a while, Aora slowed her pace down. They continued through the forest.

'Why you name dog?' Robyn said after a while.

'Because she came to me.' Aora paused, momentarily looking back at the child. 'And if I named her, she was mine to keep.' They walked further. 'But, you can't tame the night.'

After some time, Aora noticed trickles of light were coming from somewhere. A warm glow, flickering against the cracks and bumps of tree bark. When she was close enough, she peeped through a mess of leaves. Beyond her, the forest had been cut down, and mud huts with straw roofs were scattered across the flattened, dirt ground. At the centre of the huts a fire roared, maybe three or four metres high. It was the only village for miles: Robyn's home. He finally caught up to her, out of breath, and leant against a low branch. He must have been fighting his urge to sleep. Aora turned away from the village. She could safely return him to where he belonged.

'You should go back now. Go home, Robyn.'

No answer.

Aora began walking away from the village. Robyn would be fine. What could they do to a child? But before she could get far enough away, low murmurs erupted from the opposite direction.

Chanting. Escalating. She could not recognise the language.

She backtracked her way to Robyn, who watched from the cover of the leaves. Neither of them said a word. They watched.

Some of the villagers poured out from the darkness, forming a circle around the blaze. An elderly man walked inside the ring, offering a bag to each person as he passed. They dipped their hands in and threw fistfuls of powder into the air in front of them. Aora and Robyn covered their noses. It was as if their lungs were being painted in a thick, poisonous resin.

'Cer-mony?' Robyn muttered, fixated on the proceedings.

The chants accelerated and boomed, resonating against Aora's body. She placed her hand on Robyn's shoulder, willing herself to pull him away. She was paralysed. The villagers began moving: they swayed their bodies to the rhythm they created with their voices. Their shadows transformed into demonic creatures, entwining with each other, moving of their own freewill. Aora wanted to look away, close her eyes.

Then, everything ceased. The fire spat into the sky. Everyone listened. A tortured cry faded into the wake of hysterical laughs and cries from the villagers. Scarlet covered, devoured and scarred Aora's vision.

'Sacr-fice.'

Aora grabbed Robyn's arm, and dragged him into the forest. They kept running until their legs could take them no more and they knew the horror was far behind them.

'Leave me,' Robyn said. He slumped down into the protruding roots of an old tree. Aora sighed. She couldn't leave him. The village was no home for a child. Not anymore. She sat next to him.

'If only the things that happened in stories, stayed in stories,' she said. Robyn curled up into a ball. He needed to rest. As she looked at the displaced child,

Aora's mind drifted to Yu - her wolf, her sense of home. Robyn was stripped of that now.

Just as he was falling asleep, Aora whispered into his ear.

❖

Dawn was here. The first rays of sun stretched out across the sky. Aora sat at the lake's edge, watching a watery sun emerge from behind the forest. Yu slept peacefully beside her; the wolf's heat radiating against Aora's skin. Occasionally she would rub her snout with her paw and Aora giggled. The lake smiled at them, with its wobbly waves coming to rest and disappear at Aora's feet.

'You will find us where the dawn touches the water.'

She turned her head.

Robyn stood there a little way off, book in hand, waiting at the lake's edge.

~o~

'Aora's Mountain' began as a piece for a short story assignment, in year two of my studies. Originally, when I had written it, I was thinking about the effects of two worlds meeting: one full of knowledge, and the other set in its old ways, with no written language. This is how Aora and Robyn came to be.

The story deals with elements of magic realism, as well as being cryptic. Aora is a woman living in a cave, who possesses a world of knowledge. She meets Robyn, a boy from a nearby village, who is uneducated and illiterate. The villagers fear her as they believe that she is some sort of God or evil, because she is different from them. Through the course of my story, I want to convey the importance of companionship and of seeking knowledge, or the unknown. I portray Aora's character as one who is impassioned by her books, yet is very in touch with nature and her surroundings. Robyn's character, on the other hand, lacks everything that she has and yearns to know more, which is why they work as a pair. They are two halves that need each other and feed off of that.

The wolf in my story, Yu, is a symbol of freedom and life. Aora finds companionship in the wolf, but this is not enough to stop her from feeling lonely. Yu's action of running back into the forest ultimately sets Aora and Robyn free from their bounds to the cave and village, as they pursue her.

During the process of writing this piece, I was inspired and influenced by the novels I was reading at the time: *Snow Child* by Eowyn Ivey, and *Beloved* by Toni Morrison. Like these authors, I wanted to write prose that created beautiful, vivid imagery, to give off a sense of the surreal and sometimes dark atmosphere in 'Aora's Mountain'.

Over the past year, I have made changes to the original story. The first final draft of it did not deliver a satisfying, or coherent, ending, so I have nurtured it into what it is today. Also, during this time period, writing other short stories and working with my peers, I have learnt how to handle feedback and improve on my editing skills.

'Aora's Mountain' is the piece that has made be believe in my ability as a writer; it is the short story that has set me off on my own journey.

STORM MANN
PURPLE SPANDEX

Storm Mann is a twenty-year-old English with Creative and Professional Writing student. An avid reader, she aspires to become an English teacher and to have her own novel published one day. She also enjoys ballet, yoga and travelling. Storm's first novel *Hide,* posted online, reached over 24,000 hits within its first year. She is currently writing a historical fiction crime novel and a children's book for her three-year-old sister, her favourite storyteller.

Happy Hour at The Glug. The tinkling of glass on glass was lost under trombone notes that danced through the smoky air. Bent over a drink at the bar, Hudson Henson screwed up his Super-Hero Intelligence Service Official Letter of Rejection into a tight, soggy ball. A purple, M-shaped mask landed in a puddle of whiskey between himself and Earl Grey.

"Only real super-heroes deserve a mask," Hudson Henson said sorrowfully, taking a deep chug of his Fanta Fruit Twist. "I failed the interview."

Earl paused to raise a Therapist Brow and take notes on their session: *Still bald. Still an arsehole.* "What was it this time?"

"The name."

"I see. I thought we came to an agreement that your pseudonym might be slightly unsuitable for the role."

Hudson Henson groaned. "Helpful Man is modest; one of the people. Unlike those self-endorsing Hollywood sell-out twats who call themselves Superman or Miracle Man or The Hunk."

"The Hulk."

"If anyone needs government support for the protection of the United Kingdom, it's Helpful Man." He stabbed a finger to his chest, at the giant smiley face on his purple spandex bodysuit. "Seven days a week of hard work and they don't count for a damn thing if you don't have any hair. Do you know how hard it is to pee in this costume?"

"Not personally, no."

"You have to take the whole thing off which takes seven hours. Your cape gets all into your mouth. Last week, I had to cut holes for my fingertips so I can text Liz when I'll be home for tea. Do you have any idea how much that jeopardises my secret identity?"

"I can imagine that's very damaging for you."

"I bet The Hunk doesn't have this problem. He just runs around with his green arse on display and everyone pretends not to be pissed off that he's written their cars off." Hudson Henson closed his eyes and practiced deep breathing and mindfulness like Liz did that time she really lost it and killed the gerbil.

Earl clicked down his pen and scribbled in a psychological evaluation comment: *Bald arsehole expresses deep-rooted anger for failing to fulfil ambitions.*

"Maybe I should just stick to being an accountant," said Hudson Henson, opening his eyes. "It's all I'm good for, anyway."

The next morning was perfect crime-fighting weather. Hudson Henson and his dog, Henson Hudson, sat on a bench on Dudley Street eating Quavers. As a freelance super-hero now, Hudson Henson decided that he needed a new image: a vicious but loyal canine companion and a new, understated and modest costume. Helpful Man now wore a simple shirt and a little employee badge with *Helpful Man* printed in Comic Sans. Nobody would ever suspect that a vigilante was among the people of Wolverhampton. He chuckled cunningly into his bag of Quavers and scooped his Chihuahua into his arms, sensing crime.

Dudley Street was a silver haze of Christmas lights and cigarette smoke. Outside Greggs, Ethel Miller stopped picking up bus tickets from the floor to greet her neighbour. She narrowed her eyes to read Hudson Henson's name badge.

"*Helpful Man.*" She pronounced the words very slowly. "Does the company you work for not bother to learn their own employee's names? Disgusting." She paused to fold a damp bus ticket into her pocket. "How's Liz, Hudson? Are you two coping better since the gerbil died? There's certainly less noise."

Hudson Henson decided the lack of noise was down to Ethel's faulty hearing aid. The noise was ever-present. He heard Liz screeching in his sleep about what you should and should not eat ketchup with. "Liz is fine," he answered very calmly, feeling confident. He even threw a grin in for added effect. "Our therapist says she's showing far fewer signs of being a bitch and will probably not murder me."

Ethel's eyes widened, then travelled below Hudson Henson's waist. His skin crawled. His confidence disintegrated. Cold sweats broke out all over. Liz's purple spandex leggings felt very obvious all of sudden, even tucked into his most modest pair of loafers. Hudson Henson shuffled away, making a mental note to sell his house.

It was a quiet day for crime. Hudson Henson figured the criminals must all be out Christmas shop-lifting with their criminal friends, so he headed to Sainsbury's to investigate. At the entrance, the security guard narrowed his eyes in confused disbelief. "*Yes*, it's me," announced Hudson Henson, flexing his pectoral muscles one at a time. "You can take your lunch break now."

Hudson Henson strutted to the Warburton's section of the bread aisle and imagined the newspaper headlines: *One of the People: Helpful Man Abolishes Crime Whilst Shopping for Liz.* They would make movies about him, his very own comic book series; he'd be the face of Duracell. Seducing Lois Lane, divorcing the troglodyte. Hudson Henson lifted the loaf of bread above his head. He could see it now. He could see it… Liz. Standing at the end of aisle 4.

"What are you doing you knobhead?" Liz threw a pack of ten toilet rolls onto the floor and charged towards him. "Why are you wearing my disco pants again?"

"Couldn't find my work trousers in the washing basket," Hudson Henson stuttered, hiding his lower half behind a pyramid of Heinz baked beans tins. "I was running late. Just went to work. I'm an accountant, remember? I need trousers."

"*Helpful Man?*" Liz shrieked, prying the loaf of bread from his hands and pressing an aquiline nose against his name badge. "Have you been sacked?"

"No…"

"Are you now an employee mascot at Fat Lards R Us?"

"No…"

"Are you now a figure skating elf at Twat Land and your contract permits you to *wear your wife's bright purple 1980s disco pants, stressing your very small elf arse?*"

Hudson Henson thought about this for a moment. It would be a good excuse. "No…"

"This is why I need therapy," Liz sighed, "Don't come home unless you've transformed into a fully functioning human, or at least change your trousers."

Hudson Henson laughed nervously and scrambled away, Henson Hudson trotting beside him. From aisle 4, Liz shouted something about a bald prick and changed from Warburton's to Hovis.

It was beginning to get dark outside, the sky a warm violet. Hudson Henson stepped away from the empty main high street into a dark alleyway that smelled of tobacco and piss. He had to step over a drunk Santa Claus on the way.

"Suspicious," Hudson Henson grumbled, looking down at the crooked beard and Carling cans scattered around his body. "Clearly, somebody has killed Santa Claus in cold blood." Helpful Man was finally on the tail of a criminal.

"I can smell a murderer," he whispered to himself, taking a left out of the alleyway onto a car park. The smell of murderer (cannabis and Lynx deodorant), led him to a group of teenage boys huddled in a smoky corner discussing Princess Peach's boobs. *This is it*, thought Hudson Henson, *Super-Hero Intelligence Service won't be able to resist me after this.* Before he could collect himself into a professional super-hero stance, the conversation fell silent. The leader of the group stepped out of the smoke, his braces glistening in the dark.

"Lads," he bellowed, his voice barely broken. "Lads, this tosser is wearing his missus' clothes." Hudson Henson felt his cheeks burn.

"Um, well, actually, the shirt is mine," he explained very clearly, but the other four boys stepped closer too, an amused grin carved onto their pre-pubescent faces. "I'm not looking for trouble. I'm just here to serve justice." An eruption of laughter followed. They came closer. Greasy hair, acne and Futurama shirts closed in on Hudson Henson's vision. Henson Hudson began to growl, and together they ran. Footsteps hammered behind them the whole way home.

At 181 Pleasant Avenue, he lost them. Outside the house, a silver Ford Fiesta sparkled under a street lamp. He recognised it as Earl Grey's. Through the upstairs window, the faint outline of his wife and their therapist tangled in an embrace was visible through the cheap nylon curtains. Hudson Henson vibrated with rage. He knew what he had to do. He stepped out of the purple disco pants and pushed them through the letter box.

The next day, Super-Hero Intelligence Service opened its glistening, Hollywood doors and let Hudson Henson in from the rain. The smell of cleaning detergent cleansed his lungs and he felt new again. *Home,* he thought, hanging his Helpful Man blazer up on a coat peg near the entrance. "Hi Amy," he said confidently, approaching the receptionist. "I'm here to see Martin Funk for my appointment about representing the city of Wolverhampton."

With a knowing smile, the receptionist reached across her desk and stabbed three numbers into the receiver. "Hello, Martin? We've got another nerd on the ground floor in his Y-fronts. Do you want me to call security?"

~o~

Purple Spandex is a comedic short story based around the central protagonist, Hudson Henson, and his attempts at becoming a professional super-hero for the Super-Hero Intelligence Service (a wordplay on MI6). I produced this piece for my Creative Writing university course. The module was Humour Writing, which both excited and terrified me all at once. I had never written humour before this story. In fact, I was rather used to the opposite. My stories before this one had a tendency to be on the darker side. I would write crime, mostly, so *Purple Spandex* was challenging for me. I wasn't sure I could even construct a successful knock-knock joke, never mind an entire humorous piece. However, in the end, I thoroughly enjoyed the process of writing *Purple Spandex* and humour itself has become a tool I like to use in my writing now.

My inspiration forr this story came from watching a documentary about ordinary people who dressed up as super-heroes and walked the streets at night. This had me wondering: *Didn't their partners find this slightly odd? How did they send text messages with all that lycra on their fingers?* "Helpful Man" (and his spandex disco pants) was the product of this train of thought. Having been previously unfamiliar with how to write for the comic genre, I attempted to use humour techniques in my work such as comic incongruities to increase the effectiveness of my text. Comic incongruities appear a lot in this story, for example, Hudson Henson's sessions with his unprofessional therapist, Earl Grey, who deems him *"Still bald. Still an arsehole"* whilst taking notes on the session. In *Purple Spandex*, I used the idea of expectation being contrasted by the outcome in order to create humour. Perhaps this approach explains Hudson Henson himself, as a working-class, naïve, failure of a super-hero who wears his wife's disco pants and an employee badge as a costume. Hardly the Hollywood, heroic image we are used to with Superman and co.

In reality, Hudson Henson is the 'loser' archetype whose shortcomings as a super-hero are mostly due to the fact that he is too concerned with reality. Whilst his question "Do you know how hard it is to pee in this costume?" may completely contrast against our expectations of a super-hero (as does his location in Sainsbury's), it is all too familiar and relatable to a reader aware of the conventions of a super-hero text and also of the stereotypical 'little man' who is a direct contrast against this idea.

Comic incongruities, naïve voice, insults, contrasts, intertextuality and archetypal characters are all used throughout this story to achieve comedy. However, *Purple Spandex* is primarily reliant on the techniques of contrast and contradiction to create an incongruous super-hero who subverts the expectations of his role, preventing the story from being a conventional action hero text.

ABBY HOWARD
RAIN

Abby Howard is a Creative Writing and English Literature student from Telford, Shropshire. She enjoys crime fiction and blogging. Abby has been writing from a very young age and was first published when she was fourteen. She plans to continue writing in the future and also hopes to pursue a career in education.

The rain can come anytime. One minute you can be enjoying a stifling summer day and the next you're cowering in a shelter, desperate to stay dry.

They say it's irreparable, those in charge. They say that the party before them knew where we'd end up if they ignored the warnings, which they did, apparently, because for longer than I can remember it has always been like this; the rain seeks and you hide. If you don't, you die. It's that simple.

My father still has nightmares about the first storm. He says that the rain was so acidic that day his shirt caught fire. His left arm never recovered from the damage. But he tells me that it wasn't his flaming clothes or the searing of his skin screaming for relief that haunted him for years afterwards; it was the stench of the people burning around him.

I tried to imagine what it must've been like for him as I stood under the glass roof of the shopping centre. There had been a threat of it all day, town had been quiet; nervous people stayed home whenever there was cloud cover. They didn't want to get caught away from home when the rain came.

Offended by the change in weather and knowing it was likely I would be sleeping here tonight, I returned to work to see if anybody could tell me how long this storm would last. The last storm held on for two days before it gave relief; I was at work for over forty-eight hours. When I returned I found the manager in the office, a worried look on her face as she scanned the news feeds for word on what time we'd get rest this time. The news wasn't reassuring and we returned to work feeling unsettled.

My shift finished in a flurry of shoppers, stranded until the rain stopped, panic buying emergency wellington boots. The new release was meant to protect your feet when the ground was wet, fresh after an acid storm so you didn't have to wait until the pavement was dried out to go anywhere. Ordinary shoes burned and melted, these boots were what you needed if you didn't want to burn from the feet upwards.

At six o'clock, as we closed the store, an announcement came. It informed us that the underground trams were now open to ferry the stranded home. I ignored it. You had be under eighteen or accompanied by a small child to get on those trams when the rain came in for the night. Since I fit into neither of those categories I was resigned to a night trapped at work. Our company was good to us though; they had had sleeping areas fitted so we didn't have to stay in the public shelters. We could keep to ourselves within the shop.

The screaming started in the early evening. It had been raining for seven hours and I was frustrated about being stranded. The screams were nearby, close to our store. I couldn't resist going to see what had happened, my curiosity was too strong.

The manager opened the doors enough for those of us who wanted to see to slip under it and down to the source of the racket. People from all over the centre were dashing past us in a keen hurry to see the commotion. Even a few shoppers had emerged from the public shelters for an investigation. I approached with my colleagues and managed to push further into the crowd, towards the front. I weaved my way past grumpy, disturbed workers and shoppers alike until I was only a row from the source of the chaos.

I was met by the sight of an old man. He was standing in front of the main entrance to the shopping centre. The doors behind him had been tricked into opening despite the weather. Rain was sneaking inside and the back of his coat was smoking where the acid was burning a route through his clothing. The man was yelling at the crowd.

He didn't seem to have noticed his smouldering jacket; he was too busy trying to tell his audience what he thought about the rain and about what was causing it. He seemed to have an idea that the whole thing was staged.

"None of this is real!" He cried, his eyes big and watery. "They-" He must have meant those in charge. "-are just trying to keep us scared, ladies and gentlemen; they want us to *think* the rain will kill us; they want us to think we're going to die."

I'd heard all this before. At school we had been taught about a group of people, sick people, we were told, who thought that the rain wasn't acidic at all; at least, not naturally. They believed, so the teacher said, that the government who worked so hard to keep us safe, were so determined to stay in power that they had found a way to manipulate the weather and were using that power to keep us scared. These people also believed that they - the government - were using this fear to provide us with those acid proof shoes and cars in return for our undying loyalty.

I didn't get all that from a lesson at school. Most of it came from the news reports that came on after every storm. They wrote these people off as lunatics and reassured us the government was striving for a solution to our problems. I didn't see why people couldn't be happy with that; they were trying to help make our lives easier. With weather like this, we needed all the help we could get.

"It's not about protecting us!" The man screamed, so loud my ears rung. "It's about keeping us scared, keeping us submissive, from asking questions! It's about stopping us chasing them out of Olympus."

He would have gone on preaching if it weren't for the sudden commotion from the back of the crowd. People were gasping and screaming in alarm. The people around me began to shuffle and move in panic. The group around me, mostly workers from a bakery, saw whatever was going on and parted our segment of the man's audience. In the flurry I was knocked off balance. My head hit the floor with a vicious thud noise. I felt the skin tear and the subsequent warm stickiness of blood on my forehead.

I was so stunned that I lay there minutes after. Four burly men came through the split in the crowd; batons in hand, ready for use. They were police. I recognised the uniforms and blue labels on the back of their shirts through my briefly blurred vision.

Dizziness swamped my brain. I pulled in a long breath and exhaled slowly. Around me the crowd quietened and the man had stopped trying to preach about the rain and government. Instead he made what sounded like his closing statement. The sight of the police must have caused him to decide to end his raving as soon as possible.

He screamed one final cry of defiance and disappeared into the storm.

My vision cleared in time for me to see him punch his fist in the air as if in a jubilant expression of joy. The old man took a wide step backwards, his face turned upwards to the sky. He opened his palms and exclaimed one loud, victorious sounding laugh; as if the sensation of rain on his skin filled him with elation.

Moments past and the man seemed fine. The police skidded to a halt, sort of joining him out in the storm. Instead they stood as we stood; in awe of the old man in the rain; seemingly unharmed as we had been taught to believe he would be.

Then it happened. The acid took hold. His coat and hair caught first. Smoke rose from them for a matter of mere seconds before the flames came. The acid tore through his skin like it was paper. His expression of triumph was wiped from his face and was replaced with something much more awful; agony and terror. His eyes bulged from his skull as he cried out in monstrous wails of pain. He was almost completely alight when he finally collapsed to his knees screaming.

I wanted to beg the police to help him, to make it stop but I knew they couldn't. Even if they could, they wouldn't. The rain would have them burning before they could pull him from its grip. And this man was, in their eyes, insane. He was defying the government by laughing in the face of their efforts to protect him. If he chose death over heeding their advice and accepting their help, then so be it; he deserved what he got.

Few stayed to watch until the police called time on the ordeal. The old man had been reduced to smouldering mound of burnt flesh and singed bones when they finally closed the doors. I was on my feet my then. The baker who'd knocked me down had realised his error and pulled me to my feet. By the time those doors were closed the blood on my forehead had begun to congeal and I could feel the sting of the forthcoming scab.

My supervisor and I sat in the office of our shop when it was over. Another colleague joined us in the early hours suffering with an inability to sleep. She had never seen somebody commit suicide by rain until today. The image would never stop haunting her now. The old man was the second I'd seen die that way. Like my father, the most prominent memory I had from that day was the smell.

My supervisor shakily confessed the memory of seeing six at once. They were the first cult death. I remembered the news coverage from that day. Six friends with the same belief as the old man today tied themselves to a bridge railing when the rain came and what was left of them was hosed away three days later.

The rain wasn't so bad at first. It still burned you to death but the acid levels weren't so high; death took longer to come. Many got off with burns back then; it was rare to be that lucky now. The very first storm was the worst. It still holds the record for the most acidic to date. My father's left arm was so severely burnt that there was risk he might have lost it all together. It was saved but it barely works well enough to hold a pencil.

It was always the 'in' thing to be worried about climate change. Schools and newsreaders had been shoving their warnings down our throat before I was born. The government liked to make sure we knew whose fault it was this happened. The previous party, they said, knew this was coming. They said their predecessors knew the risk of water pollution becoming this strong was growing more prominent. But they ignored it, we were told, they ignored it and now we paid the price.

They had promised to protect us. That was what won them the vote in the end; their insistence that we'd be safe with them in charge. In a sense they were doing just that. Cars were acid proof and a new form of tyre had been developed so cars could be driven after a rain storm. Public areas had been fitted with underground sleeping areas for when it rained too late into the night for people to be able to get home. Many farms were given funding to have greenhouses fitted so crops weren't destroyed whenever there was rainfall. It was difficult, but manageable. And since they were the party in power they were only ones doing anything about it so we just kept them in so they'd keep us safe.

"It's stopping."

The sound of my manager's voice woke me from the doze I'd slipped into in the office chair. I glanced at the clock; four-thirty in the morning. There was still noise on the roof from the storm outside but it was lighter and sounded less like the hooves of an armada of horses. I figured I would be home by seven at the earliest if the rain continued to slow at this rate.

The shoppers began emerging just after six. They came from the public shelters looking bleary eyed and nervous. They were mumbling about the conditions outside and complaining about how much they disliked the shelters. Security appeared with them to make sure nobody started rioting about wanting into the shops or trying to get out of the centre before they were told it was safe to.

At half-past-six the announcement came. The rain had stopped and we would be free to go within fifteen minutes when they were sure that it was safe. Excitement began to filter around the centre then. Suddenly there were people about; milling around waiting for the doors to open. The activity bought out the shopping centre staff. Food serving shops opened for business, staff wandered between stores passing on the free supplies to the centre staff and the smells of coffee roused the last of shelter sleepers.

When the doors finally opened I didn't rush for the car park. I finished chewing a cold piece of toast, donated by the nearest café, pulled on my wellington boots and shrugged on my large coat. Others made their breaks for it as soon as they could; desperate to get home to loved ones and their own beds. I couldn't blame them; I'm sure I would have been the same if I was old enough to remember the days before the rain was too dangerous to go out in.

Eventually I felt that it was time that I should clear myself away. The mall was cool, the breeze flapping in through the now open doors was chilly. Outside, there were groups of white suit workers clearing away the leftovers of last night's suicide. As I walked the words of the old man rang in my head. Could it have been possible; there were still storms that were safe? I planned to go home and wait. Wait for the next story on a suicide. Wait for the next acid rating. Wait for the next storm.

I was halfway across the car park when the raindrops fell.

~o~

I've been writing as long as I can remember. It's always been a passion and I hope that I am able to continue to write in the future, even if it is a hobby. This story happened while I was between college and university and was caught in a torrential downpour under a glass roof. There were people insisting that they would not be attempting to return to their cars until it stopped and I remember thinking that was strange; it was just rain. That's when the initial idea happened. I wondered what they would do if they had no choice but to stay inside when the rain came. I'd been working on a novel at the time and, originally, that was what I wanted to turn this idea into. But whatever I did it kept coming out as a short story. When the first draft was complete I attempted to map out a larger scale version but I could only make it work in this, shorter, form. My favourite writers are the ones who make you think and I hoped to achieve that in *Rain*. I wanted it to be one of those stories that gets your mind racing.

DANIEL MORGAN
MISTER MANNEQUIN

Daniel is a twenty three year old student of English Literature at Swansea University. After working in various industries for several years, he came to the conclusion that the only thing that he could ever do for a living was write, and he hopes to achieve that through his novels. Daniel is an avid reader, and a fan of gothic literature and fantasy. He says that he takes inspiration from every facet of the world around him, as it's a bottomless well of stories just waiting to be drawn from.

Shannon is beautiful; there's no denying that.

Her skin is of the milkiest white and her shapely curves appear hewn from the purest marble. Her only downfall is that her eyes seem glazed and vacant, and across her lower back are etched the words 'keep away from fire'.

She is made of one hundred percent polystyrene, and although that may be a drawback, or even a deal breaker for some, I look at it as her greatest attribute. For, to look at ourselves in such a simple sense is inspiring: what are we made of? I myself, and I am not too bashful to admit this, am assembled from an insidious, poisonous concoction of envy, hate, pride, gluttony, zeal and sadness, besides many other ingredients that I cannot, or am too ashamed to, lay my mind upon. Oh, how I envy the person made of one thing entirely! To know in one's truest moments who and what they are with utter certitude, that is a blessing if I have ever known of one.

I have not seen the sun for a month now. I think it has been so, although all I have to go on is what Katherine tells me, and she's hollow inside: I saw it when her arm fell off; so whether or not she can be trusted is another thing altogether. Both Shannon and Katherine are aware of each other, that much I can be sure of - it is the presence of Isabella that unnerves me. She does not know of the former two and they know not of her either. I am terrified that if Isabella was to see me with them, then there would be hell to pay. She is very green; it says so on the label under her thigh - sea foam green acrylic paint with a clear lacquer - do not inhale fumes when spraying, seek medical advice immediately. And God how I needed to! When I saw her, it was a cherub's arrow straight through the heart. It punctured me deeply, to my very shaking, beating core.

Why was I looking under her thigh, you ask? Well, I don't know that I have an answer other than the simplest one: curiosity. I was, however, sorely disappointed.

I curled against her on one particularly cold night. I, a lonely, lowly night-shift security guard, could only marvel at her glory. She would never glance twice at me, I thought, but it must have been fate that her head was positioned such as she was facing me anyway; our eyes locked and that was it. Chemistry. I had been walking off my anger at the time. Both Shannon and Katherine had been distant and quiet, giving me the cold shoulder as it were, acting as though I did not even exist.

It was a dream once, a juvenile fantasy that living with two beautiful women would be perfect; oh how sorely mistaken I was. I am constantly outmatched, and on this particular evening, I had done something so terrible that it meant I was to be cast asunder from our camp. I took to the aisles, where the bodies lie hither and thither in parts. Once, I remarked to Shannon, that perhaps I could find her a new funny-bone in all the extra limbs lying about. Needless to say she greeted the joke with her usual sullen silence.

So there I was, stuck in the headlights of Isabella's emerald gaze, drawn in like a harpoon on a line, and I the flopping whale. I was her Moby and she my Ahab. She reeled me in close, bent her perfect, glimmering lips to my pink, flaccid ear, and whispered in dulcet, angelic tones that she had been searching her whole life for me. Things grew wild, and carnal insanity took hold. The snow continued to fall, creeping higher up the windows until it blotted out the last scraps of darkened sky with utter mercilessness. I shuddered, nuzzling into Isabella's naked and heaving breast. But, as soon as the deed was done, I seemed to glean no warmth from her. She was cool to the touch and exuded no heat.

I let the awkwardness linger like a wraith about a tombstone he's not quite sure is his, and then I rolled away and donned my shirt, suddenly ashamed of my modest muffin top. I cast one guilty look over my shoulder at her nonchalant face and said, "I have to go."

She said nothing.

So I left.

And here I am, now, in this moment, worming my way back to her. Another fight with Shannon, or Katherine, and back I go to Isabella the jealous Hydra. She asks where I've been and I feel myself staring down the gullet of a lascivious pit viper. She uses me and I her, all the while diving and ducking her probing inquiries. How long I can do this, I do not know.

Every corner houses more and more women who glower upon me like a tasty morsel. There is no escape from them. They see the handsome, chiselled men, smooth *down there* and useless for their wants. The men never speak to me at all. They only ignore me. Jeremy is the worst. He thinks he's so fantastic with his perfect hair and wonderful jawbone. Yeah, well, I bet he still doesn't know it was me who took his legs. Fuck you, Jeremy, you stupid prick. Not so perfect without a lower half are you?

What's that? Hmm? Nothing? Didn't think so.

I sigh, at a juncture in the frigid, inky dark, spider clad warehouse. The ceiling groans under the immense weight of the snow that sits atop it. I wish it would just collapse already and rid me of this wretched love quadrangle.

I suppose I could always… No, that's crazy. I couldn't. And yet… Who would stop me? Katherine would have me back, especially if she didn't know. Especially if she thought she was next.

Isabella first, and then Shannon. Katherine last. Yes. She's the least hateful of them all. And I'll lay them out in bits then, for Jeremy to see. We'll see if he keeps his smile when he's up to his armpits in bodies.

I go to her on legs not my own and behold her majesty one last time. Day or night (who can tell?) I was trapped here to begin with and was ignorant at that; that this place, a storage house of mannequins, would become my tomb. But, as with most horrors in life, the tragedy is laced with poignancy, that I will surely waste in time to bones alone and be held here, with them, locked in position until someone deigns to move me, or remove me. And a thought appears, in a moment of perfect creation. What if, by the time they find me, there is only a framework of bones left, with clothes still on it, and the spiders have picked my corpse so clean that they do not know, and they mistake me for one of them? And then, I end up in the window of some shop, a lovely skeleton mannequin, forever beautiful and preserved, destined to be donned with the finest apparel and freshest fashions available to mankind the world over.

A tomb perhaps, but only for now.

I take her hand, my Isabella and drag her. She moves lightly behind me, bobbing around, enthused and intrigued by my sudden optimism.

"Katherine, Shannon," I say with a certain degree of authority suddenly mustered in my throat, "I know what it looks like, but it doesn't matter anymore. We'll all be together, and that's that. Learn to accept it or leave."

I pause, and then sigh with relief.

"Good, I'll take your silence as acceptance of this. We'll all come to love each other eventually; we have all of time to do so. Now, stand here, there, and there. Perfect."

We are all in position now, in various poses of mild awe and excitement, pointing around as though at some fairly interesting thing, all looking off in odd and intriguing directions; a vague display of life, a meagre lustre of humanity spread over the tightly pulled skin and bones that write the last of my withering life.

I am halfway there, looking upon my body, ribs and spine exposed and jutting out like some sort of mad amalgamation between cactus and man.

A smile might have graced my lips, who's to say. I have joined them now, after so long; I am one of them. And as I stand here alone and stare oddly into the dusty din of darkness that drapes across the eerily empty shelves and aisles, who is to say that I was ever alive at all? That I was ever anything other than one of them. I have had three Mrs Mannequins since I have been trapped here, and it all came so easily, so naturally, as though I was only masquerading as a man to begin with.

The striking and holding of this Olympian pose comes so effortlessly. My breath does not even seem to frost before my eyes any more. My joints are quick to stiffen and my strength fast to dissipate, as though waiting for this moment of realisation.

I smile again. One I will hold for all eternity.

I can see the truth now. I am, forever was, and forever will be, Mister Mannequin.

~o~

It was during my first creative writing lecture at Swansea University that the lecturer told us that writers are magpies, stealing snippets of the world around us to piece together wonderful stories. The inspiration for this particular piece came from a single shot in a movie, where the characters walk in front of a warehouse full of mannequins. There happened to be a security guard in the shot, and just then, the wheels started turning in my head. Mannequins are terrifying objects; they occupy that sinister space between alive and dead, masquerading as people, portraying life and action. If you were to be locked in with a warehouse full of them, how quickly would madness find you? One of my peers asked me, after reading the piece, whether the protagonist was really alive, or was he just another mannequin as well; and I said that I didn't know, that he was either, or both, and that it didn't really matter. I like the abstract, and I think that short forms, like this, which toe the line between flash fiction and short story, are wonderful ways to express the oddity in literature. They need no foregrounding, no plot, and no conflict resolution; all that matters is that the reader, for one brief moment, is utterly encapsulated in the writing, and if a writer can make a reader feel like anything is possible, even for just a second, then they've done their job right. Short forms of writing, and poetry in particular, for me, are the best ways to do this. You don't have to adhere to one style, as you would with a longer piece; continuity is irrelevant in a thousand words; you can burst headlong into poetic rhyme and alliteration for no reason, delve into the deepest corners of your vocabulary bag, and slingshot from sane to bat-crap crazy in two words; and a short story or piece of flash fiction is the best place to do that. This story is meant to evoke thought and emotion, and if it can do that, then I've succeeded, and whatever happens after doesn't matter at all.

BECCA JOYCE
AND-

Becca Joyce is a nineteen-year-old English Literature & Creative Writing student at the University of East Anglia where she probably spends more time drinking coffee and people-watching than actually doing any work. A self-proclaimed narcissist, storywriter and big dreamer, Becca is currently working on a collection of short stories entitled *I Love You, But –*, and hopes to one day live in the country with her future wife and a goat named Hilary.

a woman glances over at me from across the bar red lips white teeth black hair fair skin small hands wrapped around her martini glass as if it were a lifeline delicate hands with painted nails wrapped around a glass wrapped around a mug back at my mums house when you wouldn't let go of my leg because you were scared she wouldn't approve of you back at your mums house when I wouldn't stop biting my nails because you told me you didn't think she'd approve of me oh just how right you were just like you always are always were always right never wrong wrong time wrong place wrong guy isn't that what you'll tell them wrong guy he just wasn't right for me we just weren't right together but what about this new guy have you finally found him is he mister right in his flannel shirts and ripped jeans and wire glasses and –

Becca Joyce

a woman glances over at me from across the bar shy smile in her eyes brown eyes the kind of eyes you could drown in if you let yourself drown in drowning in the sea like that time we went to the beach to the seaside to the sea and I threw you in and I laughed at first because I didn't know you couldn't swim can't swim can't keep your head above the water and I reached for you and you held on and you told me that you would never let go you let go you stopped holding on holding out for me holding out for us you let go and you let me drown in this emptiness as you held onto him for support him with his strong arms and kind heart and square jaw and –

a woman glances over at me from across the bar before taking a long drink from her glass as a man somewhere plays a sad song on a piano an old man a lonely man a man with a scar but a hell of a talent a man with a scar on his hand scars heal over time yes time heals everything isn't that what they say what you said what I've been told over and over scars heal even those on the heart your heart your scar the scar on your thigh the scar I kissed in the shower as you cried because nobody had ever called you beautiful before beautiful you're still beautiful but now you're somebody else's beautiful you're his beautiful and how could I ever compete with his beautiful face his perfect words his delicate mind his –

a woman glances over at me from across the bar wearing a knowing look and a white dress a strapless dress showing her shoulders hair falling on her shoulders black hair curled hair framing her face curls framing your face as you wake in the morning as you wake next to me the sun shines through the curtains and you smile you smile and you kiss me you smile and you say my name and you say it softly not like the shouts that came later the shouts that tore through the air that tore through my heart tore through us through whatever we had left after I left after I made my mistake it was a mistake I promise you it was a mistake to leave you it was a mistake to leave me it was a mistake to choose him and his house and his job and his life and –

a woman glances over at me from across the bar with a drink in her hand a smile in her eyes and a ring on her finger a ring on her finger on her left hand a hand she tries to hide behind her glass hide behind her smile a smile of lies and lies break hearts and broken hearts ruin lives and ruined lives find their way to the nearest bar find their way to the nearest drink the nearest bar with pretty women and full bottles and empty promises broken promises like the ones I made like the ones I broke like the ones you think you can safely make with him because you know him you can trust him you can love him and –

a woman glances over at me from across the bar and I turn away because all I see is you

~o~

And- is a short experimental piece, partially inspired by Raymond Queaneu's 'Exercises in Style' and my own interest in human emotions, which focuses on an estranged husband who has recently lost his wife to another man. Part monologue and part prose poem, *And-* has allowed me to explore the innermost thoughts of my protagonist through the method of spontaneous writing, producing a piece rather in the style of a stream of consciousness.

This approach allowed for an intimate exploration of not just thoughts and emotions, but of memories, conjuring up small episodes from the past. My original aim was to use this stream of consciousness to simply produce an interior monologue, however I decided that this freer form of prose poetry was better suited to my character – his drunk, desperate, lost state was more effectively reflected through unorganised, unpunctuated, and uncontrolled thoughts.

Writing this piece also allowed me to reflect on ideas about literature and orality as I feel *And-,* especially due to being a prose poem, is rather effective as a spoken word piece as well as in writing. Equally the rhythm, repetition and lack of punctuation within my piece encourages a speaker to continue reading, inevitably getting faster as they do so in order to reach the end of the paragraph to take a breath. This is reflective of the way in which the thoughts of my protagonist are constantly spiralling out of his control.

In redrafting this piece, I identified that repetition was copiously present. Though originally fearing it may come across as clunky, I soon embraced it as a part of the character. The repetition also successfully reflected the way in which the character wishes to move on and start over, but always ends up in the same place. To emphasise this idea fully, I decided to begin each paragraph in the same way, "a woman glances over at me from across the bar", only concluding this piece when my protagonist turns away, reflecting the way in which he is turning his back on his problems.

CARLA MANFREDINO
JOHN

Carla is from Glan Conwy in Wales and has recently completed an MA in Creative Writing at Goldsmiths, London. She reads poetry submissions for The White Review journal based in Knightsbridge. Her poem 'Betws-Y-Coed' is in November's poetry video showcase 'Force of Nature' for The New Welsh Review magazine. Her fiction has appeared in the latest Lonely Crowd anthology, and her poems in Dirty Chai and Squawkback. Carla has written reviews for The Times Literary Supplement, The New Welsh Review and The Cardiff Review. She is currently working on adapting a story into a script as part of the BBC Comedy Room.

JOHN

John shouts at Gill for things that do not warrant a shout. He shouts about the things inside the house and then he goes out in his velour slippers and he shouts about the things outside the house. Because John shouts Gill can be in any room of the house and still be listening. John doesn't shout about the people he shouts about the gate and the bins.

JOHN IS A KEEN GARDENER

He used to water the neighbour's plants for them when they went away. John took an authoritative approach to this responsibility and would extend the duty to patrolling the neighbour's garden several times in the evening. The neighbours to the right of his house had a cat flap which John would kneel down in front of and put his head through. He liked the freedom of being able to go inside it and would quietly say, Mmm periscope, as he rotated and scanned his neighbour's utility room. John does not water their plants anymore and they miss his gentle upkeep. He handled those hydrangeas as though they were the wings of a fairy, he heard the neighbour at the bottom of the garden once say.

John lost his job three years ago when he was working for a computer shop in town. In the computer shop he sold mostly adapters and memory cards and plastic cases for computer related equipment and asked, Would you like a bag with that?, during transactions. Sometimes people bought things which did not require a bag and John did not enjoy it when he saw that the item the customer was buying could be easily slipped into a pocket or accompanying bag only to be asked, Can I have a bag with that? This kind of request would upset John and shake him up and he had a hard time concealing it. His brow would get sticky and his nose and the surrounding area would turn red like a grated beetroot.

A SPECIFIC EXAMPLE

John was in bed one night and Gill was sleeping in her usual flannelly, creamy way and John was on his back with his fingers laced and resting on his enormous stomach. It was a hot night and they were sleeping on top of the sheet: a choice which begins and ends in climactic extremes; John and Gill fall asleep on a heated grill and wake up under a tray of ice. The window was open and the sound of shaking leaves came through in regular intervals. John was lacing and unlacing his fingers in a variable rhythm whilst thinking about a customer who that day had asked for a bag which they did not need. John got so angry that he tried to close himself in the bed sheet with the aim of rolling away. This motion caused Gill to drop out of bed and onto the floor. Gill got back into bed as easily as she would overtake someone in her car. Gill put her hand under her pillow and breathed like she did not need even the effect of the trees.

THE ORIGINS

John's temper that night was due to a customer who had bought a small box of mints situated on a wire stand by the till. John was annoyed that they had come to a computer shop to buy mints which were cheaper and more relevant to buy from the newsagent next door. The customer then asked for a bag to carry the mints in and this upset John further. He pretended not to hear the customer and turned around to straighten the vertical blinds behind the till area.

John carefully unfolded each section from behind the other so that the blind fell as it should. He turned around and the customer who had bought the mints was still in front of the desk. They looked down at the packet of mints and then back up to John as though their gaze were bubble gum being pulled off a table. John's manager was watching him with an expression that did not look like, Hello buddy. John looked pressured. He started puffing quite loudly and his eyes squirrelled the top of the counter. The customer repeated that they wanted a bag for the mints and John was obliged to give them a bag. After some 'thinking on the feet' he licked his finger to provide a grip as the bags were difficult to separate. Instead of pulling one bag from the pile John pulled out many bags and what happened next was called 'violent and aggressive' by an onlooker. This was before the return of John's lanyard and fleece to the manager at the office.

LOOSE CONTEMPORARY CONTEXT

John has not had a job since the computer shop. Gill comes in from work or tennis and goes upstairs for a shower and sings the same song. The steam stifles the words but John thinks they sound excited lately. Gill then cooks dinner, pours dog biscuits in the dog's bowl and goes upstairs to bed. This is after John has followed her around and shouted about the things inside the house before going out in his velour slippers and shouting about the things outside the house. You've left the rackets out, is a frequent allegation. Gill generally does not know what he means by, You've left the rackets out, but she nods and takes to moving about the kitchen in the style of putting something away that should not have been left out. Occasionally Gill slaps her forehead too and says, Oh God I am so stupid. John agrees with her and pads off into the green house. Sometimes he is in there for the whole evening.

ANOTHER SPECIFIC EXAMPLE

One time John was in the green house when there was a storm and the wind lifted the plastic cover of the greenhouse and it was flapping about like flames. The motion sensor night light in the back garden came on while Gill was washing plates. Gill had told John she had read in the newspaper that criminal-like figures had been entering local people's gardens. Gill had told John that these figures had been banging on the neighbour's windows and pulling down wind chimes and saying quite hostile but wide-ranging things. Gill went out to see what had set the motion sensor night light off. John was just standing at the door of the polytunnel greenhouse being slapped in the face by the circulating covers.

MISCELLANEOUS

John wishes Gill was still seventeen and spotty and excited. If he could go back to when she had one sock rolled up and the other loosely rolled down to her ankle he would be happy. John wishes that he could be spotty and fifteen and excited like he was when he got good grades and his only worries were his palms sweating whilst holding hands with Gill.

THE DAY OUT

John had to go to the pharmacy last year. He had a cough and there was nothing for a cough in the cupboard. John went out to start the car but when he looked out of the windscreen everything was smudged. John got out of the car and walked through the park to the bus stop. He paid for an adult return and sat at the back and watched the dog walkers on the promenade and the waves coming together from opposite sides to meet and fall forward in foam.

John walked slowly towards the assistant behind the till at the pharmacy. He had gotten shaken up by a woman riding through the aisles on a mobility scooter. She would glide around and the wind from her riding was blowing the lighter items off shelves and onto the plastic floor. She whirred her way ahead of John in the queue and one of the small rear wheels of her scooter rolled over John's foot.

John's puffing began. Instead of 'spiralling out of control' John put his finger on her shoulder and said, You can't use your legs but you can use your eyes and I am right here. The woman placed the item she intended to buy on an incorrect shelf and pressed a button on her scooter that sounded an alarm. A voice came from a speaker at the back of the scooter and said, Vehicle reversing be aware vehicle reversing. The woman did a three-point or seven-point turn on the scooter with her eyes on John. John's sweating began and his face was filling with beetroot juice. The woman rode slowly out of the shop with her empty shopping bag waving on the hook behind the head rest. John stepped forward and paid the assistant for the tin of pastilles.

AFTER SOME THINKING ON THE FEET

John felt restricted and frustrated having spoken to the lady on the scooter. He felt how he did when he was a boy and had thrown sticky weed over the fence onto a neighbour's underwear hanging on the line. This was in retaliation to them telling John's mother that they had heard him saying, Fucking idiot, in the back garden. John told his mother that he had in fact been playing a game called Ducking Indian and the neighbour had misheard him. John's mother hit him on the head with the rubber spatula she was using to pull the side of an omelette over and sent him up to bed.

John felt so restricted about the event with the lady on the scooter that he decided he would not take the bus back so that he could let the event 'breathe'. The wind was strong as the sea front is an open space. John was restricted from experiencing 'spatial awareness' however because he was busy going over and over the event in his head and stopped on a few occasions to re-enact the scene behind shelters. John noticed that the shelters had the exact scent of urine in each one. It was quite confident for a smell especially when it altered its intensity. John would breathe in through his nose and try to locate the area the smell was being released from but it would evade him. John would then drop his nasal guard and continue acting out the scene with the lady on the scooter - you can't use your legs but you can use your eyes and I'm right here - until the smell would return bigger and braver and with friends laughing at so many intersections John could not identify the perpetrator.

MISCELLANEOUS

John later gained an objective retrospection of the smell. He decided that overall the more intense smells had lent the space inside the chosen shelter a rope-like texture. John believed that the scenes he acted out in the more intense smelling shelters had been wrung of any malice that the lady on the scooter might have picked up on. He changed the scene with the lady on the scooter in the last shelter to the part when he puts his finger on her shoulder and instead says, That smell is wicked and I'm glad I'm not wicked and you're not wicked and we care for each other and the world at large. John was so busy going over the event with the lady on the scooter that he arrived at home having not logged other local amenities he had intended to log.

MISCELLANEOUS

John wishes Gill was still seventeen and spotty and excited. If he could go back to when she had one sock rolled up and the other loosely rolled down to her ankle he would be happy. He wishes that he could be spotty and fifteen and excited like he was when he got good grades and his only worries were his palms sweating whilst holding hands with Gill. John wishes Gill would still tell him about her day at work and the sandwich she ate during her break. Gill seems to enjoy driving to and from tennis most evenings and to twilight tournaments at the weekend. John once saw two rackets on the passenger seat of her parked car and often laughs at the thought of Gill playing tennis with herself. Gill also possibly enjoys driving to the shop because food articles appear in the same places in the same sections of the kitchen as though they never left there in the first place.

CONTEMPORARY CONTEXT

John wants them all to go away. The drain pipe, The grids, The gate, The bins. Gill too. And Martin. Even though he has not seen Martin for three years. Martin takes up a discernible portion of John's thoughts and grows bigger and braver with each cycle of thought. John might as well still be working next door to Martin's newsagents. John thinks Gill and Martin should go and have sex on top of a big box of ten smaller boxes of clotted fudge in the stockroom after tennis. John wants to know how Gill can be happy living with him: Gill parks the car comes into the house cooks tea pours dog biscuits in the dog bowl goes upstairs to shower and slides into bed. John shuffles about following her and shouting about things that do not warrant a shout. John then stares out of the dining room window at the purpling sky and the cars driving home from work below it.

A PATTERN IS FORMING

John's shouting is becoming louder. He shouts about the things inside the house and then he goes out in his velour slippers and he shouts about the things outside the house. Because John shouts Gill can be in any room of the house ('probably even at work') and still be listening. The drain pipe, The grids, The gate, The bins. The lady on the scooter left without John's explicit instruction. The tennis rackets on the seat of the car are still there. Gill is still there.

THE DIALOGUE

Somebody has kicked Tess, John says to Gill who is squeezing a teabag against the side of a mug.

She is always under the rosemary bush.

I think she's always done that John I think she just likes it under there.

Gill taps the spoon and steps out into the sun. John waits in the kitchen before following Gill into the front garden.

The gate is rusty, John says with his slippers walking towards Gill. Gill is now sun-hatted and pulling at leaves under a bush. She pushes soil off herself as she gets up. You can almost hear her eyes rolling like coins in a box. She looks at the craggy grey finger pointing at her.

Tess doesn't bark anymore, says John.

Gill looks past John for an answer in the pebble dash.

Gillian she is traumatised, says John.

Tess is not traumatised she is old, says Gill and walks back into the kitchen.

THE AFTERMATH

John puffs angrily and pads away from Gill and her ignorance. John walks around the side of the house to the back garden in order to log the quantities of bird food in the bird house. He thinks the birds have been uncontrolled lately. John wants to tell the birds that 'spiralling out of control' is bad but what do they care. The birds don't have a lanyard and fleece to return to the manager at the office. The birds just eat and croak and pose on apparatus before flying away. Probably to congregate and laugh about John's scattering of bird seeds whilst the dog sweeps in and out of his legs. Gill is still standing where John left her. She puts a finger in her hat which she must have shrunk in the wash because it looks tight and the sweat is curling her fringe.

Everybody knows John kicks the dog.

THE RECURRING DREAM

John dreams that he walks past the windows of the houses near where he lives and people's heads are black against the light of televisions. John hears the high tide climbing the break rocks and he dreams that he walks through Martin's gate and up to the large front window that seems too big for its frame. This gives the window a predatory aura as if it is ready to attack or restrain. Martin is watching the tennis on the television and biting his nails. John watches Martin bite his nails and store the nails in his mouth before emptying the nails into a chute in his hand and delivering the nails to the bin. The light from the television glows through the curves of Martin's thin blow dried hair. In the dream John touches the top of his own head and then feels behind both ears for the clump of artichoke-like hair. He closes his eyes in appreciation of this area of hair. John opens his eyes and remembers what he is in Martin's garden for. John is here to fight for his marriage. John knocks on the claustrophobic window but the television is at a high decibel and Martin does not hear him. John walks down the side of the house and puts his big hand over the gate and unhooks it from the outside. In the dream John walks up to the patio doors and starts banging on the glass and shouting,

Fucking idiot fucking idiot.

THE AWAKENING

John wakes up in the middle of the dream tonight and Gill is lying there in her flannelly creamy way. John is suddenly angered by the situation of being in bed with Gill. John wants to come at something directly like a ball. John wants to blame. Worse than blame John wants to share something. John gets so angry with this new need that he tries to close himself in the bed sheet with the eventual aim of rolling away. This motion causes Gill to drop out of bed and onto the floor but instead of getting up back into bed as easily as she would overtake someone in her car Gill takes her pillows and goes downstairs.

THE WALK OF SHAME

John goes down in the morning and starts shouting about things that do not warrant a shout. He shouts about the things inside the house and then he goes outside in his velour slippers and he shouts about the things outside the house. Because John shouts Gill can be anywhere ('even at Martin's') and still be listening.

JOHN

John shouts about the objects such as the bins and the gate, The bins Gill the bins, but he doesn't say what it is about the bins for example that are upsetting him. John wanted Gill to just pull him up on the whole thing and ask him what he was playing at. Tess sweeps in and out of John's legs as he stands at the window and watches the sun leak over the slate draped hills. Tess looks at her empty bowl and back up at John as though her eyes were bubble gum being pulled off a table. John bends down and looks at Tess in her accusatory eyes. John says to Tess, Why aren't you here now Gill honey? To nip this thing in the bud while it was still possible?

~o~

'The purpose of fiction is to transfigure the quotidian!' was a disappointed friend's response to reading my story, 'JOHN'. The friend was upset by the repetitions, erratic chronology and the protagonists' mundane existence; they felt I was reinforcing a sense of isolation and entrapment, when writing should be an escape from these states. You can't excite everyone. As Vonnegut put it: 'Write to please just one person. If you open a window and make love to the world, so to speak, your story will get pneumonia'.

I've always been interested in art that can reveal emotional depth to the everyday. Take Degas' paintings for instance, in particular the sequence of women doing domestic chores. Degas uses colour and lineation in a way that portrays the everyday, yet elevates it. I aspire to use words in a similar manner; I want to embrace the banal and depict it in a way that leaves space for reflection and emotion from the reader. Through writing about John's menial routine in this style I hope to transcend it, and thus change the perception of it.

'JOHN' is separated into episodes with refrains to mirror John's repetitive thoughts and the story circles back on itself. John's habits are unending as he is unwilling to express himself directly. Through reworking the piece, I discovered that I write more clearly when I trust the voice inside me. When the conscious and analytical mind came in to play, problems arose. By coercing scenes into events that 'made sense' and maintaining a linear chronology, I felt I was taking away the uncertain sadness of John and his life.

I had the idea for the story a few years ago but it took some time to come to fruition. The voice and prosody of the story came first. I had to get to know and understand the protagonist, but I couldn't figure him out: he abuses the dog yet he feeds the birds, he loses his temper with a customer at the computer shop, but he has a conscience. He is not exactly nice to Gill, but he genuinely misses their adolescent romance. I had to accept John's ultimate humaneness; to be human is to accept life's contradictions.

I used the third person subjective narrator so that I could focus on John but keep a distance from him. I think this distance allows the reader to more fully participate in the story, by piecing together what is not said. The fractured structure is to allow this too. The linguistic refrains are to show John is trapped in his monotonous existence, and also to suggest he lives by this internal poetry, one he is not aware of.

Ali Smith gave an insightful lecture on the short story at Goldsmiths last year, and she talked about its unique ability to capture the brevity of life. I wanted to do the opposite with my story by using the short form to demonstrate the stagnancy and perpetuity of John's routines. I think that is why I am drawn to the short form - it seems the ideal space to explore the interiority and actions of a particular character. I don't think the voice and form of 'JOHN' would work in anything longer, it could become rather annoying!

DANIEL WILES
JERICHO HILLS; OR, THE INDIFFERENCE OF LIFE AND FAITH IN THE HOLY LAND

Daniel Wiles is a twenty-one-year-old Creative Writing and Film Studies student. He is currently researching for his final dissertation project – a series of short stories set in the 19ᵗʰ century Black Country. Daniel is an avid film buff and hopes to be a working writer, for the page and the screen, after he graduates in 2017.

Holy Land
Geographical Name

The lands comprising ancient Palestine & including the holy land of the Jewish, Christian, & Islamic religions

Hebrew שֶׁדוֹקַה ץֶרֶא (*Eretz HaKodesh)*
Arabic ضرأل ةسدقملا (*Al-Arḍ Al-Muqaddasah)*

1:1

THEY CAME in crowded echelons of three or four, these corralled pilgrims that time has set about trying to erase but only found failure. Ages over ages.

They moved like germs under the microscope in this claustrophobic space and headed toward the sun that unfolded at the end of El Wad Ha-Gai Street.

The dry heat of the sun advanced over the crowd as it funnelled out of El Wad and into the open. We all seemed to look in the same direction almost out of instinct like a new-born calf to the mother or baby to the breast. It was of course the Western Wall. I understood why it was nicknamed "The Wailing Wall" for the cries and the chants from zealots in their strange tongues echoed all about us. Upon approach their audio was cast with a visual of messianic movement as the zealots with closed eyes kissed the wall and spoke to it as if it were alive and their reactions suggested it returned their faith in speech only they knew the meaning of.

1:2

Me, Mum, my two brothers and Aunt Jo packed into her four by four and left Jerusalem for the day.

We drove along Route One for almost fifty minutes. The cool air from the car moved through my shirt. We were heading for the Dead Sea.

'Where are we?' I said.

'Half an hour,' Aunt Jo said.

She worked, works, at the British consulate in East Jerusalem, West Bank.

I looked out of the open window and watched them. Golden desert hills dancing under the sun and moving as if some giant mole travelled beneath the surface in search for the truth it would never find.

We passed Mitspe Yeriho. The hills were dotted with shanty housing and two men, the one perhaps just a boy, stood looking out from their doorway with hands held over brows sheltering their eyes from the hovering white sun. The younger one waved. I noticed then we had slowed down and Jo was fiddling with the sat-nav. The once dancing hills of Jericho now moved in foxtrot.

I thought about living here and I wondered where these people would go to pray to their Gods or whether they believed in God at all. The boy was out of sight now and Mitspe Yeriho faded.

1:3

We stopped in Jericho city and we took the cable car up to the Mount of Temptation. It was a sparse land but a forgiving one. There were farms full of crops, green and life. I saw the mountain and studied it still from afar, a whole monastery carved into the rock and its appearance that of something so alien and something you would see only in dreams yet possibly more mystical still. I thought of the Christ and I thought of Lucifer. It seemed to me that of all this land and all the Judean Desert, this mount was truly His domain and the feeling getting closer was that of no return.

Later we decided to go deeper into the Judean Desert and visit Hisham's Palace. Old ruins of yesteryear were becoming commonplace in our lives and by this time the heat had become worse. At the lowest point of the earth we were being fermented by 45 degrees Celsius. Hisham was a ruler in the 700s. On site is the mosaic of "The Tree of Life" depicting a giant tree bearing fruits and deer eat from the tree in peace on the near side but on the far side of the mosaic a lion sinks his teeth into one of the bucks. The awareness of life and the actuality of it bestowed in the soil of this place bears truth and power. Could it surpass any belief system? The palace was an Islamic complex yet these ancient inhabitants proposed answers to questions far beyond belief. "The Tree of Life" was truth and truth to those pilgrims was and is God also. I studied it and wondered if either was any different. Life and faith. Both truths.

1:4

We returned to Route One and had taken a left off Route 90 toward Beit HaArava. Here the landscape seamlessly changed. Salt white plains stood motionless like castaways of the Jericho hills. Unmoving and old and ready to die alone. They gleamed under the sun and I studied the lunar like moulds and craters that cast half shadows and formed alkaline colours offsetting the talcum splayed surface.

We passed a sign reading:

דרך יגנד

غاندي طريق

Gandhi's Road

Even in this landscape where God would himself suffocate there are roads named after Gandhi.

'We're going the wrong way,' Jo said.

'How do you know?' Mum said.

'We shouldn't be on Gandhi's road.'

We turned around at Beit HaArava and headed back. The cool air in the car wasn't enough to ebb sweat from palms and frowns from eyebrows. We shuffled in the car like jigsaw pieces each trying to sit snug yet only making the fit more awkward.

We took a left. The landscape was changing again. What once seemed like the surface of the moon was now littered with trees and shrubs. It wasn't a rainforest, or even Lichfield. It was Death Valley with greens. It was Almeria. It was *A Fistful of Dollars*.

We reached a turnoff and on the corner a pale white house that looked transported from biblical times. I contemplated whether it was transported at all and thought maybe these times are biblical unto themselves as two centuries ago Yusuf and Zekharyah would not have labelled their times biblical, but simply their times. But would our awareness of those times implicate those of our own? And implicate those in a further 2000 years from now? Or would the consciousness not matter to those brains at all as time will have passed and for that we shall be labelled. They will have moved on. But still perhaps those times themselves would be biblical to those even further in the future and this concept of time and faith could be just a cycle we as memory makers concoct out of pure phenomena.

1:5

'Can you see Jordan?' Mum said.

We looked through the windshield. A distant and long mirage of land floated in a halo of baby blue below the rich Prussian sky. It looked odd, almost as if the land was rising and being chivalrous unto the sea.

We travelled to the Dead Sea and floated in the cordoned shallow lagoon; like melting butter in the pan we slid around the salty surface. We raised and sunk in the underwater mud to our knees and clambered and laughed, each at one and other and upon exit we were soon dried by the sun.

On the way back we stopped on Route One, just past Beit HaArava. There were chains of sparse stalls selling goods, from pottery to fabrics, and wicker to clay ornaments. They sold olives and olive trees and palm and pine and even Christmas trees. There were date farmers and camel herders that congregated and conversed.

We walked to a stall that looked dilapidated as if abandoned but all around it bunches of dried fruit hung from the tent rafters, each waiting in solemn silence. The dry air evoked a smell of heat and antique wood and brass. Jo called out and a farmer emerged crumpling a tea towel. He had gunmetal grey hair which curled on his skull. He smiled and asked what he could do us for and she asked for twenty dates. He obliged, passing us each a date to try as he spoke of date prices in Tel Aviv. Jo explained that she lived in Jerusalem and he asked if she knew Arabic. She did not. They spoke of prices again and disagreed, half agreed and disagreed again. He smiled and moved his palm up his forehead and wiped it on the back of his white trousers as he turned to his till and offered a conclusion to the business.

'Twenty for twenty, madam. They are forty in Tel Aviv.'

'OK,' she said.

The salesman handpicked and placed the dates onto a polystyrene board and bagged them in an off-white paper slip with the opening cut into asymmetric spikes. We thanked the man and I took his picture as he smiled. I asked him why they named a road after Mahatma Gandhi.

'That is not named of Mahatma Gandhi of India. It is Rehavam Ze'evi. He was known as Gandhi. He was killed.'

Rehavam Ze'evi was Israel's minister for tourism. Before that he was a general and served as a platoon commander during the Six-Day War. When he formed his own political party, he advocated the transfer of Gaza and West Bank Arabs to neighbouring Arab countries such as Jordan and Syria. In 2001, four Palestinian gunmen assassinated him in a hotel on Mount Scopus. When he was younger, he shaved his head and entered a food hall with a towel around his waist and people laughed and he sat and ate and he was no longer Rehavam.

2:1

In Bethlehem we made our way to the small Milk Grotto through the streets behind the church of the nativity. We passed a small building where with open doors men sat in heaps of sawdust at work behind machines carving wood. They looked as if they were plugged in at the wall behind them, slumped and still, drowning in their lives.

We bought water and passed another open-door shop, this time with a lone man hand carving objects of the Virgin Mary and Joseph and Jesus Christ. Spread out in front of his work space were finished products in peach-coloured varnish and he smiled and grimaced at the heat and spoke something in broken English none of us understood. We watched and moved on.

We saw the Milk Grotto. It was here Mary nursed the baby Jesus during the Slaughter of the Innocents and where a drop of milk fell to the floor and turned the dirt white. Inside there were murals cut into rock and no sound could be heard. I wondered whether the visitors of this place were seeking refuge of their own and maybe even attempting to enter Mary's shoes, or whether they just needed somewhere to cool off.

2:2

They shinned over one another and moved with an awkwardness that fell onto us like plague upon pigs.

'It's mainly Russian Orthodox, I think,' Jo said.

They fought one another as if they were heading for salvation and only one of them could make it pure and unsoiled as if the light from this star would cleanse them and change the very fabric of their beings and there will be more of them and only more for with time comes legend. It was a six by six underground room with two entry points. Tour guides shouted. People scuttled. The sound of sliding feet upon the clay floor like ocean waves before impact. It was the Church of the Nativity. Christ's birthplace. There was a marble star under a small shrine ensconced in royal blue fabric and the golden tassels fell down hovering like that fabled star that drew them, sent by word of mouth, to this point. The marble was surrounded by metal forming the star. This was where the pilgrims fought to be, to touch, to smell, to pray. We stood at the back of the squashed room and watched them, and then we left.

2:3

The next day we visited The Church of the Holy Sepulchre. This was where Jesus was laid down after the crucifixion. The rock still lays in place and that is where pilgrims rubbed their sentimental objects on the cracked ancient stone as if they were hoping to transfer the very blood of Christ onto them thus saving them for whatever meaning or reason.

The Church itself was looming with energy as if He was watching from the high ceiling above and the adjacent murals were looming high and smoke eked from atop low hanging lanterns that looked formed from pure silver and studded with emerald, ruby and gold. People lit candles and the collective smoke would rise and blend with the lantern smoke and interact with the sunlight and cast sharp shapes that tried to force their way in through the entrance like projections of the past where once the Roman infidels of Jerusalem had come to sight vengeance upon Christ for being the one He chose and the deep bellowing hum of the priests singing in their red robes of the Church echoed through the halls as we circled the epitaphs and some people hugged and some people fell to their knees and we passed one woman who cried to her kin and it was then I had realised we were not in a world of men anymore but something else entirely.

2:4

On our return we passed a lone horse grazing. And I, Daniel, set my gaze upon it and in its eyes the Jericho hills danced and with its jaw revolving it studied us only for a moment before dipping back down to graze again.

~o~

My story was originally conceived for a module at university. When I received positive feedback from peers and tutors, I decided to sharpen it up and submit it.

My main aim was to take the factual travelogue and break the form open, creating a narrative short story that could be identified as a work of fiction as well as the travelogue. All of these events happened, but I tweaked and fictionalised the majority of the text, and all of the dialogue.

For example, I wrote in the section on the "Ghandi" character: In reality, the date salesman did not tell me who Ghandi was, (in fact I didn't even speak to him) I created that fictional back and forth to allow me to add a factual element and also make the story flow as a work of fiction.

The Holy Land is a powerful place. I felt compelled to write about the strange underlying feeling I had when I was in the area. Similar to how I felt the facts and historical elements were needed in the piece, I remember thinking it would've been very remiss for a writer to go to the Holy Land and not to write about the otherworldly atmosphere, and what creates it. So that's what I did. I took various locations, different churches and sites, and tried to dig under the veneer, the veneer that anyone can see on a travel guide, and offer something more. To achieve this, I tried to write the piece in a fractured, dreamlike style and present the action in forms of reflection and contemplation. I also felt it would be ideal to write the piece in as biblical a fashion as possible in order to make its tone reflect the subject matter.

I decided to write the story as a road-trip. 'We got in the car and went here… and 'from there we went here…' I believe this is another aspect that gives the piece the patina of fiction, making it able to sit on both the factual travelogue and creative fiction shelves.

Overall, I learnt a lot when writing this piece of work. I learnt that travel writing is flexible. You can implement things deeper than their face value, such as thoughts, perceptions and atmosphere – not just things to see and places to visit, and through that, create a story that meshes different forms and genres effectively.

Of course the main objective is to create a story, and one worth reading. I hope that I achieved this with *Jericho Hills*.

SANIA RIAZ
VIOLETS AND LILLIES

Sania Riaz is a 21-year-old student currently studying English Literature with Creative Writing. She enjoys writing thriller and suspense stories, as well as the occasional romantic comedy. Sania aspires to one day publish her own novel and work as a full time writer.

1. Growing up different

From the age of ten I knew there was something wrong with me. Most children would spend their time playing with trucks or dolls, and there I would be laying in the grass with my magnifying glass burning any ants that came into sight. There was something about the way they would react; first they would freeze unaware of their impending doom, then the 'sizzle' as the ray of sun pierced through their tiny shelled backs. Their squirming is what captivated me the most, it intrigued me how I was in control of their destiny without them even knowing. I had the power of life in my hands- like a God you could say.

God. God was involved in my life more than my own father was. Every Sunday we would go to Church and as always mother would sit on the front bench, and like always, I would beg her to sit a bench or two behind otherwise I would have to sit next to Mrs. Tessie. Mrs. Tessie was a large woman in her sixties with a bosom even larger than her behind, not that I looked often.

Whenever I sat beside Mrs. Tessie she would squeal and comment on how 'ravishing' I looked.

What does ravishing even mean?

Whilst everyone was finding their seats she would turn to me and ask me if I had found a girlfriend yet, and like a record on replay I would respond with "Not yet Mrs T, I'm only ten, and Mother says our eyes are only to read the Bible, not to glance at girls." Mrs T would laugh and turn away mumbling "A cute boy like you? You must be joking." But I wasn't. The truth is, I didn't like girls. All the boys in class would chase them during recess, trying to give them a peck on the cheek, but I always stayed inside and painted. Girls just didn't appeal to me.

Walking home from Church, mother would always ask me what I learnt and sarcastically I would reply "God is good and God is great." That always put a smile on her face, "That's right! Now remember, your eyes are *only* for the Bible!"

Mother needn't worry, my glance never fell on girls.

At school I was invisible, and to those who saw me, I was known as 'bug boy' with hair stuck up like antennas and eyes always roaming around searching for any possible danger. When it came to classes I always sat at the back to avoid any confrontation. I felt at peace knowing there was no one behind me that could harm me in any way.

"Okay class, we have a new girl joining us today, her name is Lilly and she is very shy. I hope you are all welcoming and make her feel comfortable. Toby, I would like you to be her partner and show her around."

Me? I had hardly spoken to anyone in school and now I would have to talk to a *girl?* What would I say to her? *How* would I speak to her?

An hour later Lilly arrived. She walked into class refusing to look up. Lilly was a short chubby girl with tanned skin and brown curly hair that bounced off her shoulders. She wore a purple cashmere sweater with ripped black jeans and red sneakers, there was something about her that fascinated me, but I couldn't put my finger on it.

Lilly and I got on extremely well, she wasn't shy, in fact, she was the opposite. She always knew what to say and without a doubt she would make me laugh until I had stitches in my stomach. I finally had a friend, someone who didn't think I was weird or that my hobbies were creepy, *and* she was a *girl!* Of course I never told mother about her because then we couldn't be friends, and I wanted Lilly to be my friend forever.

Five summer holidays passed and my friendship with Lilly had blossomed. We did everything together and there was never a secret about the other that we didn't know. As Lilly began to settle in with the rest of the class she made many new friends which made me jealous. Watching her talk and laugh with the others made me envious as I would never have the confidence to do such a thing.

I no longer burnt ants with a magnifying glass. I had moved on to spiders. We would set traps to catch them, and once caught, we would rip each leg off individually before squashing their bodies with a rock. Lilly told me that a quick death was not painful, so we were doing them a favour.

She was perfect! Everything I wanted in a friend and more.

After destroying any moving creatures we could find, Lilly and I lay on the grass,

"Why won't you tell your mom about me?" She said. "It's been five years and you haven't mentioned me once to her, and you always take me to the field furthest from your home. "

How could I tell her? Mother still told me that my eyes were for the Bible. She would never accept my friendship with Lilly. Even though it was completely innocent, it was impossible.

I explained to Lilly that my mother was extremely religious and that in her eyes, even a friendship between a boy and a girl was a sin. Lilly nodded and she seemed to understand. A few moments passed and she turned back to me to ask what I thought of the girls in our class.

"What do you think of Cindy? She's totally pretty right?"

"Meh."

"And Stacey, the way her hair is so long and glossy?"

"It's okay I guess."

"And Annabelle? All the boys have **major** crushes on her."

"Never took notice of her."

"And… what about me?"

I paused, confused by what she meant.

"Yeah, you're great."

"Great?"

"Yeah…great."

"Do you think I'm pretty T?"

"I think you're… appealing… I guess"

"What is going on with you?"

"Nothing! Nothing is wrong, stop asking me silly questions!"

One look at Lilly's face and I knew I had said something wrong. Why did she care if I thought she was pretty? Why did it matter to her?

Truthfully, over the past few months, I had been confused about who I was. Since I was a child I never saw girls the way all the other boys did. I never saw their long hair and big eyes as seductive, or their short skirts as a tease. I saw them for what they were, just girls. But when I looked at boys I felt something. Whenever Jacob Moore walked past me at school I couldn't help but stare. His chestnut hair combed back behind his ears, his strong jawline defining his tanned face, and his body already at least 6 feet tall, with his broad shoulders towering over anyone he spoke to. I was entranced by him.

At that moment I knew what I was: a sinner. And I knew no one would accept me, especially my mother.

2. Planting the first seed

After grasping what I was, I decided the only thing I could do was change myself. No one at school, church or home would accept a homosexual integrating with them, so I had to change. Since our last awkward encounter Lilly's behaviour towards me had changed. She no longer rushed to hug me at school, nor would she hold my arm as we walked through the fields. Instead she seemed shy and recluse, avoiding eye contact with me at all times.

As we sat near a willow tree, Lilly gave out a large sigh.

"Okay T… I have to tell you something or I will lose my mind. Ever since I met you I liked you. When we were just ten I knew I made a friend for life who I could always trust. Growing up I realised I felt more than a friendship bond with you, but I stayed quiet not wanting to ruin what we had. Now we're nearly sixteen and I just can't keep it hidden from you anymore. I love you Toby Parker, I really love you, you're different from the other boys, and that's what makes me love you... Say something then! Don't just stare at me! Tell me, do you feel the same way?"

I felt confused, unsure of how to respond. I always felt a strong connection with Lilly, just not a romantic one. I was attracted to boys, but I knew I could never be with one, that would remain a fantasy in my mind. Maybe if I dated Lilly I would forget my desires towards men and feel an attraction towards women? Surely if our friendship bond was strong, we would be stronger in a relationship. It had to work.

Looking back at Lilly I smiled, her hands were nervously rubbing against each other as she waited for my response.

"I love you too."

Dating Lilly was a lot harder than I had imagined, I never knew how sexual she could be and in some ways it frightened me. Any chance she got, she would slide her hands towards my crotch or nibble on my ears. I never pushed her away in the fear that she may ask why, but I never enjoyed it.

On my sixteenth birthday on the way home from school, Lilly asked if we could go to the fields to sit and talk, so I took her to our favourite spot near the willow tree. As I sat down Lilly jumped on top of me and sat in my lap, "I have a present for you, you're really gonna like it."

She began unbuttoning her shirt revealing a blue lace bra holding her swelling breasts. She moved my hands to her waist and told me to relax. Her physique had certainly changed from the first time I saw her, her chubby body was now slender and toned, her hips had widened creating the perfect hour glass figure that any boy would enjoy. Any boy but me.

As she removed her shirt she smirked at me and bit her lower lip, "this is all for you, birthday boy." She removed her bra and leaned in towards me, I was terrified, unaware of what to do next. I knew what she wanted, but I couldn't give it to her, not this way.

Lilly moved my hands and put them on her breasts, they were soft and bounced as she giggled and kissed my neck. Her hands began to unbutton my shirt and slowly moved towards my belt, she slid her hand into my trousers and I winced as I felt her grab my manhood. As I uncomfortably shifted, Lilly got off my lap and began to pull my trousers down.

"Why aren't you... you know?"

"What?"

"Enjoying this?"

"I am."

"Then why aren't you..."

She pointed to my crotch with a look of disappointment. It was clear I was not enjoying it as I showed no sign of arousal. Lilly stood up and put her shirt back on, "it's me isn't it? Is there something wrong with me? Am I not good enough? I thought you would have enjoyed this! Clearly I was stupid to think that!"

"No Lilly, it's not you... I just... I don't know how to explain it to you."

"I thought we could tell each other anything T, that we were best friends who never kept secrets from each other. Tell me! Please! I beg you."

"Okay... the truth is... I am attracted to boys. You are beautiful, but I just can't love you physically as I would a boy, I am so sorry, I never meant it to be like this."

"So you used me?" Her voice began to break, "you used me to try and hide the fact that you were gay? How could you?! How could you betray me like this, I thought we were friends and that you loved me, you are an evil person Toby!"

"No, it's not like that, I thought you would change me!"

"Change you? I can't change you, not like this! I can't believe you." Lilly began to cry "today you showed me that you were never my friend, and never will be, I will hurt you the way you hurt me, but a thousand times more. I'm going to tell your mom Toby, tell her exactly what you are!"

"No, you can't! Please!"

Lilly had already put her clothes back on and picked up her bag to leave, "and don't worry, I won't leave out any details. She will know all about you Toby Parker!"

Fear filled my body with adrenaline, suddenly I felt out of my own control and lunged towards her grabbing her by the neck.

"You will not say a word to my mother, I will make sure of that."

Lilly struggled trying to escape the strong grip I had on her neck. There was no way I could let her leave knowing my secret, she would tell Mother and my life would be over. Lilly's skin had gone from tanned to a light shade of violet. She was still trying to push me away but it was no use. Looking around I saw a large rock. Grabbing it with my free hand I lifted it above her and slammed it down on her head. There was an eerie silence as Lilly stopped trying to push me away. I fell back, looking at the sin I had just committed, but it was okay, because as Lilly said, a quick death was not a painful one, so I was doing her a favour.

Looking down at Lilly's lifeless body I regained my senses. What had I done? How could I do such a thing? She was my best friend and I murdered her! If anyone found out, I would be sent to jail. Mother would live her life in shame. I couldn't do that to her. Lilly made me react that way, she gave me no choice. Looking around I tried to plan what I could do to hide Lilly's body. I couldn't just bury her, that would be too obvious. There was no way I could hide her in our house, someone would surely find her. As I paced the fields I saw a small shed we kept next to our farm, inside was a furnace that we used to burn large materials. That would have to do. I dragged Lilly's body to the shed constantly looking over my shoulders in case someone had seen me, but no one had. My forehead was dripping with sweat as I lifted her body. She was a lot heavier than I had imagined. Looking into the furnace all I could see were red flames. The thought of what would happen to Lilly's body sent shivers down my spine. But I had no choice. Lifting her body over my shoulders I pushed her in and she fell with a loud thud. Sparks shot out the furnace as the sound of sizzling and crackling filled the room. I couldn't bear to stand inside as the smell had become noxious.

I re-entered the shed once more thirty minutes later and looked into the furnace – all that remained was a large heap of ashes.

I picked up the remains and put them into the nearest box I could find. After cleaning out the furnace I picked up the box and headed back to our home. As I approached the front door I tried to plan where I would hide the ashes, then it occurred to me… our garden of course.

Our garden had always been a mess as no one bothered to clean it. The grass was overgrown and filled with junk. I immediately began picking up rubbish and cleaned out all the mess. After what seemed like forever, all the junk was gone and I began cutting the grass and trimming the bushes. Our garden looked completely different, as though it did not belong to us.

Then it was time to plant Lilly.

Mother always kept a box in the garden filled with flower seeds. I decided it would only be suitable to plant Lily seeds in Lilly's memory so I picked up a few packets. After digging a hole at the back of our garden I scattered Lilly's ashes and planted the seeds on top of them. Every day I would return to water them and soon enough my Lillies had begun to grow strong and beautiful. Even mother praised me on my hard work and told me that she had never seen flowers so beautiful and sturdy.

I couldn't believe it; an incident so awful had created something so perfect. I felt a sense of pride for what I had done. It gave me a rush that I had never felt before.

3. Addiction

Four years passed since Lilly's death, and everyone assumed that she had run away. I was pleased that there were no suspicions towards me and even 'helped' the search party look for her.

The Lily flowers I planted remained sturdy and beautiful as ever. People would come from far and wide to see 'the flowers that never died'. During winter, they remained bright and not once did they wither. I had found my calling.

Although my flowers were beautiful, I wanted more of them, I wanted all of my garden full of flowers that people all around the world would talk about. Mother told me to plant some more as I had done before, but I knew the secret behind why they were so strong. When I planted the Lily seeds in the ashes I felt a rush I had never felt before. I felt powerful and in control, and over these past four years, I could not stop thinking about it. I knew it was wrong. But if something so beautiful could come from it, surely it couldn't be that bad? I had to plant more flowers. But how?

I was approaching twenty years old and Mother told me I had to attend college no matter what. The thought of going to college made me anxious. I never enjoyed school so it was impossible that I would enjoy college. As I was reaching adulthood Mothers attitude towards me began to change. She would constantly ask me when I was looking to settle down, or if I had taken a liking to anyone. All my life she had told me my eyes were only for the Bible, and now she wanted me to settle down? Deep down I knew that would never happen and that angered me even more.

Once I had gotten used to college I truly realised how people my age behaved. Boys and girls were constantly running after each other. The smell of promiscuity filled the walls of our dormitories. I could not believe the amount of sinning that occurred in a place supposedly made for education. Nonetheless, I remained alone in my dorm avoiding any contact with the others as much as I could.

One night as I lay in bed I received a phone call from mother telling me there was to be a county fair. All the people from our town could enter showing off their famous gardens. I knew I had a chance of winning if my garden was filled with more flowers, but how could I? I had already used up all of Lilly's ashes. I had to make more.

From that moment onwards I became more sociable, speaking to anyone who approached me and attending all the awful parties. Once in a while I would hook up with a girl who would inevitably leave disappointed. When her clothes were removed, I would go into a state of panic and not finish what I had started.

The summer before our first year ended I decided to throw a party at our farm to lure in as many people as I could. Mother seemed hesitant at first, but after many days of pleading, she gave in.

Preparations were in full swing as I ordered plenty of food and alcohol as well as the local band.

The night of my party arrived and people turned up in the masses. Boys and girls from my college that I had never seen before entered my home.

It appeared that my party was a success as my home was filled with the sound laughter and music. Something that I had never heard before. As I walked through the farm I saw people running to and fro enjoying themselves with drinks in their hands. I felt a sense of pride, I was throwing a party and everyone was enjoying it, I just couldn't believe it. As I smiled walking back into my home my eyes caught sight of the Lily flowers and I was reminded of the real reason for my party. I was not to be distracted like that again.

It was now 3am and the party was coming to an end, people began to leave, some without their shoes, some without their clothes, most without their dignity. As they entered their taxi's thanking me for the 'awesome party' I waved them goodbye and went to my garden. Most people had gone home but a few remained. As I walked to my Lily patch, I saw that a group of two girls and a boy were sitting beside them. They seemed to be amazed at how tall the flowers were, but it was most likely the alcohol. They looked up at me and complimented me on how well I had maintained my garden. I thanked them and asked if they wanted to get another drink. Of course, they did not decline and we headed back to my kitchen. As I filled their glasses to the brim I noticed the boy staring at me. He introduced himself as Bart Dixon and his friends as Alice Draper and Violet Maddison - they were exchange students from England.

As the drinks kept flowing Bart and I got to know each other and I was perplexed at how confident he was with his sexuality. He told me he was an openly gay man and his two female friends were also attracted to the same sex. As I looked over to them I was shocked at the sight of them kissing and pressing their bodies close together- mother would be enraged. Looking back at Bart he had now moved closer to me and was eying me up and down. My heart was pounding in my chest as he moved his lips to mine and pulled my waist closer to his. I felt his erection against me and could feel myself slowly submitting to him as we passionately began to kiss. A moment later the thought of my mother entered my mind and I pushed Bart away surprising him and shocking the girls.

"What the fuck - why did you push me away?!"

"I shouldn't be doing this, I'm sorry."

"Seriously mate, you need to lighten up."

They were laughing and calling me frigid as they left the room heading for the front door.

"Wait! I shouted. "I'm sorry, let me make it up to you, don't leave just yet."

They looked back at me and then at each other. Reluctantly they decided to stay and followed me to the fields. The three of them walked timidly behind me as I led them into the cabin. It was now 4am and the sky had turned into a mixture of black and purple. Clouds moved ahead showing signs of rain as the trees blew gently in the wind.

As I went to light the fireplace the two girls went and sat on the sofa together whilst Bart came up behind me and kissed the back of my neck. Why was everyone so sexual? Their lack of self-control sickened me. I had to play them at their own game. It was the only way I could gain control.

Looking around my cabin they asked why it was filled with so many tools. I was amazed at how stupid college students could be, and told them that because I live on a farm we did a lot of agricultural work, so the tools came in handy.

As everyone got comfortable I knew that it was the right time to set my plan in action.

"So I've heard of this game you play, where everyone sits in a circle and spins a bottle. If the bottle ends up facing you, you go into a dark closet with the person and you make out, or more, for 2 minutes. Shall we give it a try?"

Of course, the girls were over the moon that I suggested such an idea and squealed at the thought of a game so full of mystery. I spun the bottle and it landed facing Violet. She giggled and said that a boy who looked so feminine couldn't be that different from a girl. I got up and walked towards the closet knowing this would no longer be a painful challenge. As she entered the closet I looked at her skinny body under the unflattering satin mini-dress she wore and dreaded the thought of kissing her. As she leaned in towards me I switched off the light and grabbed the nearest shovel head I could find. Her breath reeked of alcohol and as she moved her hand towards my crotch my first impulse was to swing the shovel against her head. There was a thud as she fell to the ground. Unsure if she had died or not I swung the shovel against her head a few more times, ensuring she would not wake up. As I walked out of the closet

Alice asked me where Violet had gone. I told her that Violet did not feel well and was calling for her. Alice then entered the closet as I shut the door behind us. Looking at Violet's limp body on the ground Alice turned to me in shock. Before she could say a word I struck the shovel against her head and she too fell to the ground. By this time Bart had become impatient and wanted to know what all the noise was about. I grabbed a rake and just as he opened the door I pierced it into his stomach.

That morning I planted all the violet seeds in my garden with the enormous pile of ashes I had created.

4. Emily

Death - the act of dying, the end of life; the total and permanent cessation of all the vital functions of an organism. All that my life constantly revolved around.

A few months after I graduated college Mother passed away. After burying her, I visited Mother's grave every weekend and knew that my garden was all that was left for me, and I was never going to let it go.

Mother's dying wish was to 'see her boy settle down' so I got into a relationship with a woman named Emily. Emily and I did not get along, she despised me as much as I despised her. But she never left the relationship out of fear.

My garden was now the equivalent of heaven on earth and had won countless awards for its beauty. There was one remaining space which I had saved for Emily, but with Emily her death would have to be different. Emily was an intelligent woman who, although I was not fond of, I had grown accustomed to. We were very similar.

Emily's death took one week of planning.

Monday morning

Emily woke up at 7:45 for her daily shower, drank her coffee and left the house. On her journey to work, she stopped by the local post office to see if her parents had written back to her; as usual, there was no response and she continued on her way to work.

Monday morning

I woke up at 6am and made my way to the post office. As always, I retrieved the letters from Emily's parents and disposed of them.

Tuesday evening

Emily prepared dinner as the doorbell rang, she answered the door and found a large bouquet of flowers addressed to her. Smiling she found a vase and filled it with water. Emily loved flowers.

Tuesday afternoon

I arranged for flowers to be sent to Emily's home: chrysanthemums, a large bouquet, her favourite.

Wednesday evening

The phone rang and Emily answered, she heard a faint voice and made it out to be her mother's. Immediately, the phone was disconnected and all sound was muted.

Wednesday evening

I tapped into Emily's phone line waiting for someone to call, at 6:52 the phone rang and it was her mother. She pleaded for Emily to return home and leave her 'psycho boyfriend'. However, by this time, I had disconnected Emily's phone and she was unaware of all that her mother had said.

Thursday night

The neighbours were awoken by yet another argument between Emily and I. A loud thud was heard and all became silent.

Thursday night

I accused Emily of deception and we fell into an argument. Irritated, I slammed her against the wall and proceeded to kick her into unconsciousness.

Friday evening

Emily laid the table for dinner as I decided we would 'move out' together later tonight after we had eaten.

Friday evening

I prepared dinner as Emily packed her suitcase and penned a letter to her parents telling them of our decision…

~o~

My initial idea when writing 'Violets and Lilies' was to show how a child growing up questioning his sexuality could be affected, especially when surrounded by religion and doubts. I wanted to pick up on how an insecurity can trigger someone into doing things they would never have imagined doing.

When writing chapter one (*Growing up different*), I wanted to include different aspects of Toby's life. Due to this, I started the story with Toby aged ten, showing his naivety, then switching to age 15 where he had begun to question everything around him. By including Lilly in his life I felt that the reader would be able to see his innocence change from burning bugs for fun, to mutilating them with no remorse.

Looking at chapter two (*Planting the first seed*), I wanted to show a development in Toby's character. By this point my aim was to show that he had slightly matured and accepted that he was gay. However, I also wanted to show his innocence as he thought he would be able to 'change' himself into a straight boy.

The idea of a strong male figure preying on 'weak' women would come across as misogynistic and stereotypical. For this reason, I twisted the story into the idea that Toby was extremely insecure with himself, and when approached by women, he did not know how to react. Because of this insecurity with his sexuality, he could not control his anger and his mental stability weakened.

When writing about how Toby would hide Lilly's body, I had many ideas but felt they were too gruesome and would not appeal to every reader's taste. So I decided that as he lived on a farm, I would include the machinery and equipment in the murder, as it would allow the reader to imagine the scenes and the farm he lived on. When deciding what Toby would do with the ashes, I once again wanted to incorporate his lifestyle and farm into the story, so I decided on planting flowers in the ashes. I felt that the contrast between something seen as natural and beautiful being buried in something so unnatural and creepy would give the story an eerie presence without being too gruesome.

I did not want Toby to become a cliché (lonely boy turned psychopath) so regardless of him being antisocial, I thought it would be best to show him living a normal life and going to college. Despite the fact that he has sexual inclinations towards men, he still despises the act of sex, showing that his religious upbringings still affect him to this day.

In my fourth chapter (*Emily*), my aim was to show Toby as a real psychopath. When planning Emily's death, I changed the structure of the story (where he explained what was happening each day of the week). I felt it would be more cold and methodical showing the switch in how his brain now worked.

BEN RAMSEY
CYANOPHOBIA

Ben has been writing for four years, and hopes to go into writing for television and radio as a future career. His inspirations are Douglas Adams and Steven Moffat, and is currently studying at the University of Salford. In 2015, he won the under 18s section of the Walter Swan playwriting competition with his play *Following Orders*, about the events and aftermath of the Vietnam war.

Cyanophobia. Noun. The irrational fear of the colour blue.

Blue. It was everywhere. The sky, the sea, the horizon, everywhere he went, everywhere he looked. Blue. No matter how hard he tried, how far he ran or deep he hid, it was always there, always waiting for him. Blue. The colour of his friends' eyes and families' tears. The colour of his books, his door, his clothes, his food, his everything. It was in everything. It was everything. Blue.

He woke as uncomfortable as he had slept. Hands clasped firmly over his eyes, arms folded before his face and legs tucked up to his chin. Slowly he pulled his arms away from his face, letting the morning light fill his eyes, flooding them with radiance. He blinked painfully, the scene before him just a hazy blur.

His first leg fell out of the makeshift bed, soon joined by the other one. His hands collapsed onto his knees, bracing him and propping his body up like an errant marionette. As he swallowed, his mouth, having been starved of any hydration all night, clenched and rasped sorely. Sooner or later, he'd have to face it. He'd rather later than sooner.

On the floor beside him was a pair of glasses, tinted with rose-shaded lenses. Feeling around for them, he turned his gaze towards them. Just in the corner of the frame, he saw the reflection of the window. He'd forgotten to close it last night, the idiot! And now, in the glasses, he could see the outside.

Blue.

His breathing was the first to go. His chest convulsed, growing tighter and tighter until not even the shallowest of breath could escape. His eyes filled in a harsh red blaze, consuming everything around him. His senses shut off, everything from touch to smell to sound fading away from him. He fell to the floor, panting harshly and rapidly. Blue. It was all around him.

The first day had been the hardest. He had woken as he normally had, restful and refreshed from a good night's sleep. He had practically leapt out of the bed, strolling leisurely towards the window. His hands had grasped the thick linen curtains and pulled them open.

He was met with a pure sky of beautiful blue, dotted with the occasional cloud here and there, a bright sun beaming out over the surroundings.

And it almost killed him.

By the time he'd come to, it was gone noon. What had just happened? A fit? A seizure? He felt fine now...

He rolled across the floor to his feet, staggering clumsily into the hallway.

On the wall before him was a picture. It had been there for years, ever since a drunken friend had bought it for him as a last-minute Christmas present. 'Whitby at Dusk,' it was called.

It was a marvellous little painting of a seaside resort, with a boat just off the horizon and fishermen drawing in nets by the docks. And across every corner of the canvas was the sea, painted in a lovely shade of...

He keeled over again, squeezing his eyes shut, desperate to press out even the remotest hint of it. His hand shot out instinctively, meeting the picture and knocking it from the hook. It clattered against the ground with a smash.

What was wrong with him? Why was this happening? Fervently he cast his mind back, searching for an explanation.

By now, he was well used to the experience. But that didn't make it any more tolerable. Each time it happened, it was as horrendous, as terrifying as the first. And it always would be.

All of the windows in his home had been boarded up, save for the one in his bedroom. Through trial and error, he had discovered that, at night, it was safe to look out at the world beyond his safety, at the endless black, grey and white. He could look as far and as long as he wished, and he wouldn't see a single glimpse of-

He couldn't even phone for help. That had been his first instinct; police, ambulance, fire brigade, anything! But he could even come close.

As he stumbled into the living room, still-half blind from the ordeal, he fumbled around for the phone. In the exact same second he opened his eyes to look for it, he realised his error. It was that colour. A strangled cry dragged out of his lungs as he fell forwards, colliding with the phone on the way.

There was a brief crash, and a few crunching sounds. And then the phone was no more. He was alone.

Outside his kitchen window was a pile of crockery, a pile of shattered plates, mugs and bowls, just where he couldn't see them. On that first day, back before the roots of his affliction had dug into his mind, he'd been naïve enough to decide to eat.

Acting purely on instinct, he'd opened a cupboard and reached for a plate. And one of the plates, a pure shade of cobalt, had sent him back down to the floor, gagging for futile breath.

Eyes tightly pulled shut, he reached for the window, unhooking it and throwing it as wide as possible. With one hand over his eyes, the other grabbed at the offending articles and flung them towards the window, hearing the discordant crashes and smashes as they landed unceremoniously.

At last, he was able to eat and drink. He gulped down the first few glasses of water only slightly slower than he could pour them. As he slammed the glass down for the fifth or sixth time, he realised his mistake.

In the curve of the glass, the whole kitchen behind him had been reflected. The chairs, the cupboard... the window.

The fear had grasped him, its tendrils wrapped around him as if squeezing him for juice. He had clawed at his chest, hoping to tear the terror out of him, rip it from his body and leave it behind forever.

Atephobia. Noun. The irrational fear of ruins. Iatrophobia. Noun. The irrational fear of doctors. Ombrophobia. Noun. The irrational fear of rain. Elurophobia. Noun. The irrational fear of cats.

Why couldn't it have been any of those? They would have been impractical, yes, kindling building towards a fire, but they would have been manageable. But this... this was beyond his imagination. Beyond where even his most fevered nightmares had dared to tread.

Every day, he found new fears, infinite other ways he could have been punished. Athazagoraphobia. Noun. The irrational fear of being forgotten. Enetophobia. Noun. The irrational fear of pins. Pupaphobia. Noun. The irrational fear of puppets.

If he had the chance, he would have chosen one of them, any of them, in a heartbeat. He was too terrified to even leave his own home, to venture into the outside world, just in case it found him again.

Rupophobia. Noun. The irrational fear of dirt. Genuphobia. Noun. The irrational fear of knees.

But he knew he didn't have that choice. He knew that, no matter how hard he prayed, how long he begged, sobbed and screamed, it would stay with him, until his last breath, until his dying days. Forever.

Phobophobia. Noun. The irrational fear of phobias.

Grimacing as he did so, he slipped on the glasses, letting the rose lenses shield his eyes. It was a blessing that he even had the things. The belongings of a slightly mad aunt, sent to him after her passing and otherwise forgotten about. But in his desperation, the memory of them had come to him.

He rummaged through the box, tossing aside books, jewellery, other random bric-a-brac that had been flung together seemingly without rhyme or reason. And at the bottom, covered in dust and slightly scratched on one lens, were the glasses.

They didn't hide it completely. At most, they dulled the pain, reduced the colour to a calmer shade. He knew it was out there. It would always be out there, waiting to pounce at him and attack. It still ate at him, but it at least this way, he could cope.

He was still trapped in his house, though. It was the only safe haven he had, the only place he could be sure, absolutely certain that he wouldn't find any of-

It had been his favourite colour. Before... this had happened, he'd loved everything about it. The various shades, the way it always seemed to help calm him, soothe him in times of trouble. All throughout his house was countless azures, cobalts, teals, cyans, ceruleans, lapis, navies, aegeans, more shades than he could name or remember.

As best he could, all of them had been removed, either hidden from sight or simply thrown from the house. And so, as a result, his home had become barren, bleak, devoid of any life or love it once had possessed. It was practically dead. A mausoleum.

Every time he saw it, it reminded him of his curse. Every bare wall, blank space and empty crevice sent thoughts of his burden rushing into his mind. The whole time he was awake, he was aware of it. And whenever he was asleep, his mind was intent on dreaming up even worse horrors.

On the table in the living room was a dictionary, bound in gorgeous red leather and filled with crinkled yellow pages. It had cost him a fortune when he had first bought it, and now he was getting his money's worth.

All day, every day, he'd pour over it, scanning through each word, finding new phobias and fears he could imagine. Soon enough, they were all he could think about – he couldn't take a drink without imagining the hydrophobia; he couldn't eat without thinking of sitiophobia; even the dictionary itself brought to mind bibliophobia.

The fears had started to consume his life, swallowing him whole. And every time, it would come back to his own phobia, his own menace that would hound at his heels and follow him wherever he went. It was like a spectre, hanging over his shoulder, weighing down around his neck to impede his movements and weary his body.

No matter how long he lasted, or how much he could take, one thing was certain. It would be with him for the rest of his life.

The silence was almost unbearable. Every day, he'd be alone in the house; every day, there'd be silence. As even the slightest mention would send him into cold sweats, he stopped all music and broadcasts immediately. Nobody came to see him anymore – if their eyes were the wrong colour, he couldn't bring himself to look them in the face at all. He was alone, and the silence only went to show it.

There wasn't any more knocks at the door, or footsteps in a different room. There was nothing to break the solitude, to provide some relief. He was alone with his fear.

Red, he had found, often calmed him down. As far from the source of his panic as he could get, it would bring him back to normal, or as close as he could get.

It was the sunset at night, heralding the end of another day he'd survived, the departure of that damned colour from his world. It was the colour of the clothes he now wore; of the food he now ate. It was the colour of the blood that trickled from his body whenever the panic got too much. A momentary flash of pain, and then the relief brought by that blessed crimson flow. Scratches, nicks, cuts and grazes were littered up and down his body, wherever he could reach at a moment's notice.

He had stormed through what little supplies of food he still had over the last few… days? Weeks? He couldn't tell how long it had been. The affliction seemed to change time, making it feel both as long as a lifetime yet no longer than a moment at once.

Whatever food he had left after his purges, it was slowly diminishing. Any that wasn't decaying he was eating, and any that was he avoided. Sooner or later, he had realised, there wouldn't be any food left. And then what? He had a choice. Brave the outside world, risk abject terror, or remain in his safety and die ignominiously.

He still had some time left to decide. But no matter what he did, that choice would eventually come. And then he would have to go one way or the other – confront his curse or pay the penalty.

Perhaps just trying would finish him off. Perhaps walking in a world with it surrounding him, with it endlessly above him and ready to pounce every way he glanced. Perhaps dying quietly, safe for a short while and then forever, would be the better option. Perhaps.

Could he? It would mean accepting defeat, to confirm once and for all that his curse had bested him, eroded him down until he was nothing. And no matter how terrifying the prospect might be, how much the thought of it nagged at his mind, he knew he would have to face it. He knew he would either fight his curse or die trying. He knew he would make it.

The glasses rested on his hands, which trembled beneath them. They would be his shield, his only protection against the horrors before him. It was a fool's gambit, of course; the slightest tremor or shake would mean the end for him.

But he had no choice.

It was even in his memories. A school trip to the seaside, a family picnic, a shirt he wore to his graduation. The happiest moments of his life were now tainted with it. Singed with the flames of his terror, forever.

This is what the rest of your life will be like, his mind told him. The same rancid memories, only yet to happen, cast in stone before he could even comprehend them.

What sort of a life would that be? A pale imitation of what it could have been. A mere shadow of its former self. Nothing. Everything was muted, dulled, numbed away from him drib by drab. That's why this curse had been chosen for him; this fear, of all possible ones. It wouldn't just take away his colour, or his home, or his safety.

It would take away his life.

Slowly and surely he positioned the glasses before his eyes. The sight of the red calmed him somewhat, but it still wouldn't be enough. For a brief moment, he scoffed at the thought. Seeing red. A phrase often associated with rage, or terror, or hysteria. But now, it would be his calm, his serenity.

Just the thought of it was enough to worry him. He held himself up against the door, slamming his eyes shut. Red. Think of red. Desperate, he opened one eye, looking down at his open palm. Cobwebs of veins and arteries ran just beneath the skin; which was which? He must have been told in school, but the memory evaded him.

The key was pulled from his pocket, the jagged edge placed towards his hand. He jabbed it forwards, pressing the sharp metal into the flesh. It stung as the flesh tore open, and then a soft stream of blood flowed free. Red. He was safe. He would be safe. As long as he had his beloved red, he would be safe.

The glasses were in place. He blinked once or twice, adjusting to the sensation. Taking in deep, soothing breath, he blew out his cheeks. It was now or never, he told himself.

One or two droplets of blood fell to the ground as he curled his hand into a fist, pressing on the cut. It would distract him if nothing else.

With his spare hand, he unlocked the door, before twisting the handle. The tumblers clicked as one, the only sound in the house echoing seemingly forever off of the walls and floors.

He felt himself shudder. The door creaked as it opened, sunlight casting over him. Despite the tinted glasses, he winced, his eyes still failing to adapt to the sunlight. Like a vampire, he told himself. More dead than alive.

One foot stepped through the door, and then the other. He took a second footstep outside, followed by a third and then a fourth. The door swung shut behind him. He was doing it. He had no idea how, but he was doing it.

It wasn't easy. It would never be easy. That's what he had to keep telling himself, what he would always be telling himself.

Maybe one day, he could make it as far as he wanted and back home again. Maybe he could live in the world of viridian and periwinkle and zaffre and sapphire without fear. It would always be in this world, he told himself. No matter how much he avoided it, it would always find him.

But he had a chance. He'd made it this far; he was stood in the world once more, eyes shielded and muscles tensed. And for the rest of his life, for as long as he would be able to remember, all above him, all around him, would be incredible, wonderful, astounding, beautiful…

…blue.

~o~

It was a weird experience writing this story. It came together from a few different ideas – one using a curse as a metaphor for depression, another about all the different phobias. Some elements came, no pun intended, out of the blue as

I was writing, such as the colour red being comforting, which then lead to the blood scene. I didn't even reveal the name of the main character, which helps both make the story more relatable, and avoids getting it bogged down in exposition and backstory. Overall, I'm pleased with how it turned out, and hope you enjoy reading it as much as I did writing it.

ISABEL MARTIN
PATIENT

Isabel Martin is originally from London and is currently a second year student at the University of East Anglia. She grew up with a love of reading, filling countless notebooks with stories, and was eventually inspired to study Literature with Creative Writing. After graduating, she hopes to pursue a career in the publishing world whilst continuing to write stories of her own.

1

You enter the park. The gate swings shut behind you, the guttural clank of metal on metal resonating through your skull. How many times have you walked through that gate? Thousands, probably. But you never noticed until now how loud it was.

You need a rest, a break, a chance to get out of the house. Not that you do much anymore, so you're not sure what exactly it is you're taking a break from. Still resting. The change of scene doesn't seem to have had much of an effect on you. You're just cold.

Kids are on the pitch that you and your mates trampled at their age. Scruffy-haired boys with muddy shins, their names and faces long forgotten now. The children shriek into the sunset, their silhouettes chasing the black dot that bounces across the grass.

A dog charges past you, Frisbee caught between its jaws. You had a dog once, but it died. Cancer.

Your mother told you it was sent to live on a farm. You were four, and you believed her.

You had decided that you wanted to live on the farm, too.

You watch the dog recede into the distance.

You locate an empty bench. Sit down. Breathe. Groan, as quietly as possible.

You taught kids here once, when you volunteered at the holiday camp. They boasted about your contributions years later.

A woman passes you, toddler hanging on to her hand. She glances back at you over her shoulder, and you grit your teeth. She recognises you, but she can't quite place you.

You close your eyes. The light makes your head throb. You don't spend much time in the sunshine any more.

"Mummy, why is that man asleep?"

"Don't point, darling, it's not polite."

You do not open your eyes. You listen to the child's voice piping away down the path, and you are still, staring into your eyelids. You stare for so long that you forget the blackness is there; it merges into one blind spot. Maybe this is what death looks like.

The pain is still sawing at your brain, but the medication would just make it worse. It clouds your head, stops you thinking straight.

You hear the battering of wings, and open one eye. A seagull has stopped to investigate, but takes off once you shift position. There in one breath, then gone.

You wish you'd brought a jacket. You wonder how long you have to spend here for it to "do you good".

Your phone buzzes, but you ignore it. The kids from the pitch are filtering out of the gate now, and the day has dimmed. You contemplate standing up. You groan internally. You heave yourself to your feet. Your legs never used to shake like this. You look at the empty football pitch. You sigh. You walk away.

2

I keep tripping because the floor is all squeaky and slippy. Mummy hasn't been in any of the rooms, I think she went home in the car and left me maybe. She will be cross because I ran away, I didn't mean to be naughty but the needle was massive and I didn't want it in my arm, all sharp and digging. Maybe I missed my injection time and I can go home now. She said it isn't meant to hurt you, it's to protect you against nasty diseases. But it can't be good if it hurts, so I think maybe she made a mistake.

There's posters with people looking worried and there are funny words and sometimes the people look happy maybe because the doctor made them better but it's all wrong because I'm lost and they're laughing at me.

I want to shout out for her but I might start crying and then they will laugh at me and I can't cry because I'm not a baby, I'm five and I have to find her before the hospital closes and I get locked in.

My throat is all funny and hot, like my breath is trying to run away, and I feel all watery and like I want to make a big noise but I can't. I can't.

There are footsteps but they're like shuffling, Mummy's feet go tap tap tap.

"Are you all right, sweetheart?"

That's a lady and she's smiling at me, I haven't seen her before but I think she's a doctor because she has a card with her picture on it and she's wearing the funny necklace they use to listen to your heart. I don't think she's meant to be wearing it now, maybe she forgot to take it off. I have to be careful in case she secretly has a needle in her pocket but I don't think I will mind if she listens to my heart, I just don't want a sore poked arm.

She asks me if I am lost and I nod my head yes. She holds my hand like Mummy does and that makes me feel sad but I don't know why. She takes me to a big desk and there is Mummy looking all messy and annoyed like when she's trying to do work and I want to play. When she sees me she makes this big breath like the wind going *whoooo* and shakes my shoulders but not hard, and then she gives me a hug and I can feel my chest going back to normal. Like something was squeezing all the time but now it's letting me go. She says: you had me worried sick. It's a funny thing to say in a hospital when there are doctors and lots of sick people. I say can we go home and she says promise me you won't run away again, and I say I promise.

3

The waiting room is a wash of blue, a desperate reach for tranquillity: blue chairs spilling their foam upholstery, a faded seascape hung lopsidedly on the peeling wallpaper, a chipped blue plant pot.

The plant is dying.

There is a murmur of whispered conversations, with no real reason for the hush.

Besides a stack of mismatched pamphlets, crumpled magazines are strewn across the little table in front of you: celebrity gossip of two summers ago; a torn electronics magazine; copies of Gardening Weekly. People steal the good ones, apparently.

Questions about cancer?

You snort, and the woman opposite you glances up.

The word patient originally meant "one who suffers". It was Greek, or Latin, or something. You don't remember.

Patience is a virtue, and yours is being worn thin. You can always rely on the doctor to be late. Have patience, patient. You almost smile.

The little girl's heels scuff the leg of her chair, dangling at least a foot above the floor. She rubs one ear of the threadbare rabbit squashed within the crook of her elbow.

"How many?"

"One's more than enough, Emily – do you want to have false teeth when you're older?"

The child sticks out her bottom lip. "Four."

"*Four?*"

"Five."

"Don't be silly, sweetheart!"

"For my age – one two three four *five*." She beams.

"I'll let you have two treats, how does that sound? Now, are you ready to be a brave girl and get your injection done?"

The mother glances at you, smiles, rolls her eyes knowingly. You stare blankly at her, and she falters, dropping her gaze. Your mouth twitches in a delayed attempt at a compensatory smile.

You wonder how many sweets you would get for being brave.

An obnoxious little ping sounds from your mobile. The tinny vibration sends sharp twinges to the back of your eyes, scraping against your sockets.

Five missed calls.

People spare a thought for you every now and then, remember that you exist. The sad friend, the dying friend, the object of their pity. They think of you occasionally, think that they ought to make the most of you while you're still there. You switch off your phone, stuff it into your pocket.

Your name flashes up on the panel on the wall, as the first brutal twinge snaps at your chest. It makes your head spin, the few paces to the surgery.

You should be honest about how bad it's getting, but what good would it do? They'll just prescribe you more drugs. More and more drugs to clog the dregs of your mind. They can't save you.

You glance at the scans on the desk, the illness mapped out like spilled ink. It seems to cover most of your body at this point. You're not hearing the words spilling from the doctor's mouth. It's time to start thinking about more effective pain relief. You have to understand that these are often life-shortening, but the *quality* of life will increase significantly. We have to be thinking about balance at this time.

Will you consider the options over the week?

You want to go to bed, to lie there until your heart finally splutters to a halt.

You pass the child again on your way out, still happily babbling about sweets. And then pain.

It is a supernova, clamping down on your heart, your head. It seizes you, gripping your chest, pummelling your brain as your legs shake, spasm, and suddenly your limbs are knocking against the floor and there is nothing but darkness, and alarms, and shrill voices, a wailing child and the thud of running feet, so many of them, and

4

It is never an easy thing, losing a patient.

He had become numb to the fact that he was dying. He had been terminal for months. He gritted his teeth and ploughed through each day.

She knew who he was, of course. She recognised his face the first time he walked into her surgery.

She had slyly Googled his name later that afternoon.

He was a footballer, once. It was hard to imagine, the way his disease consumed him now.

If he had been in one of the bigger teams, the press wouldn't have left him alone. It's fortunate for him, really, that he retired years ago.

It's hardest for the loved ones, usually, but he has – *had* – no family that she needs to tell. She had pitied him, but in a strange, perverse way she can't help feeling that it is a blessing. It is an impossible feat, having to wrench the hope from the tear-stained relatives, having to tell them what they know already, somehow. They are the ones who will feel the weight of the loss, the blow that strikes again, and again.

He was always alone. She asked him, once, whether he would like to have somebody there with him for his next appointment. Somebody you trust, she had said. A friend, or relative, or - ? He had snorted, and she had not asked him again.

Nobody to tell. She straightens the file on the desk.

"I'm afraid Anthony has passed away," she informs the empty room.

Her gaze lingers over his file. Gently, she closes the cover.

~o~

I am fascinated by the concepts of time and mortality, and wanted to explore these themes with highly contrasting perspectives; those of a terminally ill ex-footballer and a small child terrified of having an injection. The story centres around pain and endurance on different scales and in writing it I hoped to overlap these very different lives – a child who has his whole life ahead of him, and a man who is disconnected from the world, exhausted by his illness – too exhausted, in fact, to tell his own story, which is narrated in the second person. I set this in contrast with the childlike stream of consciousness which follows, and ended the story from the perspective of the doctor, the only person who truly knows Anthony now that he has cut himself off from the world. The final piece of narrative was intended as a feeble attempt on the part of the doctor to achieve some sense of closure, with some small acknowledgement of the death of a man who has nobody to mourn him.

LAUREN WILSON
KALE LEAVES

Lauren is nineteen years old, born in Essex and currently in her first year studying History and English Literature at Bangor University. She enjoys travelling; spending a couple of months in Ghana volunteering early in 2016. She has had an interest in literature since she was young and intends to continue writing as much as she can in the foreseeable future.

In a world full of Kardashians and kale leaves, embrace your appeal as a sexy, smart, sophisticated spud. Be the potato among troops of spinach and detox drinks, skinny lattes and diet soda.

That's what I tell myself when I leave the house. As I look in the mirror and beam rather majestically at myself. You *are* exactly what you want to be. Potatoes aside, I'm looking pretty damn fine.

I'm twenty-five. Tall, curves in all the wrong places, short sighted and naturally blonde. Now, after years of bleaching and chemical warfare on my locks, I'm more of a dreaded brunette, with some fluffy stray strands glinting a nice swamp-green in the sunlight. Dull beads and old gold hoops wrap and curl around my matted hair and overall, I'm feeling rather avant-garde.

I'm selling myself, I know, but it's best to get the worst out of the way during our first interaction, don't you think?

No 'I didn't realise she wore makeup' or 'she looked different under the layers of silk and chiffon' type things. This way, you're not going into this with any false expectations. You, with your big eyeballs, scanning across my life as though it's a page in a book.

I don't, thankfully, have spots; never have. I did, however, have a nice big shiny forehead and pearly whites forced together with tracks of gleaming metal as a youngster, so I didn't miss out on much.

As a late developer, I had a beer belly before I had breasts, and while most of my fat has disappeared into the void, I can just never shake off the few extra pounds. I have more important things to focus my time on, like eating a family size packet of pasta in one sitting. A few of my friends, Daisy and Heather for example, would describe me as rather 'dead end'. Lovely people, they are. You'll soon learn that most of my friends are named after rather beautiful flowers, while my name, Lilith, is reference to a demon. It's a conversation starter, at least.

I own a shitty flat in London, where I can only afford the rent because of the obscenely loud squeaking and scuffling that comes from inside the walls. My landlord can hear it as loudly as I can, and while he insists he fix it, I insist he wait until the mouse-orgy is over, as it would be rather rude to evict them during the main event. For now, at least, he's left them in peace to continue their escapades, and I get rent sliced neatly in half. It's quite nice having company, anyway, and the mice listen to me better than most of my friends. They're at least twice as smart, too. Now, don't judge me on that. I see the raised eyebrow and the questioning look on your face. My honesty about my friends' intelligence isn't a judgement on their character. Nor on mine, I'd like to add.

Anyway… I work in a retail store, stocking clothes and gifts and jewellery and smiling at customers whose heads are so far up their own arses I'm surprised they can walk straight. Or comfortably. I suppose you can get used to anything if you are exposed to it for long enough.

I have no opportunity for promotion, and as I buzz around daily on minimum wage, it takes a lot of effort to force myself to give a shit.

First impressions are everything here and somehow, I managed to tame my rather strong Essex accent into something more broad. More soft spoken. Is she English? Is she Welsh? Is she mocking my accent? Probably. I unknowingly do that a lot.

I scrape the beast (the name I gave my hair when it was baptised) back into a relatively satisfying bun, though now I can't whip passers-by 'accidentally' when they get too close. This is one negative of taming the beast for work. Ten hours a day, five days a week.

Today was as uneventful as any other. I spent the morning unpacking, smiling, hanging, sorting, smiling, changing, running, smiling. Sweating, a lot. The afternoon, I spent with a customer, mourning the loss of a stolen dress in the public loos downstairs. Never leave a posh bag in a blue-lit-to-prevent-druggies-injecting bathroom.

When I finally signed out, twelve seconds after my shift ended, I practically ran outdoors, leaping about like a gazelle listening to the sound of music. I stopped when I noticed the tourists taking photos and filming my song and dance piece, and was reminded that London is never quiet, and probably isn't a suitable venue for an unplanned recital of 'the hills are alive'.

This, however, was a slightly substantial moment. I'd finished performing 'the hills are alive', and was onto an improvised version of 'doe a deer' when I crashed into a rather lovely looking lass, and my life as a straight, white, privileged woman living in London like an alley rat ended. Don't get me wrong, she didn't rob me of my nationality or run off with my purse. She simply caught my eye in more ways than one, changed my view on the female species entirely, and drew me into her incredible, crazy life.

~o~

I wrote this introduction to a longer story in the middle of the night a few months ago, and after a few revisions and showing it to a close friend, I decided I'd like to submit it. The intention was to begin writing an amusing story, with a comical narrative, whilst also maintaining a theme that currently isn't as mainstream or popular within novels; LGBT themes, and rather realistic first person narrative, with the speaker seemingly beginning to understand that there is someone 'watching' or 'reading' her story. The attempt was to create a realistic central character, with both relatable and slightly over dramatised personal features. I have less time to write at the moment, but it meant I was far more invested in this piece individually, and I spent more time working on and revising it.

CJ FORRESTER

APOLLYON

Christopher Forrester is a twenty-two-year-old writer and gamer. Currently studying his final year of a Creative and Professional Writing and English Degree at the University of Wolverhampton, he is working on his first science-fiction novel and a short story based around his early life. An avid Game of Thrones and Warhammer 40,000 fan, he also enjoys football, boxing and volunteering his time in the community. He plans to pursue a teaching career alongside his writing and aspires to have a novel published by Black Library.

My Dad tells me to go into the cupboard beneath the stairs. He doesn't join me. I think it's because he is too big. Same with Mum. They are moving quickly, pushing boxes in front of the grate. I wriggle around, trying to find a more comfortable position. I come to my knees, feeling the cold metal through my thin trousers. It feels strange. There are gaps between the boxes, tiny ones. I can see my parents still rushing around, trying to hide Mom's jewellery and money that has been left out. I can just about see the front door.

The gunfire gets louder, the snapping sound coming more often. I can hear the deep rumble of engines coming down the streets. They sound like tanks. The engine sound is the same as it is in the movies. I can hear explosives thumping into the other houses, the bricks falling and glass shattering. It almost drowns out the tinny voices of their crews shouting over megaphones and loudspeakers. I whimper, covering my ears as I curl up into a ball. Gunfire. Glass smashes. More gunfire, a *ratatata* sound. Wood splinters. Screams follow.

I can hear the neighbour's doors being kicked open. Gunshots. Screams. Begging. I turn in the small space, pressing my ear against the wall. I hear people falling, kicking and scraping at the floors and walls. They shout, begging not to be thrown into the street. They stop begging. They start wailing instead. They must have been thrown out.

The front door crashes open. Five men in grey-green uniforms charge through it. Four of them carry big guns and the other a smaller gun. My parents back away, hands raised. They shake their heads, tears trickling down their cheeks. Their lips move but I can't hear what they are saying. Tanks continue to rumble past. Planes howl overhead. Bullets are fired. Bombs are dropped. There's shouting and screaming everywhere.

It never ends.

I loosen the grate, shifting the boxes out of my way. The soldiers don't notice. My parents don't notice.

"Loot the place," the officer says, smiling. He raises his pistol. Two shots fired. Mom and Dad. Dead.

I want to scream. To run to my parents and shake them back to life. Yet I know I can't; they're gone. Nothing can bring them back. My veins burn. My teeth are clenched. The murderers put bags on the table, and begin to fill them with rings, necklaces, pretty picture frames and other expensive things from my house. One of the men leaves their gun behind. I rush from my hiding place, reaching for it.

Scooping up the weapon I struggle to hold it right. It is so heavy my knees begin to shake. I find the trigger, two fingers fitting easily into the curved metal. He half-turns around. His eyebrows rise. He freezes, like one of those action heroes in movies.

"You got balls kid," the man grins. He raises his hands, fingers open and palms flat. "Now put it down and just leave. You hear me kid? Put the gun down."

Something in me snaps.

A sharp, silver knife rips into his belly. The man's eyes roll up to the ceiling, and he drops to the ground. Another man comes rushing in. I squeeze the trigger. A shot echoes in the empty room. He dies too.

The gun makes a clicking sound. I pull the trigger again. Click. Click. Click. Click. There is a slide on one of its sides. I pull it, hoping something will happen. Click. Pull. Click. Pull. Blood runs across my sweaty palms, deep cuts on my palm and fingers stinging, torn open by the metal of the gun. It shines on the metal. Click. Pull. Click.

A man stands in the doorway, laughing. He wears a more impressive uniform than the others. His pistol is drawn. I look into his eyes, sharp green and very cold as he moves towards me. The skin around the edge of his left eye crinkles with a scar running down the side of his face. My body wants to shudder but I refuse to show him I'm afraid. The gun is close to my face.

I drop my own weapon. Tears stream down my cheeks. They sting my eyes. I am shaking, fists clenched. The smell of my parents' blood makes me gag. I open my mouth and vomit gushes upwards.

The soldier laughs, the sound dark and booming. In his laugh echoes every crazed cartoon villain rolled into one. In it, I hear the devil my parents often spoke of. I want to run. My muscles burn with new energy. I could run. But I know I won't make it.

"No," he chuckles.

He raises the gun above his head.

He brings it down rapidly.

He strikes my temple.

I wake, surrounded by doctors in white masks, to find a skull-mask hanging over me. They are taking blood. I see it in syringes and plastic tubing. They scrape me with cotton sticks while explaining what happened to me. An assassin found me in the wrecked house. Someone from the Western Alliance. They saved me, and now, like all children who lost their parents, demand that I fight for them.

Needles stab into my chest and arms, burning water of many different colours flooding into my body from clear plastic tubes. I feel more awake now than I ever have. My muscles burn with energy I feel driven to use. The urge to hurt people bubbles up in me though I cannot remember why I feel angry.

I can see everything around me. The hidden observer seated behind the glass screen. The sweat running down the masked doctor's face while he checks the squiggly lines on his machinery and the clear plastic tubes. Training weapons and dummies carefully placed at one side of the hall. Targets and sandbags at the other end.

They train me with something they call flash-memories. My instructor said that the memories of dead warriors and assassins make it easier to learn everything they need me to learn. I don't think so. They force me to repeat every move, again and again and again. They make me do it until I get it right.

When I succeed, they hurt me. They say it's a reward, the pain. That I need to embrace it, see it as a precious gift to motivate me. They say I must move past feeling pain before I can unlock my full potential. This 'reward' often comes from the instructor's baton, beating me where it will hurt the most but not damage me beyond recovery. Their other 'reward' is several punishing hours working through the assault course. I have never got through it once without going back to my room in lots of pain.

If I fail one of their exercises or tests, if I'm one second off a set course time or miss a predicted score by a single point, they hurt me even more. These punishments change as I grow older. They starve me, cut me, beat me with shock batons and burn me with fire or mark me with brands. Sometimes they hold me down while buckets of water are poured over a damp cloth forced down hard on my mouth and nose by another instructor. Other times they strap me to a metal rack, sticking electrodes across my chest and other soft tissues, sending electricity coursing through my body while they shout my failings at me. It ensures I remember them.

Every few months my instructors insist on fighting me. I last longer every time, a few seconds or maybe a minute. Yet I am always sent to the medbay covered in cuts. My body, once so pristine and innocent, is now a tapestry of healing cuts and old scars.

I no longer recognise myself in the tiny mirror they permit me to keep. I barely remember my own name. What I do remember, what I force myself to remember, are those eyes. That scar. Those memories push me onwards when all I want to do is give up. They keep me alive when all I want to do is die.

"You've done well," my training master tells me. His face is hidden beneath the leering skull-mask of our order. "The person you were when you arrived here as a boy is a distant memory. Like me and all those before you, you have become a Headsman of the Western Alliance, your name shed in place of a code-name: Apollyon."

I knew the name from ancient mythology. A demon of terrible power. The hubris is almost amusing. Still, it is a word in place of the name I no longer remember.

The list of my colleagues and predecessors stretches to hundreds of names. Each one is engraved on the walls, the gold lettering glittering in the artificial light.

I, at last, meet the architect of my forging, an overweight man with wrinkles and grey hair. He carries himself with an air of superiority, waddling arrogantly into the room and looking down his nose at me. Yet his piggish eyes are narrowed in terrified condescension at the two assassins in the room. My training master bows to the fat man, taking his leave through the door on the left.

I wait for the fat man to give me my mission. He takes a seat, sweating profusely. I suppress the impulse to sneer at him. He pulls a photo from the inside pocket of his suit, tossing it onto the table. He draws a cigar from the same pocket, lighting it despite the smoking warnings on every wall. I take the photo, ignoring the rancid puffs of smoke spilling from his mouth.

"You are to eliminate this man, a high ranking officer in the Eastern Coalition. He is a war criminal and a traitor," he tells me, exhaling a puff of smoke. His voice quavers, jowls shaking with every word. I hear the rhythmic beat of his heart and see the corners of his eyes twitch. "He was our hidden eyes within the EC for years but has since turned rogue. He works exclusively for them now. His men fill mass graves with the results of his purges."

Photos flash up on the screen in front of me. Men and women, children and elders tossed into shallow pits. Blood mars the keepsakes taken to comfort them in death. Toys. Necklaces. Books. Figurines. Treasured possessions taken from their homes.

The fat man puts a hand over his mouth, trying to cover his retching. I resist the urge to smile at the strangled gagging sound he makes. His skin is tinged green and the repulsive smell of vomit hangs over him like a shroud.

I feel nothing.

"Our forces are marshalled and ready to invade," the fat man continues. "Our initial landings will be in his province. His death will cause military forces in the area to lose cohesion and send a warning to any other agents who consider defecting."

I look at the photo, absorbing every detail of my target's face. Middle-aged, bearded. A faded scar running down his left eye. Those eyes…that scar…I've seen them before.

I leave.

Without a word.

Several days pass. I am at my target's home town.

The same town where the boy I was died so many years ago. Memory tempts me to visit my former home, to see where my parents fell. To try and find their graves, if they even have graves. Training shuts this down immediately, banishing the thoughts from my mind. The mission comes before anything else. According to the locals, my target is to speak today. He is to address the public in an open square at midday.

The sniper rifle feels heavy in my backpack. An appropriately weighty feel, yet the shoulder straps are digging in. It doesn't hurt. It just irritates me. The drugs in my body start to lose their effect: my vision becomes sharper, my mind clearer. I take a deep breath, feeling excitement course through my body. It infuses my muscles with fresh energy; they feel lighter. Stronger. My chest burns and I feel a smile spread across my face. I can almost taste blood on my lips. I lick them, knowing nothing is there but savouring the idea all the same. Its copper stink fills my nostrils.

The sun approaches midday.

I slip into a library, abandoned for the festivities. A guard patrols it, no doubt part of the secondary cordon patrolling all buildings around the square, weaving between the bookcases with his rifle held across his chest. His inexperience is obvious, not checking every angle before he moves and missing out several obvious potential hiding places. A raw and eager recruit or a terrified conscript.

I slit his throat, removing his radio. He bleeds: drip, drip, drip. His face is white. Eyes wide. He collapses onto his back. Blood gushes from the wound. A thrashing arm reaches out for me, for his weapon, for the radio now in my hand. The light dies in his eyes, they become glassy and still. Fixed on me. The last of his life flows onto the black-tiled floor.

Beneath the skull-mask of my order, I smile.

Three more die before I reach the stairs. They were no more aware than the first, bleeding out from opened throats or eyes pulverised by small-calibre bullets. I pause for a moment, checking the thermal scans of the building on my wrist-computer. No heat signatures beyond my own. Building clear.

I place traps as I ascend. I tuck proximity charges behind old books, carefully shaped for an outward blast. I place anti-personnel mines beneath rugs or underneath loose floorboards.

The sun reaches its peak. I reach my nest, a broken window on the fifth floor with a clear view of the square. I unpack the sniper rifle, assemble it and take my position at the window. The barrel rests on the plastic bottom of the window frame. I look down the scope and wait for my target to appear.

The sound of trumpets echoes in the square, almost overpowering the cheers. I wonder briefly how much he paid these people for such a reception. Probably a lot, coupled with an unsubtle threat to their families. On cue, my target waltzes onto the stage, waving and nodding in random directions. A mob of officials and bodyguards in suits trail him. A woman, demure and beautiful, sits next to him. Two small children sit beside her. They share his green eyes, the bulbous nose and thin-lipped mouth.

I wait for a moment. They deserve one last moment with their father.

I train the scope on his face. Anger bubbles beneath years of mental conditioning. The urge to growl, scream and snarl wars with the ingrained need for silence. I can feel my eyes, my mouth, twitching, facial muscles pulling my lips into a bestial snarl. I suppress the scream I feel building in my throat.

Beneath it all there is a sense of satisfaction. The crosshairs zoom over his cheek. My lip curves up. Slightly.

He takes a sip of water and then adjusts the microphone on his uniform. His lieutenant's insignia is gone. The rank bars and shoulder pads of a general stand in their place. They taunt me, his prosperity and my pain. Two dozen medals glint in the sunlight. It almost affects my aim.

Almost.

I load a single bullet into the chamber. The copper gleams in the sunlight. I pull the slide, chambering the round. Flick the safety off.

I move my crosshairs over the children for a moment. I sigh, moving them back to the general's cheek. My finger tightens around the trigger.

I squeeze it. Tighter. Tighter. Tighter. Click—bang.

His head snaps back, the round tearing through his forehead into his brain. His body hits the ground with a thud, rolling onto his stomach. The cheap metal of his decorations scrape against the stone. His wife runs over, screaming. Her children are inches behind her. Blood pools across the sun-warmed stone. Civilians turn their heads and guards cock their rifles. Screams ring out. Cries of 'assassin' and 'murderer'.

'Daddy'.

Someone triggers a trap, a muffled explosion and angry yells drowning out the wounded man's screams. My wrist-computer beeps a warning. They're on the first floor, climbing to the second. I'm already moving.

There's a crossing between the library and the next building, an old college, abandoned years ago. I skulk down the stairs, stepping gingerly around the trip-wires and proximity mines I've placed between the stairs and the door to the crossing.

I slip through the first set of doors, moving quietly across the corridor. Barely any daylight gets in here; the windows are taped up or boarded over. No chance of being seen. I break the lock chaining the second pair of doors shut. The shouting grows louder, the clattering of jackbooted feet too. My pursuers are drawing near.

I ghost through the dilapidated building, a shadow in the darkness. The stairwell is nearby, the signs barely visible under years of dust. I rush down the stairs, hearing faint echoes of screaming and shouting through the thick stone walls. I reach the bottom, vaulting the railing. Momentum carries me through the stairwell exit.

The door is a few steps ahead of me, opened slightly by a broken hinge. A small chink of daylight beckons me outside, where the sound of sirens, screaming and angry yells is a welcome relief. Ninety seconds have passed according to my wrist-computer.

I move towards the daylight, sliding through the open door. I hide the skull-mask in my pocket, seeing people running in every direction, yelling and screaming. I slip in amongst them, glancing up to where my sniper's nest was. They're in there, looking about. More traps are triggered. Fire and shrapnel burst out a window. More people scream.

Hood up, I move with the crowd.

~o~

My inspiration for writing has always been my emotions. They fuel my imagination, helping me to guide the narrative and I have always found that I produce my best work when writing from a place of emotion. I always know roughly what path I want my writing to take, key events within the narrative that drive the characters towards their destinies or determine the course of the piece, but I find free-writing based on emotions will make the journey between these points more interesting and compelling than if I had written it without using my emotions.

For Apollyon I wanted to create a character in who personal desire and emotions constantly war with his duty or his mission, a conflict between what he feels and what his mind tells him to do. It was a situation I often encountered as a youth, the war between what one feels one should do and what one knows one should do. My choice to have him focus on the mission was meant to reflect that, inevitably, the head wins over the heart. His name was a nod to his position as an assassin, the choice of a mythical demon's name meant to reflect his lethality and the taste for violence created in him. I also intended to infuse the piece with a small amount of irony in that Apollyon may be serving people far worse than his parents' killer but that is for the reader to decide. I wanted them to read it and the character in the way that suited them best, as a monster bent on revenge or a wronged child that was stolen from his home and voluntarily subjected himself to inhumane treatment to avenge his parents. Having him bear witness to his parents' deaths was the only catalyst I felt was strong enough for the rest of the piece to be plausible and would engage the reader with his situation and having him kill one man and try to kill another was to show that the potential resides within us all and can be brought out under the right circumstances.

I loosely based the two superpowers in the narrative on the Soviet Union and the United States, asking myself what it might have been like if they had ever engaged in an extended conflict. This idea drove much of the subtext in the narrative, two powers that had been at war pretending to be friendly whilst all the time readying themselves to strike. This in turn gave me the idea of having a young victim turned into a weapon through years of training and conditioning. It is something explored in science-fiction but I wanted to give it a more real-world feel and the choice of target being the same man that killed his parents was intended to demonstrate that vengeance, whether on a personal scale or an international one, is simply an endless cycle, hence why I decided that this character's children should bear witness to his death.

HEATHER MUSSETT
SWORDSONG

Heather Mussett is twenty-two and a recent graduate from Newcastle University earning a degree in English Language and Literature. Heather is currently working on her fantasy novel, as well as contributing to her own blog and writing about wrestling at Intergender World Championships on Wordpress. In her spare time Heather bakes and rides dressage with her ex-racehorse, Socks.

Today was the day. Terra stood with the rest of her tribe in the Minai clearing awaiting the pairing of the Amorata who had finished their training. The pine trees fidgeted in the wind, towering over the gathered Inai tribe who were all discussing one thing: this spring's candidates for pairings were an odd number, and everyone knew who the odd one out was.

Chack waited with the other soon-to-be Amorata. Terra watched him as he fumbled with his new hide bracers. A strand of Chack's sand-coloured hair had come loose and fluttered by his shoulders. Today, Chack faced two paths: pair up with an older Amorato, who had already lost a partner, or fail. It was Gaia's choice. He was too proud to let anybody see how nervous he was, but Terra knew he'd been dreading this day.

Terra had only been this nervous once before, at the Reading of the Ways, eight years earlier. It was the day her future was decided, where Karian, the chief Shaman, would draw out of the fire an idol marking her as a Builder, Gatherer,

Shaman, or one of the intuitive warrior protectors, the Amorata. She'd dreamt of whizzing about the forest with Chack, masters of the larca blade, scourges of all the Inai's enemies. Just like her brother and his amorato, Anoro. But when Karian had plunged her hand into the flames, she had drawn out a carving of Terra holding a basket, not a blade. She would be a Gatherer, like her mother. Her family had tried to console her. Chack had tried. All she had wanted was to ask to try a blade, just to see if she could have been Amorata. But she knew that even that much would be forbidden.

Terra pushed her dark auburn hair out of her eyes, rich as the mahogany heart, as her mother would say. The gathering jostled her to the front of the group and she fought to catch Chack's eye, to offer any sort of comfort. His eyes stayed fixed on the dirt. A hand squeezed her shoulder.

"It is good to see you here supporting your friend, Terra. Gaia bless you." Anoro, the smith, stood behind her. A slit of a scar sliced from his cheekbone to pucker at the tip of his kind smile. Terra tried to return it. Her gaze was pulled back to Chack as Anoro moved away. 'Gaia, bless Chack,' Terra prayed.

"Inai! It is time!" Tucin welcomed them all with open arms, opening his cape and displaying the full splendour of his chief's attire. Today, it was arrayed with blooming spring flowers in varied pastel shades in honour of the occasion. Tendrils of his long white hair blew across his beaming smile. "My favourite day of the year!"

Behind her the Amorata trainer, Atter, nudged her and sniggered. Terra turned angrily to hear what he might say, but Anoro had already come to her rescue. "Gaia is at work today, Atter. Watch and learn what a little humility could grant you." Anoro slapped Atter's shoulder in a show of mock camaraderie. Terra watched with amusement as Atter fought to regain his breath, his eyes bulging.

If Tucin noticed, he didn't grant the disturbance any of his attention. "It is that time of year again, Inai! Springtime! And as the stag readies himself to protect his doe, we in turn welcome new protectors of our tribe!" The Inai cheered.

"Gaia knows that we fight stronger together than we ever could apart, and so today she grants the intuitive connection we rely on so well. The catching of the larca symbolises the pair's unfaltering trust, and the second throwing proves Gaia's blessing on the connection. So, Inai, if you please…"

Tucin raised his arms to shoulder height, asking the tribe to part to form a path through their middle. It was not too much wider than a warrior. "Trust in your future Amorata starts now, I see!" Tucin chuckled to himself as he made his way down the path to stand behind the crowd. 'He's right,' thought Terra, 'if any of the second throws are off-target then we'll have need of the Shamans.'

"Let us begin!"

Four pairs had become apparent from training, Terra knew. And then there was Chack.

Don, a lithe, agile, red-haired fighter stepped out first. He centred himself, launched the larca blade high into the air, and began walking. The crowd watched it spinning, glinting in the morning sunlight as it reached level with the canopy of the forest. It seemed to hover for a moment before it plummeted toward the ground. Prena shot out of the ranks of the trainees, raven black hair streaming, and caught the blade deftly by the handle, raising the blade in her other hand and sending it on its way toward Don's turned back. Prena's eyes glittered with elation as Don's arm raised to catch the larca. She let out a scream of triumph, running down the gap and leaping on Don in glee. After approaching Tucin for their second pair of larca blades, they turned to Anoro to receive their rata rings in private. Terra applauded with the rest of her tribe.

Kenna was next, finding her centre before she made her throw. Terra gasped as she started walking before she'd fully completed it. The blade veered off backward, over the heads of the waiting trainees and into the forest. Asca, Kenna's twin, swore and took off after it. Terra watched Kenna walk through the tribe. The crowd held their breath. Sooner than they expected, a flock of birds scattered out of the trees, screeching indignantly at the spinning blade which chased them. The crowd broke into cheers as the blade sailed into Kenna's waiting hand. Sprinting into view, Asca hit the flat of her palm against Kenna's in triumph. Arms around each other and swaying with relief, they, too, received their blades from Tucin.

Braid and Lana completed without a problem. Miri and Danna, too, fulfilled the ceremony, shouting with joy. Now it was Chack's turn. The tribe began to mutter.

He stepped forward. He looked at his single larca blade questioningly, then up at the sky.

"He isn't going to go through with it!"

"Well, would you want to?"

"Give it up, Chack."

'Don't give up, Chack!' Terra pleaded silently.

Chack looked at the blade again. He seemed to rise to his full height and Terra watched as the tension melted off his shoulders. Then, as if it were red hot, threw the larca up into the air and began walking. The crowd shuffled as the blade soared upward, whirling. It started to fall. No-one had moved.

'Gaia?' Terra questioned.

Still, no-one moved. Somehow, Terra noticed, Chack was serene. The blade was halfway back to the ground. She heard the *shick-shick-shick* as it span in the air.

Terra shot out of the crowd, moving faster than she ever believed she could. Eyes fixed on the falling blade, everything was heightened. She saw every detail, felt every force acting on her body as she sped toward the hurtling blade. Next instant, the blade was nestled in her hand. She stared at it in disbelief. 'How could I do that?'

A motherly voice came to her, barely a whisper on the wind.

I have need of you, child. Now, make the final throw.

Terra panicked. Suddenly the blade felt heavy, and sharp. An image of Chack stumbling toward the ground, the blade embedded in his shoulder flashed in her consciousness. She cried out.

Do not despair. I am with you. Make the throw.

Terra's hand raised itself and flicked the blade toward her friend. She watched, pleading in her mind as it whistled down the walkway. It whizzed across the gap, toward Chack's left side. Terra watched it, praying. Without looking round, his left arm swung back and caught it. It was as if a dam had opened. Chack's consciousness poured into her mind, revealing every facet of his consciousness. His triumph exploded like an opening bloom, mingling with surprise and the tiniest glimmer of worry, quickly forgotten under another surge of satisfaction. Terra shrieked with relief and ran to him, just as he turned round to catch her. They laughed, reeling as they acclimatised to their new connection.

"I can't believe you caught it!"

"Did you know I was coming?"

"Not at all! What were you thinking?"

"I didn't! It just happened! I can't believe I did it!"

It was a moment before they realised they were the only ones talking.

The crowd were shuffling in bemused silence. A breeze sidled through the clearing, rustling the pine trees in embarrassment.

Tucin broke the silence first.

"This is unprecedented," he boomed.

Terra suddenly grew hot as her heart pounded. Her hand slipped from Chack's arm but he held it tight. She felt his determination. They had completed the ceremony. That had to prove something.

"But this I cannot question!" Tucin beamed at them both, holding out their larca blades. The crowd began to clap confusedly.

"Praise Gaia!" Anoro roared, punching his fist in the air. "Today we have seen a miracle!" The tribe roared with him, whistling and stamping their feet. Terra allowed herself to smile as she felt Chack relax.

Atter stalked past them, eyes like a storm. "Just like Elith. No respect," he snarled.

Terra was too stunned to reply. What did Atter know of her sister? She felt Chack's indignation and was relieved to see Anoro beckoning them away from the tribe. Terra approached the pious smith tentatively, only to see her own wariness reflected in him. As they neared Anoro he turned to the iron box next to him and the final two rata rings. He presented Chack's first. Despite it being made of solid iron and forged with the blessing of a goddess, Anoro handled the ring delicately, as if it might fall and shatter at any moment.

Chack's ring was a thick band etched with an intricate design of intertwining branches and leaves. He slipped it onto his thumb.

"I pray the design foretells good fortune," Anoro inclined his head respectfully, and Chack followed suit. Terra hoped he could feel her pride over his own. He stepped away, admiring the design.

Next Anoro produced Terra's ring.

"I expect you're wondering why I never doubted the outcome of today," he began. The ring was slightly wider than normal for a female rata ring, and the etching so delicate that Terra couldn't make it out. "As you know, the rata rings of fallen Amorata are kept and placed on the branches of the trees they lived in," Anoro continued. "Last night, however, Gaia had me remove one to make a new ring. Your ring, Terra."

Terra understood. "Dain?" Anoro nodded. She could see his hesitance. Her brother's rata ring had hung with his ancestors' on their family tree for the last six years. It was her mother's only comfort. Her mother, who this day would be sitting alone with her memories, communing with their Amorata ancestors. The implication hit Terra full in the chest. Gaia had had Anoro desecrate her brother's memory, his honour, in order that she could live the life she wanted.

"I would never have disrespected your family's tradition in this way if Gaia hadn't asked me to. Your brother's death was a tragedy for us all." Anoro had been accepted as part of her family after Dain was murdered. As his Amorato, he had known him better than any of them.

Terra remembered nothing of her brother's death, save for the wisps of images that haunted her sleep: The large man with his charcoal-black hair and piercing blue eyes. The rushing of white water. Dain smiling as he speared a fish. An axe shearing through skin, a dull crunch as it hit bone.

Anoro's next words shook her from her memories. "Not least because of the problems it caused with the Kuraia."

The mention of the Kuraia shocked her. She had vague memories of bloody skirmishes after her brother's death between the Inai and the mountain tribe, which, after half a year, ended abruptly. The Kuraia had withdrawn to their own tribelands and no-one had seen anything of them since. She faced Anoro, unsure what to answer with. Terra still didn't take her ring from Anoro's hand.

"I don't know what Gaia has decided for you. I do know that she wanted you to wear the metal from your brother's ring. I can only hope that she plans to end this."

Years of mistrust and hatred, ended?

She felt Chack's interest, and eagerness. He at least believed that they could make a difference. Terra looked at him, grateful, then back at the ring.

"Please, Terra. Take it. Gaia means for you to have it." Anoro held out the ring again. This time, she could see the etching. Infinitesimal swirls and counter swirls and every so often a small circle. Deafening white water.

She hadn't been near the river since.

Terra took a breath and took the ring, pushing it down to her thumb joint as quickly as she could. She saw Dain laughing as he celebrated the fish he'd speared. Tears forced themselves out.

~o~

Swordsong was a piece I originally started working on in my mid-teens and only started to meaningfully engage with when I decided to make it my dissertation project, for which I was lucky enough to be supervised by Ann Coburn. The story in its first instance is a reflection of my love of fantasy fiction. As a child I loved to get lost in made-up worlds, loving the freedom of Tolkien's Middle Earth, Paolini's Alagaesia, and the Cornelia Funke's Inkworlds in particular. *Swordsong* has matured with me, and likewise I want the story to follow Terra and Chack's coming of ages in their own different terms, focusing on their different personalities and how they will clash and come together again.

In terms of audience I aim for a crossover audience of both young adults and adults, in the same way that Philip Pullman's *His Dark Materials* appeals and speaks to both on an emotional level. This is in part because my protagonists themselves are young adults and I'd like to show their growing maturities as they grapple with more adult themes: in this case, their home and way of life being threatened by a technologically superior civilisation. Another reason for wanting to aim for a more adult audience is to avoid the cliché in some young adult literature of the overly romantic relationship being at the centre of the narrative. I worked hard to make my characters rounded and driven, and almost didn't want the distraction for them: I wanted more for them! Terra and Chack's relationship is very much inspired by Eragon and Saphira's in Christopher Paolini's *Inheritance* cycle: a telepathically linked pairing who care a lot for each other and fight as a cohesive unit. Also, issues surrounding gender roles were constantly on my mind in planning this novel, and I've presented the Inai tribe as a culture without gender roles. This in part harkens back to the freedoms I used to admire so much in literature as a child, but also means that my characters are free to achieve what I want them to without having the constraints of gender and relationship expectations. Gender politics is something I write about in terms of sport and sports entertainment in a nonfiction setting so the opportunity to create my own rules regarding gender was an interesting one for me.

While gender politics were a consideration in my writing, I primarily wanted (as most writers do) to tell a good story. This particular story has undergone many twists and turns, characters have died and been resurrected, relationships built and then torn down. Although I have been known to get frustrated with myself, I feel it helps to think of my story as a living, growing thing, and it's been a pleasure to work with so far.

ROBYN WILSON
CARTOON CHARACTERS

Robyn Wilson is 20 years old and has lived in rural Warwickshire her whole life. As much as she loves it there, she hopes to someday travel the world in body, and not just in her writing. She is currently studying American Studies at university, and is pouring inspiration from her travels in the United States into a poetry anthology, which she hopes to publish upon its completion.

The sky was the same grey as hospital curtains as I laid my path beneath it. *Crunch crunch crunch* – the grass I flattened with my footsteps provided the only soundtrack required or deserved. Spring was on its way, no doubt, but, as always, it approached slowly and draped still in winter's shroud. In my mind, spring was long over and I reclined on the lawn in a new bikini from Fifth Avenue, sipping fairy dust from something long, thin and poisonous. The grass wasn't crunchy, it was positively *verdant*, and the only frosting that remained was the sugar on my lips… Ah, dreams. How they indulge us! In a blink of a weary white orb, the surge of the hill up towards the house was once again barren; the twinkle of the city was coy behind its smokescreen, and the house was a faceless blob of bricks, with only the complete blackness of the storm cloud it crouched beneath to distinguish it from the shadows.

An empty glass awaited me in the kitchen when I went to fetch a drink. A whole line of them, actually: seven daintily arranged bridesmaids. All had a crusty residue of sticky brownness swamping up their insides and I suspected that more than half had been waiting some days to be cleaned. Desperation for a drink turned quickly into desperation for a very specific sticky, crusty, brown drink as I scrubbed with a clenched fist until all seven tumblers were clean. Then I took one and emptied my husband's bottle of Jack Daniels into it. Then I smashed it into a million tiny little diamonds against the wall and left it there for him to find.

Crack. Vacuous and vague, grey as a gathering storm, eyes stared back at me through a white kaleidoscope. Blinking in a hundred different places and reopening to the same world. Crack. Darkness, a wink of it, was all it took for angles to change, to tilt, and for everything to slide to the edge of the world and fall off, freefall into another version of reality, one only 90 degrees away. And it swirled. And it swirled on. Crack. Flecks of red glitter exploded into my vision from either side and the kaleidoscope twisted faster. Everything was red, then orange. Soon it was yellow, and it remained so for several whiplashes of blinking darkness that tried to unknit the yellow tapestry. It's lumpy stitches held fast. Try as it might, the kaleidoscope couldn't spin through them and for a thump of a fist, the world levelled out in the vision of the kaleidoscope's oceanic white eyeballs. Crack. Before those eyes could adjust to the flat surface that sprawled out before them and level the world as they saw it, the kaleidoscope clattered through the yellow stitches and they unravelled in endless streams. Crack. The panels melted away in slow motion. The kaleidoscope dissolved. Sugar, sugar, sprinkling across the floor, up the walls; angles and fragments of colour, turning grey as the eyes let them into their vision and they turned to glass. Glass on the floor. Glass up the walls. Glass under my fingernails and in my hair. Glass. In my nostrils and up my sleeves and inside my shoes and under my skin. Crack. Crack went the mirror. Crack.

My husband's singing woke me up. It was not loud, nor abrasive, but I had not heard the sound of it in so long that it startled me into consciousness. In the bedroom, the air was very thick. I reached for the glass of water on my bedside table and my fingers came back covered in gin. I frowned, and scraped them dry on the duvet. The curtains were closed, but I was aware of a thin, lemony light making them twinkle. What an odd time to wake up. The light I could see was, I presumed, a dying one but nonetheless, to be light at all at this time of the year it must still be before 4. Doubtless, then, whatever coma I'd enjoyed could not have been a deeply substantial one. As for the singing, it was a treat. As sweet (almost) as awakening to the birdsong. It almost sounded like spring. You don't need to furrow your brows like that: your husband is a musician – those furrowed brows strike downwards into my mind like forks of lightning! – so why wouldn't he sing? He's a miserable musician, that's why. Caged birds do not sing. Or do they? I forget the facts. I suspect they sing only when forced. Making music gives him nostalgia, and nostalgia gives him crippling depression. Can you understand now why it was such a surprise to hear him sing? With such lightness of tone, too, almost as though he relayed the bars through a smile. Of course, it would be all the sweeter if he sang something from the same neglected vault that he hid his fond memories inside – *not* the Velvet Underground songs that performed their exhausted cartwheels through the clouded landscape of our existence with dizzying continuity.

"Rusty," I called to him as I flopped out of bed, "Where are you?"

"Right next to you."

"Ah!" My eyes swirled all over the room, the faint yellow light making watercolour paintings of it. I looked blindly for him. Skeleton claws clutched at my face and I shrieked as my husband's big, olive eyes floated into my vision.

"What are you flailing around for? And screaming? You're hysterical."

"Oh, I am not," I flicked his hands to the side and dragged myself erect, "You're singing!"

"Well, it's a beautiful day."

"Where did you go this morning? The gates of heaven? Have you seen the light? My god." I cackled, and despite *his* good humour, *mine* fell upon a flat-lining grin.

"I went out," he told me, "It's warmer than it's been in a while."

"I went out too. I was unmoved."

"Aaah," he smiled woozily as his cactus fingers extended towards me like a hungry zombie's, and pushed a strand of hair back. I watched, suddenly unable to move all over again, "There's my immovable object."

My lips were stiff, but I was still able to meekly demand what he was doing. There was a moment of levitation where his hands swung away from my face and dangled in a suspended pocket of time, his mouth motionlessly gawping like a dead fish. All of a sudden, his hands crashed into his lap and he straightened up, time sprinting to catch up with itself.

"Oh," said Rusty, "Nothing."

He left, and I surged forwards with the intention of following him, the world wavering happily around me like it'd had too much to drink, but found my legs were too wobbly to support the enormous head of air on my shoulders. I slumped back down, and compensated with a loud shout.

"RUSTY! Why have you poured this glass of gin?"

"It's for you," he replied, voice taking on that tropical, nasal harshness that I loathed so much, "Because you looked so dehydrated when I found you."

"Yes, I wanted water! When you found me? Found me? Was I lost?"

"You'd fallen asleep on the settee drinking whiskey." The doorframe was rapidly flooded with shadows and out of them emerged a crackling, scowling Rusty, standing on the threshold. "There was glass all over the floor."

"I smashed a bottle", I told him.

"You never stop drinking. Why don't you ever stop drinking?"

"What are you talking about? *I* am not a trained alcoholic."

"Frankly, I don't care what you drink. Just clean up after yourself."

His pupils floated around in the olive emptiness of his vacant stare, glittering with a gossamer sheen, draped across his face like fairylights. There was an absence of all feeling in them. No discernible emotions but many, many questions, all unanswered and many unanswerable. His pupils, as they bounced off the walls of his soulful Mr Rochester unseeingness, were as black as ink blots and I wanted so much to squeeze them from his eyeballs and demand what they wanted to know. *I will answer your questions if I can. I will. I will.* Beneath his eyes, his mouth swung agape on its hinges and all of his silent words joined the haze of my confusion as it fogged up my brain and dizzied my sight. No words – audible ones, at least – passed between us for what was probably only a few seconds, but felt like many minutes. Confusion reflected back at confusion and the sight of its crooked countenance shocked it to silence.

Rusty gargled. Whatever he wanted to say came out as mush and he shut his mouth immediately and frowned, apparently at his own unintelligibility. Patiently, I allowed him to try again.

"You, uh… You don't… Never mind, Elvie. Get some rest."

"Well… I am rested. Aren't I?" Spoken with a grin painted sloppily across my face to give respite to his evident discomfort, this was really the musing of a caged tongue, trapped behind teeth that attempted to restrict its hostility.

"Right. Well, I need to change the record so—"

"Yeah, asshole, you do. Wait – change the record?!"

"Turn it over."

"Rusty… Rusty!" All I could feel of his face against my fist was a dusty fuzz of soft skin. Every other bitter angle, unfeeling feature, down to the gasp of pain that the screaming in my head nullified, was lost beneath the vibrations that made my whole body throb like an active landmine. The slow-motion sinking of the room around me consumed everything and I was barely aware enough to feel either satisfied or horrified by the crimson glamour of the blood on my knuckles. He staggered backwards with elongated steps as his mouth slowly swung open and his hand glided upwards to cradle his nose in its balmy palm. My body remained still, fizzling and crackling, but still. Then, with a twist of the kaleidoscope, the world burst with haste and colour, dizzying the galaxy as it rushed to catch up with time, moments lost to its slow-motion staggering regained under the time constraints of a blinking eyeball.

Rusty was grabbing me, clawing at my shoulders whilst I screamed. The click-clack of my gnashing teeth made my jaw hurt. I tried to stop, but could only continue deliriously thrusting my teeth together as my husband forced me backwards onto the bed and climbed on top of me. I screamed. I gnashed my teeth. I screamed. Or did both. Or did nothing. I lay there, graveyards in my eyeballs, as he straddled me, hands on my hands. Hands on my hands. Face so close, so close and saying: "You are not well, Elvira."

He whipped his head one way, then the other, as though seeking someone to whom he could address his panting breaths.

Noises tumbled free from my mouth, roars and screams that wouldn't sound out of place beneath the Amazon canopy, and I listened with a sense of detachment to them. I wondered if they sounded to Rusty as they sounded to me: the bleeps and whirs of some alien lifeform, communicating only the emotions that rumbled between its ears with no knowledge of human communications. As my body thrashed and my mouth foamed with feral words, my mind wondered why it was so far away. It had the power, but not the resource, to stop this. To lie my body still. To steady the flailing of my lips and restore my senses. So where was it? Where? Where? Where? Where? Where? Where? Where? Where? Where? Where?

Blood dripped into my open mouth and I gulped it back and screamed into the mouth of the red river. I was told: "You are not well! You are not well!"

The pressure that mounted on my wrists hurt. I attempted to push talons forth from my fingers and scrabble free. I made claws of my fingers. But the pressure increased. It pushed me down, down into the covers and my lips, open to beg softness, were suddenly still. How? What silenced them after all my private struggles to seal them? And now some external power in control? Still though they were, they were suffocated. Something was pressing against them, forcibly silencing them. I struggled, as best I could, against this oppressive presence and when it finally released me, my lips were left scorched and sticky with something I couldn't immediately name. Senses spitting at me particles of themselves from all angles, Rusty gradually became visible to me, hovering above. I frowned. He frowned back, a red blur still to my recovering sight. And then he kissed me again.

Crack.

~o~

Cartoon Characters is the novel I am working on. This is an extract from it. It chronicles a week in the life of Elvira Stratton, a famous musician stuck in a creative rut, in which her life spectacularly explodes. Her husband, Rusty, is a toxic wasteland of a human being. Insecure and unstable, he spends his days binging on drink and drugs and listening to The Velvet Underground's debut album on loop. In this extract, we catch up with them on Wednesday of their week from hell. The cracks are beginning to show. Over the course of this confrontation, their relationship plays out an entire life cycle, from awkward interplay through bitter disagreement, before it is dubiously rekindled. With the action never leaving the house, there is an intense sense of claustrophobia: Elvie doubts her husband's sanity the whole time, whilst never suspecting that she might be the crazy one.

This novel is about famous people, but in it, as in all my writing, I try to pluck things from the human psyche that speak to all of us. Based on rock 'n' roll's greatest Power Couples, and some parts of my own brain, it assesses the price we pay to 'live the dream', and asks what the difference is between dreams and delusions.

MICHAEL CONROY
RED PEOPLE

Michael Conroy is a 21-year-old English writer. A postgraduate student in Creative Writing at the Manchester Writing School, he's also a ravenous bibliophile and would like to apologise for all the adverbs in his work (he's clearly read too much Lovecraft). He's working on lots of writing projects, including a dark fantasy novel about a necromancer who resurrects Vladimir Lenin, and an erotic science fiction retelling of *The Iliad* from Aphrodite's POV. He also has two jobs – one as a copywriter, the other as a sales assistant. He occasionally writes for a blog online at suchandsuchmag.wordpress.com.

Words of Warning

"I say one Communist in a defence plant is one Communist too many. One Communist, on the faculty of one university, is one Communist too many. One Communist among American advisors at Yalta was one Communist too many. And even if there were only one Communist in the State Department, that would still be one Communist too many."

There are many ways to spot a Communist.

If anyone is seen reading or advocating the views expressed in Communist publications, then they're more than likely a Communist; if someone supports organisations that reflect Communist teachings or are labelled Communist by the Department of Justice, then they, too, may be a Communist; if someone defends the activities of Communist nations while consistently attacking the domestic and foreign policy of the United States, then they may also be a Communist. And if they do all these things, or have done in the past, then they undeniably must be a Communist. If you have any sort of feeling that someone may be a Communist, then they probably are a Communist.

But be warned, there are those who refrain from showing their real faces, choosing to work more—silently.

Conditioning

Strolling yonderly past the Woolworth building, remarking to myself how it was once upon a time the tallest in the world, I reminisce about first meeting Betty.

I had a bit of a crush on her all the way through high school but I could never work up the courage to ask her out until our prom.

After that, our relationship blossomed. And now we're married!

I enter a large department store, impulsively deciding to buy Betty a gift, to keep her happy and quiet, although, I'm at a loss for what to purchase for her.

Round and about are all manner of people – families shopping, old folks dropping from the sheer stress of it all; young people loitering, socialising, debating the joys and woes of teenage life – all sorts of folks. I'm still a little perplexed as to what I should buy, but a swift wave of euphoria envelops me as I—

Dark, dark, can't see anything. Head hurts. Is this real? Am I dreaming? No, dreams don't—Ow! Hello, Sally, that hurts! I think I'm bleeding, I know it, bleeding, I can feel it.

Oh dear.

Something's biting at my already sore wrists, can't move them, abrasive – feels like rope. Tied to a chair it seems – hands and feet bound.

Can't move chest so much either, hard to breathe, wheezing, tangled in rope's rough embrace, in the dark.

Where am I? How long have I been held here for? What's going on here? Somebody better tell me or I'll—Holy hell, I've been kidnapped!

"Hello!" I call out. "Hello, is there anybody there? I demand that you untie me, you scoundrels. Let me out of here this instant, you hear? Somebody help!" My voice echoes back to me. It's no use. I don't think anyone can hear me, wherever I am. It smells wet, damp, like we're underground.

Waves of consternation send my mind reeling about on choppy waters; sweat rolls fearfully down my forehead as I frantically try to loosen my ties but a sudden explosion of light blinds and hinders me from doing so. I squeeze my eyelids shut like a bear trap, trying to block out the piercing white glare that's stabbing at my retinas. A burst of pain shatters against the side of my face, leaving my vision blurred and hazy. My eyes, straining to adjust to the impossible brightness, can barely make out the two figures in front of me. They hit me again, once across the face, then in the gut, my throat burning as I spew up my lunch into a tepid puddle on the floor.

A third enters the room, wheeling in an ominous looking machine, something between a polygraph and an electroencephalograph. As the men attach suction cups wired to the machine to strategic points around my face, and strap on some tightly fastening headphones, as they flood my veins with some unknown substance, I notice that they are all wearing the same suit.

In a panic, I try and shake off all their paraphernalia but they hold me still in a vicelike grip. One wheels a chair in front of me, sits down, and holds up a rectangular red card. He notes my response down on a clipboard. Someone holds my head back while another pipettes a few liquid drops into my eyes; they then shine bright red lights intermittently at me, dictating mantra-like instructions and—

Fyodor Andreyevich Theodore Anderson. Fyodor AndreyevTheichodore Anderson. Fyodor AndreTheyevodoichre Anderson. Fyodor AnThedreodoyevreAichnderson. FyodoTherAnododrereAyevndeichrson. FyTheodoodorAnredreAndyeversichon. TheFyoododorreAAndndereyrsoevnich.

TheodoFyoreAdorndeAndrsoreynevich. TheodoreAFyondedorrsoAndnreyevich. TheodoreAndeFyorsodornAndreyevich. TheodoreAndersoFyondorAndreyevich. Theodore Anderson Fyodor Andreyevich.

—finally I'm blindfolded.

Shrouded in darkness once again, the throbbing pain imploding in my brain increases tenfold as I begin to drown in terror – fearing I might soon be dead. The levels of cortisol in my blood must be staggering, but why would I be thinking about that right now? High-pitched whining is emitted from the headphones, beneath which eerie whispering voices resonate, making me weak and lethargic.

I don't know how long my ears are raped like this, but eventually I give in, lapsing into catatonia and, finally, sleep.

—come to a decision before a chic little store window, deciding to buy her this lovely mauve, belted pea coat that she hinted, not-too-subtly, at wanting a few days before. It's very in vogue, and cost me a pretty penny, too. Polly wants a cracker – so that's what she gets, as long as it shuts her up for once. Golly, women can nag. Am I right, fellas? Of course, I am. Still, I hope she likes it. I hope it's the right one. Well, I'm sure she'll be happy, which is all that matters really.

Awake

The sun screams. The sun screams maddeningly through the wooden blinds that bar the bedroom windows, sickeningly yellow in the darkness. It pierces my eyelids at 6.30am. Betty, my wife, my beloved, lies in the foetal position. She stirs next to me but soon falls back into her slumber, or so it seems. And I dare say, she cowers, slightly. It is quite chilly in here. It enfolds me, envelops me, claws at me, tears me to pieces. Like a man, I get up and bare the chill of early morning, and pad my way to the bathroom to shower.

I turn the handle and fluid gushes out of the head like a severed artery. Scrubbing my face, applying soap to my not-so-muscular-as-it-could-be but still well-toned body, and then shampoo to my deep dark wood hair – shades of earth and oak with the occasional glint of red, like Autumn leaves falling to the floor – I wash out and away all the sweat and other oily accumulations that come with a good night's sleep.

When I'm done, dripping like Richard Carlson stepping out of the black lagoon, I step onto a carefully prepared towel laid down a few minutes earlier. Drying off, I glance at myself in the mirror and ponder whether I should shave today. Betty's been nagging me to grow a bit of stubble. She says it'd make me look even more handsome. She has a real hankering for that rugged lumberjack look. But I doubt I would suit it. It just wouldn't be me. Still undecided on the matter, I wrap the towel around my waist and squeeze a sliver of toothpaste onto my toothbrush, commencing another daily ritual.

Afterwards, I make good use of the hairdryer, and then I apply Brylcreem to my flawlessly spruce hair, slicking it back and combing it until it meets my preferred style. It is *very* important to have a good haircut and a good hairdo. It can make or break a job interview, make you appear weak or authoritative, and can lose you a nice gal. That's why I use Brylcreem. It's the best pomade I've ever used. It gives the hair a nice shine, has excellent hold, and you don't need much. *A Little Dab'll Do Ya!* as they say.

I opt to put on the Monday suit today, although, it's really more an action of automatism. The ensemble: a woollen three piece, the jacket and pants of which are a light, chocolate shade of brown, and the waistcoat a much darker, earthy sort of colour, accompanied by a wonderful golden coffee-coloured tie with a pale cerulean-blue paisley pattern. The coffee matches my shirt and the blue the pinstripes on my suit. The tie in question I got as a Christmas present, last year. And a very good year it was.

Half-dressed, I slip on some socks that match the waistcoat's colour and then into my fabulous russet half-brogues. Sliding into my jacket, a single-breasted, two-buttoned number with a notch lapel, I then head downstairs to see what the woman's made for me: a selection of muffins, toast, bacon and sausage, yogurt, fruit, cereal, etc. Uninspired, not too imaginative really – I'm underwhelmed.

I make do with the most important meal of the day, half-heartedly kiss Betty goodbye (I can't say much for the eye shadow she's wearing; far too dark for my taste, and only around one eye; what, did she forget to do the other one?), and popping on my dark beige Chesterfield overcoat, head out the door.

Tod Trivisey, neighbour, waves to me from two houses up while collecting his newspaper from the lawn. I return a reluctant wave. His mailbox is—

If they have a Red *mark upon their skin, upon their clothes, or on their property, then they are indeed a* Communist; *and you will not suffer a* Communist *to . . .*

—hideous; I can't believe I've never noticed it before. An overpowering urge to go over and paint it a different colour pours over me, but I hold back. That would be rude.

Blankly, I stare past Tod – through him, and into the distance. This overwhelming subtle sensation begins to take hold. It's bizarre, like I'm being wound up like some sort of toy robot. I feel cold and detached, dichotomous, sort of separated, and not quite aware of my surroundings. I feel rather like a marionette. I think my heart stops beating for a minute.

I return to planet Earth and Tod's no longer at the mailbox. Mrs. Carleton waves to me from across the street. I don't wave back, repulsed that her kind should have the nerve. So, inserting key into door, and entering my Barbara, I make the drive to . . .

Soviet Abduction

I'm driving along, to work I think, only it's dark now, real dark and I'm not sure where I am. Then, as suddenly as when a bomb hits, a great explosion of light from above (is it heaven, am I dead, are great American angels come to ferry me to the other side?) blinds me and almost has me swerve off the road into a ditch but I wrestle with the steering and gain control of the car but I still can't see and then I can see again and I'm about to go over a cliff somewhere in the desert but I'm floating, the car's floating, Babs is floating and she's screaming, "Oh my God, what's going on, Theo?" and I'm screaming, "Oh my God, I don't know!" and Uncle Sam and Joe McCarthy are in the back screaming too, although there is no back seat in this car so how could they be, but we're being lifted up, up, up to somewhere in the sky. I roll down the window and lean out. I can't make out what it is at first, but then I see it, the craft, a real flying saucer! the spaceship hanging as if from a string like a child's toy airplane you hang from a ceiling fan or lighting fixture that spins round and round. We're being lifted up as though by magic, but I know it must be some unthinkable alien technology and it is – damn Soviets, always kidnapping you and lifting you up in their *traktor*-beams like it's nobody's business.

Steadily, we ascend to the little Russian spacecraft and the underside opens up like a great mouth and we're eaten alive, but not really, just taken inside to what looks like a cargo bay/vehicle hangar of some sort, full of farming machinery and crates and vehicles. Oh God, it's all so beige and chrome, and boring and decidedly low-tech, like we're in the hold of an *actual ship*, almost anyway, with pipes and plumbing snaking about everywhere above us and furnaces here and there on the ground. Smells like sawdust and manure on fire in here. There are pictures of tractors and farms everywhere, great big agricultural posters, and framed photographs of Uncle Joe (Stalin, that is) like family portraits of him and his Commie bastard buddies, him standing around with his comrades, arms around their shoulders or shaking hands with someone only there's no one else in the picture because they've all been purged, erased from history – a damn good job they did of it, too – but it's still pretty easy to tell that there was someone else in the picture originally, like that one over there – Uncle S shaking hands with some phantom, a great eerie void in the middle of the picture – and on others it's even worse, their faces have all been replaced with Stalin's, rows of S-men just standing there, and he all looks happy as punch.

A siren starts wailing like an air raid is about to happen and Russian soldiers in their fur coats and fur hats burst into the room from some other room and start pointing their AKs at me and Babs and the boys and I slide out of her real slow like, and kneel down on the floor like they tell me to. Sam and Joe do the same. When they get closer to me, I realise, they're not Russian soldiers at all, not even human, the bastards are Goddamn aliens! Little green men in Russian hats and coats with great big heads and bulging eyes and long fingers like straws with little flat suckers on the ends where their fingertips should be. Sticking out of each of their big furry hats are two insect-like antennae too. And their weapons aren't AKs even, same basic shape, yes, but the contours are all weird and alien and made of this weird bluish-green metalloid unlike anything found on Earth. I punch one in the face as he approaches and he wails something in his garbled alien tongue, just gibberish, not a real language at all.

One of them comes forward and punches me, but it's completely laughable 'cause it doesn't hurt, like being punched by a baby wearing a boxing glove, but then they shoot me with one of their space-alien-guns ZAPF! and it's like being electrocuted and then I'm asleep.

Sometime later, I don't know how long, I wake up to Lassie the Golden Retriever licking my face, and Joe saying, "Goddamn Commie-Socialist un-American, Commie-Soviet-Russian bastards. It was like this in Korea," to which Sam replies, "It was like this at the Alamo, only worse. Goddamn Mexicans." Lassie barks his assent, while I stroke the back of his neck.

I see that Joe looks puzzled, says, "But you weren't at the Alamo, you're not even a real person like I am, just the personification of American Ideals—" and Sam interrupts, "I ain't no personification, Joe, I *am* America, Goddammit! Always have been, always will be. Yes, I may be named for Samuel Wilson, American Hero, who died in the War of 1812 (Goddamn British bastards killed him), but I'm also all soldiers, all true Americans, even you, even Theodore here (a fine name, son, a fine name indeed), all the time, all at once, as well. That's why I wear this suit of stars and stripes. It's not just for show, Joe. It is what it is."

Joe ponders this and tries to get his head around the idea of Sam being all Americans, all the time, all at once, but he doesn't seem so sure.

We're in what looks like a perfectly ordinary nondescript waiting room with only one door: chairs against the walls, table in the centre covered by magazines and newspapers (only there's a great big window looking out into space on one side), but none of them are in American (English, that is – the American kind) so they're useless. Nevertheless, with hands that are not my own, I pick up an issue of the futurist magazine Tekhnika Molodezhi and marvel at the miraculous images of the speculative Soviet space art, laughing ironically at the rather far-fetched predictions being made in the articles and stories printed there as well.

"Put that crap down, man," says Joe. "We're approaching the big Mother herself." This gives me a bad feeling in my gut, so I take a look. Lassie starts whining, sensing, as animals do, that something's up. I feel it too.

Oh no. Looking out the window into the vastness of starry space, like a big old American flag streaked with comets and asteroid belts and planetary rings, I see it.

They're taking us to the Motherlandship.

Things just got a helluva lot more complicated. I don't think I'll be home in time for dinner.

I turn around, looking for anything to use as a weapon and Uncle Joe says to me, "The chips are down, son, so what are you gonna do about it?" and Uncle Sam says, "Lets blow this joint, sonny. I want you! . . . to blow this joint." They hand me a Thomson machine gun and some grenades, and we hunker down, ready to burst out and surprise these bastards soon as they open the door.

I watch out the window as we are taken into the behemoth craft, entering the wide mouth of an open hangar as though being swallowed by a giant woman in the shape of a spaceship. Soldiers are everywhere awaiting our arrival.

It doesn't look good.

The ship shakes and judders as we land. I can hear voices now, alongside hurried footsteps, clacking against the floors outside the door like little tiny horses, rushing towards us, getting closer, about to swing open that door, and then they do.

Uncle Joe and Sam cover me as I sprint forward at the enemy, laying down a hail of suppressing fire that has them cowering in their poorly-made boots, so small they look like children's shoes. Lassie growls and leaps at one of them, going for the throat, snout drenched in their Red and yellow blood. I knock a few of them down and blow a few of their heads off, Red and yellow Commie alien insides exploding everywhere like confetti, splattering the walls of their big beige-chrome spaceship, and me, Lassie, Joe and Sam sprint away. A great big bolt of plasma or something splatters in front of me and some gets on my forearm and it burns like hot lead. I nearly fall over but Joe steadies me and we keep moving, our alien enemies shooting after us with their space-weapons PEW PEW, PEW PEW, ZAP ZAP, ZORK ZORK! They keep missing and we're away, scot-free nearly, I can tell.

But then, we're stopped in our tracks, as a line of alien Soviet soldiers file out from behind a corner, blocking our escape. In the middle of the corridor, we turn round again but another line of soldiers blocks the way back.

We're trapped. The Commie alien soldiers aren't moving. Just watching. Waiting for something to happen, but what? My answer walks out in front of them and it's—

M-G-M Proudly Announces An Entertainment Event of Exceptional Importance

---

The
teaming of the
celebrated star
Miss
KATHERINE
HEPBURN
with
one of the most
distinguished
actors of our
time—

Oh my golly God, it's Katherine Hepburn in *The Iron Petticoat*, which also starred Bob Hope. But, wait, wait, wait a moment, now. That doesn't sound right. Just hold on . . .

Katherine Hepburn *and* Bob Hope, you say?—

Stop the projection machine, there must be some mistake!

NO! there's <u>no mistake---</u>

The star team the world has

    NEVER EXPECTED!

BOB HOPE

    KATHERINE

    HEPRBURN

    IN

"THE IRON PETTICOAT"

COPYRIGHT: MCMLVI IN U.S.A BY ©HOPE RECORDS, INC.

AND BENHAR PRODUCTIONS, INC.

NARRATOR: Yes, Bob and Kate, they're simply great. In The Iron Petticoat *Kate portrays an air force captain no less, who is forced to land among friendly enemies—*

But wait a minute, that film wasn't released until 1956, so how could I have seen it? This doesn't make any sense—

176

KATHERINE HEPBURN: I kisz yoo az ay soldjah . . . Vhat iz wrong?

BOB HOPE: I'm not used to kissing soldiers.

NARRATOR: You know, the Iron Petticoat isn't really iron. It's black silk. And it isn't a petticoat. It's a negligée.

KATHERINE HEPBURN: It is for svimmink?

UNKNOWN ACTOR: It can be worn in the water.

KATHERINE HEPBURN: You vear it in frant or in beck?

UNKNOWN ACTOR: In front.

KATHERINE HEPBURN: You are foolink mee, id iz not for svimmink, id iz ay falzse boozum.

UNKNOWN ACTOR: Bra, for short.

KATHERINE HEPBURN: Zso zhat is zhe vay id iz darn.

BOB HOPE: You're amazing.

KATHERINE HEPBURN: Zhat iz beekoz Amehrikan vooman arr sooperfishul. Theyr eenterested cheevfly in nayl pollizsh end falzse boozums.

BOB HOPE: Yeah, they're inclined to make mountains out of molehills.

NARRATOR: Yeah, the whole world over, a dame's a dame, air force captain or not. This is the kind of propaganda our side is looking for. But it looked like im-propaganda to the girl Bob was actually engaged to marry.

BOB HOPE: You told that I—

KATHERINE HEPBURN: Eddie—

BOB HOPE: Ah-I—

KATHERINE HEPBURN: I vud lyk ivf you vud gi— I em zsorry to introod.

BOB HOPE: Oh, how's Ivan, have you heard from him lately?

KATHERINE HEPBURN: Noh.

BOB HOPE: Fine looking chap, Ivan.

UNKNOWN ACTRESS: Do you sleep in those?

KATHERINE HEPBURN: NATDURALLEEY.

UNKNOWN ACTRESS: What are they, good conduct medals?

The New Look –
in HOPE hilarity!
The New Laughter –
in HEPBURN histrionics!
BOB HOPE
   KATHERINE
   HEPBURN
"THE IRON PETTICOAT"
   An M-G-M RELEASE
IN VISTAVISION · TECHNICOLOR®
BOB and KATE
SIMPLY
GREAT—

The film borrows heavily, almost to the point of plagiarism some have said, from Ernst Lubitsch's earlier 1939 film *Ninotchka*, which starred Greta Garbo, but several close comparisons can also be drawn to *Jet Pilot* which starred Janet Leigh and John Wayne—but wait, hold on another minute, that film came out a year later than Hepburn's in 1957, although principal photography was finished in 1950, so maybe I saw it somehow, but that still doesn't account for how I could have seen Hepburn's film before. Hmmm. Maybe this is a dream, but that still doesn't explain anything so—

Katherine Hepburn as Soviet Pilot Captain Vinka Kovelenko, in full costume/uniform, starts talking in her phony Russian accent, so bad at times, (almost German-sounding, although it's all more or less the same garbled nonsense to an American ear) it's difficult to listen at all, saying, "Vell, vell, vell, vhat hev vhee heer? Fvree Amehrikan spiyz, eh? Zhat iz zhe vay id iz darn, eh?"

Lassie snarls and barks at her, and Hepburn-Kovelenko shoots him a manic-terrifying glance and the poor dog runs behind me, covering his eyes with his paws.

"I em Keptin Vinka Kovelenko," continues Hepburn-Kovelenko, "and yoo arr nohw may prizonors. Tek zhem avhay, but tek zher veapons avhay forst!"

Damn, they have us right where they want us. I should have seen this coming. Our weapons are snatched away from us by some invisible force and they clack against the Lenin-picture-and-Stalin-picture-and-Hammer-and-Sickle-picture-lined beige-chrome walls of the corridor we're in and stay there suspended in air, defying gravity. Damn Russians, they don't have gravity over there so they wouldn't know.

"Sorch zher poketz, in caze zhey are hiydink enythink."

A trio of the little green Commies comes forward and searches our pockets and the insides of our jackets for any hidden weapons but we have none so they return to their posts satisfied.

"Tek zhem too zhe inderrogayzion rroom. Vhee zshal ekstrakt zher zekrets fhrom zher braynz!"

We're taken to different rooms. Alone somewhere on the ship with the alien bastards, I'm restrained, held back against the most uncomfortable chair I've ever sat in in my life by big metal clamps, while the aliens prod and poke at me, making fun of my manly American features, snickering to themselves while they prepare one of their alien instruments of torture, no doubt.

I feel as though I've been here before, but I can't say when, as they fasten me into an ominous alien machine that defies any more detailed description, it's just so *ominous* and, and, and *alien*. I can't describe it any other way. In front of the chair I'm fastened into, the alien machine opens up and out comes a great long mechanical proboscis of sorts, that starts to circle my head like a shark, brushing against me like an insect antenna, and then they jibber and jabber at me in their Russian-alien voices, high as a kite and lower than a swinging chariot at the same time, like two different voices talking over each other at once, and it is just plain horrible to listen to, I'll tell ya that. And then they start prodding my head with their finger-suckers and it's, it's—oh God, they're – I can understand them, they – they want to suck out my brains! Oh God, no, they're going to suck it out through a straw! Scramble them like eggs and put them back in! That's what it is, the proboscis, a great big straw, oh God! And I can hear their thoughts inside my head saying, *You will tell us your nuclear secrets. You will give them to us, just like the Rosenbergs, you will betray your country, you will betray yourself. You will give us what we desire . . .*

"Screw you, buddy," I yell, and I boot him in the face. Then one of them steps forward and hits me with the butt of its space-alien-weapon and it hurts a helluva lot more than their baby fists do. My ears ring and I go dizzy and faint, my cheek numb where they hit me. I can feel it start to swell. They press a few buttons on their brain-sucking-straw-machine and it moves forward ready to empty my head, but before it can do anything to me, there's a big rumbling sound from outside the room, and then BOOM! A great big hole in the far wall is blown open and there's Uncle Sam, Lassie and Joe gunning down the alien bastards like little ducks at a shooting range. The enemy shoots back PEW PEW PEW, but it's no good. BLAM BLAM BLAM, go our American bullets and they're dead. Sam, Joe and Lassie greet me but there's another great rumbling throughout the ship and a loud wrenching-squealing sound. The ship's been damaged by the explosion, I can tell. The whole thing's gonna blow! So we're off and on our way again, just about ready to escape this Godforsaken Soviet spaceship.

"Well done, Joe. Just where were you hiding those grenades?" asks Sam as we hurry down the beige-chrome corridor from earlier.

"Ahem, um, nowhere . . ." he says. "My pocket, they were in my pocket," stammers Joe.

I begin, "I thought they searched all our pockets when they—"

But Joe interrupts me, "They were in my pocket, for God's sake. Nowhere else, just my pocket, that's where they—"

Joe doesn't finish. Standing before us is the dread Soviet Space Pilot Captain Katherine-Vinka Hepburn-Kovelenko. "Yoo vhill noht gedt oudt ovf hehr aliyvf, Amehriken skumm! Keel zhem!" she screams and more of her minions start to charge, all of them shooting off their space-guns at us. We return fire until they're all dead, but the Captain's left standing, and she's blocking our exit.

Lassie looks at me as if to say, *Go, Theodore-Master. I will sacrifice myself to save America. Because I am a good boy, yes I am, yes I am*, and then he leaps at the Captain, biting and clawing at her, tearing her to pieces as Joe, Sam and me rush past them both to make our escape. At the door to the hangar, I look back at Lassie as he fights the Captain to the death, and he looks back at me for a moment, and I know he's saying *Go, go! It was an honour to serve you, Theodore-Master.*

Babs is there waiting for us, which doesn't make sense but it doesn't have to, and she's shouting, "Come on! Get in!" and we do and she revs her engine and bats her eyelashes and, tires screeching, burning rubber, she zooms out of the hold and into space where we head back to good old America, on good old Earth.

Behind us, the Motherlandship explodes in a silent flash of colour, lighting up the starry night of space like fireworks on the Fourth of July. Suddenly we're back on the ground again and—

I'm driving along and it's dark now, real dark.

~o~

The novel from which these extracts are taken began life as a short story I wrote in college. At around 60,000 words, the plot is less a plot and more a suggestion of one. It follows Theodore Anderson, a successful advertising executive in 1950s America. He's charming, funny, well-educated, and lives the American Dream. Then he's brainwashed into an insane anti-Soviet secret agent, intent on stopping the communist threat by any means necessary. Considering America's current political climate, I think it's quite relevant (but maybe I'm just tooting my own horn).

We watch as Theodore's mind unravels: suspecting his wife, friends, and neighbours of being sympathisers and spies, experiencing hallucinations of Uncle Sam and Joseph McCarthy – whom I paraphrase in the opening extract. He is likewise pursued by his evil Russian doppelganger Fyodor Andreyevich (who may or may not be the same person as Theodore), eventually turning to espionage and violence. He also talks to his car, a 1953 Chevrolet *Corvette*, which he names Barbara – it talks back to him too. The novel explores other 50s social issues as well, like homophobia, sexism, marital abuse, and xenophobia.

I love Virginia Woolf and Bret Easton Ellis's work, so stream of consciousness was a big influence on my writing. I'm also a huge fan of Vladimir Nabokov and the literary games he plays, both overtly and more subtly. As such, I've incorporated anagrams, in the form of character names, and hidden messages into the larger text. I'm similarly interested in the unreliable narrator, and there are times when Theodore reaches beyond his own POV to explore this. Furthermore, in keeping with the Modernist/Postmodernist influences, and themes of espionage/subterfuge, certain sections of the novel are censored. Additional narrative voices will sometimes interrupt the text halfway through a sentence, with entire scenes playing out before returning to the original line. Certain words are written in red to illustrate Theodore's POV, with the colour of someone's shoes, blood, etc. justifying his violent actions. At one point, for instance, he realises a little girl with a red balloon is a communist spy, and decides to interrogate her.

I chose these particular extracts because they give you a good idea of the overall style, with a glimpse of Theodore before his kidnapping/brainwashing, plus the Soviet alien abduction hallucination, with its metafictional presentation of the film trailer to 1956's *The Iron Petticoat*. Theodore is a caricature of 50s America, spewing out references to popular culture, the story being as much satirical farce as it is an exploration of psychology. The text was as much influenced by Dostoyevsky as by the weird fiction of H. P. Lovecraft, and the uncanny, particularly the doppelganger, figures into the story in different ways. I'm toying with the idea of writing a companion novel from Andreyevich's POV (looking behind the Iron Curtain to focus on Russia). It may not be for everyone, but for a first, though unpublished, novel, I'd say it's pretty good.

IMOGEN MYERS
OPENER

After training as a dancer, Imogen studied English at the University of Cambridge on a Winston Churchill Memorial Trust Bursary. She appreciates an eclectic variety of fiction, ranging from medieval literature to cult horror films of the 1960s and '70s. A Performing Arts enthusiast, Imogen has worked with both the National Youth Ballet and the National Youth Theatre of Great Britain, and was recently awarded a place on a new playwrights' programme at the National Theatre. Imogen aspires to write for page, stage, and screen, and enjoys directing both Dance and Drama.

As the opener shut, DELL plucked up the courage to perform the most painful, and also the most criminal, act known to him at that point in time.

DELL ATSIV Y2223 was nothing remarkable when standing as little as ten metres away from him. He was relatively small for a Y model and stood at a mere 68 X 10 X 4 inches. He was naturally pale skinned, although, as global temperatures had risen, his skin-tone more regularly resembled that of a tommy-toe, as opposed to maintaining its natural sanguine tint. His square-rimmed see-ers were not stronger, nor weaker, than those of the regulation model, and his silver 3 X 4 inch DELL control box fitted snugly into the left-hand pocket of his grey overalls, and was wired into an insertion made halfway down his left hearer-riverbed.

DELL ATSIV Y2223 was nothing remarkable when standing as little as ten metres away from him.

If you happened to move any closer, however, and to look him square-on, you would notice that DELL had a freckle on the grey tulip of his left peeper. A spot of brown. A mark against the normality of metallic modernity. In that freckle you could see everything that had happened to DELL, and everything that was going to happen. You could make out the ups and downs, the highs and lows and the inevitable pain that comes as retribution for being slightly different in a network which strives for uniformity and punishes individuality.

Just like his peepers, DELL ATSIV Y2223 was a non-conformer.

On this particular day, 29/02/2232 to be exact, DELL was sauntering back to his cubic-living-space during the midday heat of the sweltering sun. He was returning from a repair job which his line-manager, MAC KOOB Y99, had sent him through his hearer-piece at precisely 9:21:46 that morning. DELL had never seen his line-manager. All he knew was that he routinely sent orders down his hearer-piece, and that he was a MAC, meaning that he was high-up in the network - possibly even an Administrator. Although he had never met MAC KOOB Y99, DELL knew that to be a MAC his line-manager must be immensely intelligent, as well as being an exceptionally committed Monitor. It was down to these two facts that DELL respected MAC enormously and went about his orders with a sense of duty and zeal.

This particular job, however, was not so gratefully received.

As DELL ambled home he was struck by an immense surge of passion. Forgetting his wasted muscles - an endemic problem in these days of little exercise - he broke into a run and continued breathlessly, darting all the way up five flights of stairs to his personal cubic-living-space.

As he stared into the laser peeper-reader at his opener, DELL reflected that it had not been wise to run with his hearer-piece in - one of the Trackers would be sure to notice a change in his in-built pedometer stats and suspect something out of the ordinary. As his opener shifted sideways to reveal his cubic-living-space, DELL, at war with the surge of feelings threatening to overwhelm him, decided it was safest to remove the hearer-piece before any chemical imbalance could be observed.

As the opener shut, DELL plucked up the courage to perform the most painful, and also the most criminal, act known to him at that point in time.

Without hesitation, he tugged brutishly at his hearer-piece, trying, unsuccessfully, to suppress his screeches of pain, until, reluctantly, the hearer-piece surrendered and followed DELL's touchers, spitefully bringing with it a large and semi-circular chunk of DELL's inner-hearer. Red-oxygen-carrier splattered everywhere - all over DELL's touchers - and pummelled at his naked hearer-tambourines. But DELL didn't care. All he felt was intense elation combined with insurmountable anger, now made all the more immense by electrifying pain.

DELL knew what was bothering him.

DELL knew who was bothering him.

DELL had arrived at the X model's house at 10:03:46, forty-two minutes after receiving MAC KOOB Y99's orders through his hearer-piece. Her cubic-living-space, he was instructed, was fifty metres forward and seventy metres to the left of his own. She lived at Number Thirteen. For some irrational reason, unknown to even himself, DELL felt slightly uneasy at the number thirteen. He concluded that it was probably something to do with his creator once removed on his X side who had always had crazy ideas. Nevertheless, disregarding his instincts and inhibitions, DELL utilised his control box and sent a message to the resident of Number Thirteen signalling them to open their opener.

The X model was an AVIVO ORCIM X121 with a faulty information browser. She also, DELL noticed, had long and strikingly red head-warmer, and her peepers were not the regular grey colour. In fact, they were an indescribable marriage of green and brown, the likes of which DELL had never seen before. She was also slightly larger in the first dimension than DELL was, standing, to DELL's guess, at approximately 70 inches vertically. Her manner seemed cold and disapproving. She was haughty and, regardless of the fact that models were not permitted to communicate through their devourers, she made an audible tutting noise when DELL sent the message to her hearer-piece that it would take him approximately twenty-six minutes to fix her.

Everything about her was distasteful. And yet she was irresistible.

DELL hurried into his cubic-waste-space and shut the opener behind him.

As the opener shut, DELL plucked up the courage to perform the most painful, and also the most criminal, act known to him at that point in time.

Free-breeding and other such stimulation were strictly forbidden, but DELL could not stop himself. As his right toucher slid up and down his tiddlewiddle, with the lubricative assistance of his own red-oxygen-carrier, DELL could not help but feel a sudden surge of fear. If he was caught fiddlinghiswiddle he would be deleted for sure.

DELL heard the opener to his cubic-living-space opening.

DELL stopped fiddlinghiswiddle and let it drop with a surge of adrenaline that threatened to stop his ticker tocking. He zipped up his double-leggers quickly and watered his touchers to remove the red-oxygen-carrier.

Tentatively, DELL opened the opener.

She was sat at his eater. AVIVO, with her long red head-warmer and unique peepers, was sat at his eater.

Silence.

She see-ed at him in a disapproving manner, before stating through her devourer,

'You have a freckle on the tulip of your left peeper.'

~o~

'Opener' is the opening chapter of a dystopian novel which was originally borne out of a last-minute coursework rush for AS Level English. The ideas having stewed for a while, I pressed 'START' on my timer and scribbled it down as fast as I could. Coming back to it with a good few years' distance, I rearranged and developed parts of the piece, as well as altering some of the sections and vocabulary, which, with hindsight, definitely needed a rethink. Some such sections remain and continue to perplex me, but perhaps I'll return, newly enlightened, in a few more years' time (!).

The piece is heavily influenced by works such as Orwell's *1984* and Burgess' *A Clockwork Orange.* In both works, I admired the authors' flexibility with language and their ability to merge standard English with neologisms in a manner that retained comprehensibility, whilst adding a futuristic bite. As a reader, I appreciate non-linear structure and find it exciting to have to piece narrative together, particularly in works such as Heller's *Catch-22,* and in films including *Pulp Fiction* and *Mulholland Drive* (although I'm still not sure I've quite got my head around the latter!). Having found such inventive structural experimentation engaging, I undertook to try it myself, hence the use of repetition and single-line paragraphs.

I chose to set my piece in a world in which the boundary between humans and technology has become indistinct as, at the time, I found the pace of technological advancement pretty disconcerting. I wondered what it was that made us innately human and what it would be that would continue to differentiate us from machinery, and decided that both passion and fallibility featured highly on the list. Humans are far less logical than machines, and are, consequently, significantly more likely to mess up under pressure. Machines, on the other hand, are far more likely to detect any such errors. Sadly, it seems that the threat of becoming slaves to technology is looking less far-fetched than it did at this piece's inception six years ago.

As a reader and viewer, I am gripped by pacey, quirky, zippy, action-fuelled work, and I strongly admire the directorial styles of Kubrick, Lynch, Tarantino and Luhrmann. I enjoy experimenting with writing plays and screenplays, as well as short stories and narrative poems.

FIONA BREWIS
AN INCREDIBLE FIGURE

Fiona Brewis, 18, is currently studying German at the University of Warwick, where she manages her degree alongside her duties as Arts Editor of online youth newspaper Young Perspective and President of German society. Her love for writing stemmed from an insatiable thirst for reading as a child, and she hopes to one day publish a novel. Out of term time Fiona can be found on the streets of her hometown, Edinburgh, tucking into the revered Scottish delicacy of a deep fried Mars bar.

Bob Cheeseman had the sort of ridiculous name that meant no one could ever take him seriously. Bank managers chortled at his name, the postman snorted at his name, passport control giggled at his name. They could never resist trying it out, testing, as if it were a foreign swear word. "Welcome to Scotland, Mr Bob Cheeseman," with a knowing smile or wink. Mr Cheeseman just smiled back. He didn't mind being the subject of hilarity, which was just as well, as combined with his name, Bob Cheeseman's sensational figure made for a headline hit.

His shape was unbelievable. Rolls of fat stacked above his belt like cake, the suspenders on his trousers acting like a bra for his belly, supporting an immense mass which was otherwise in danger of sinking to the floor and pooling around his feet. Every time he looked in the mirror to appreciate his entirety, he seemed, impossibly, to have acquired an extra bulge, and every time, he gazed with a mixture of pride and revulsion at the offending monstrosity, marvelling at his innate talent to simply keep putting on weight. Mr Cheeseman never called it obesity, he called it fatness. Obesity was why you went to the doctor, fatness was why you went to McDonalds.

Sometimes when he was tired of the strain on the suspenders, and when there was nobody else around, he would physically lift his belly onto the table, and sigh at the relief he felt from taking the burden off his shoulders. In this position, he would often wonder about the very foreign concept of slimness. What would it feel like, buying an ice cream without a flake? What would it feel like to be within the range of ordinary bathroom scales, and not have to use the one at the zoo which they used to weigh the hippopotami? What would it feel like, to be able to stand on the second floor of a building, and know that there was absolutely no risk of falling through the floor? It was a staggering thought, and if it weren't for the effort associated with losing weight, he might've given it a go. What he needed, was motivation.

He was not ashamed of his stupendous mass. In fact, he almost cherished it; it was a measure, in all manners of speaking, of his successful career in business. With every victory in his business, no matter how small, he would allow himself to indulge his craving for food, and as his business rapidly expanded, so too did his waistline. Whenever he mentioned, casually, that he was a business boss, people reacted rather rudely.

"I've always been a fan of fast food," they'd say.

To which Mr Cheeseman would draw up his bulk and haughtily reply,

"Obviously. I take it you're not a gym regular?"

Nobody would ever have guessed, that he was in fact the co-owner of a multimillion pound gym chain, which extended to forty-three countries and several cruise ships, had created special pet gyms for hypocritical Americans who had difficulty feeling their pooch's ribs, and had invented a radical crockery range, including "The Common Sense Plate". This consisted of a plate with half the surface area of a normal-sized plate, tricking unsuspecting fatties into consuming healthy-sized portions. His specialised luxury gym chain, a series of clinics which catered specifically for the needs of the weighty, was so revered, it was rumoured people actually put on weight so they would qualify for membership.

Mr Green, the co-owner with whom he shared the business, was the polar opposite of Mr Cheeseman; in as many ways as Mr Cheeseman was extraordinary, Mr Green was ordinary. It was as if the two men had invisible fat channels connecting them; every time Mr Cheeseman put on a stone, Mr Green lost one, resulting in a partnership than that was more comical than it was financial. Whilst Mr Cheeseman handled the advertising, Mr Green held the company's best economic interests at heart, and it was with this in mind that he approached Mr Cheeseman.

"A very important potential investor refused to buy our shares, because he "couldn't go into business with a fitness company captained by a whale"."

There was no more to be said. Mr Cheeseman was not in the habit of being compared to enormous stodgy sea-dwellers, and it was something he had no desire to encourage. Admittedly, there was one time he was lying face down on the beach and a concerned walker phoned the SSPC about a beached walrus, only for an SSPC representative to arrive and declare it – he – was actually a malformed whale. He had decided it would be too embarrassing to reveal himself a human, so he let them bundle him up in a net and tow him back out to sea using the local rescue boat, where he then had to float around pretending to be a whale for a while. He got sunburnt.

Over the next few months Mr Cheeseman exercised like he had never exercised before, which, actually, he hadn't. First he went for the obvious choice; his gym. He broke a running machine, and never went back. Mr Green took care of that particular gym thereafter. Next he tried a spin class, which jellified his legs to the extent he had to be stretchered off. It took six men to carry the stretcher. He had never been so mortified. Then he tried ice-skating and sank through the ice until he was as stuck as a big-boned seal in a smaller-than-previously-thought icehole. The whole rink had to be melted and he swam out the door in shame.

Finally, his salvation came, in the form of a dance class. The class itself was an embarrassment – he went a bit wild when the overenthusiastic teacher shouted "Shake everything you got!" – but it was after this, that he noticed the sign which was destined to lead to an extended career as a sports champion.

"Sumo Wrestling – Not For Cowards." He didn't take any notice of this sign. Sumo wrestling was far too mainstream for people of exceptional girth, so he went for karate instead. From the very beginning, he was outstanding. The karate fighters would dance around him for hours, tiring themselves out whilst he stood there eating a burger, his soft belly absorbing every jab, and when they had drained themselves of all energy he finished them off with a soft poke to the forehead and they keeled over quite happily.

A few fights and three championships later, Cheeseman didn't regret his choice in the slightest. His technique had made him world famous, promoting his company massively, and giving him further reason to celebrate his accomplishments by ingesting yet more food. Jealous competitors called him "representative of Britain in every way" to which he just chuckled and chopped their competitor in the face. The secret to his success, was the very thing he had been trying so hard to rid himself of; brilliant, reviled, fat.

Of course, he never did lose any weight, but took comfort from the fact that if his life was to be shortened by diabetes or heart disease, at least he would have lived it to the full; eating, earning, and revelling in the art of gaining weight.

For those of you who tried and failed, miserably, to get fit as a New Year's resolution, allow Mr Bob Cheeseman's story to lift you out of your wallowing pit of despair. Cast off your hatred towards your pudgy thighs, and remember, that fat can be a wonderful, life-enhancing, blessing.

~o~

As a somewhat overactive optimist, I admit I have absolutely no time for people who take life too seriously. To me, a good read is a book which totally and completely immerses the reader, to the point where they forget their environment – perhaps a bus, a waiting room, or the living room of their fiancé's parents – and snort inappropriately loud with laughter.

It's a real shame that only a fraction of young people nowadays would choose to settle down and pick up a book in their spare time. There is a simply uncountable number of brilliant escapes guided by authors from each and every background; a complete inferno of imaginations just waiting to be harnessed. The inevitable escapism of a good story is what I hope to achieve in my writing. I hope to bring a little joy and laughter into people's lives, or a slight release at the end of a tiring day.

"An Incredible Figure" is the product of a fascination with body image and the way society perceives those who fall outside the perception of a "normal" weight. I am all in favour of promoting confidence regardless of the shape of your body, but obviously not in favour of people becoming a gargantuan wad of fat like the title character in the story. On the one hand, putting on a little weight is not necessarily a bad thing, as it is, after all, reversible. However, I had so much fun playing with descriptions that I reached the point where I was almost encouraging people to get fat, which is unequivocally not to be encouraged.

Yes, there are more obese people nowadays than ever before. Yes, we need to do something about it. But there is too much idealisation of the thin body, meaning that people with anything more than skin on their bones learn to hate every cosy fold of fat adorning their chin, and I believe this is not the correct way to go about reducing waistlines. Rather than rounding on people's failed efforts to lose weight, we should be distributing rounds of applause for the effort, in the hope that eventually they will have more success than dear Mr Cheeseman in reaching their goal body shape.

My aim in writing the story, however, was not entirely to make a grand statement, but also to provide a piece of writing to which people can relate and hence enjoy the silliness of. A scrumptious overload of potatoes at Christmas, one chocolate cake too many at Nan's birthday, a slightly too cheeky "cheeky Nandos" – we've all been there.

Sure, we all want to look good and not roll our way to work each morning. But we also want to buy four doughnuts for £1, because who isn't excited by that bargain? We can't help it if our housemates are conveniently not in and we have to eat them all ourselves before they go stale.

Let's enjoy a guilty conscience, and the last biscuit in the tin.

AMBER JENSEN
THE ETERNAL MAN

Amber is an eighteen-year-old aspiring writer from Devon, England. She has a twin sister who inspires a lot of her writing, although after suffering from depression and anxiety a few more philosophical focuses became present (such as in this piece). Her dream would be to publish at least one successful book and work with animals of all shapes and sizes.

Death, people would say, was a mean master. Theodore disagreed. Death did its job; it killed indiscriminately and treated everybody the same. Of course, it treated them poorly, but the same nonetheless. Theodore's bad luck simply meant he got that treatment many more times than the average human being.

Death was a funny creature, really. It made games out of the job it had occupied for centuries: with Theo being the only person on Earth who could see Death, hear Death and live on after death, Death took it upon itself to tease him. Someone would be sentenced to die, Death would sit in the chair next to them, fake a big sneeze as Theo watched, and then that person would have a heart attack as though shocked into cardiac arrest.

Of course, seeing a man dying is not funny. But after years and years of rebirth, Theodore could see the appeal to making light of such things, and when he laughed as that man was rushed to hospital and all the occupants of the café stared at him, he wondered why they were so profoundly affected by the death of a man they did not know and had not spoken to, even once.

However, the manner in which Death took life in Theo's presence became much less amusing when Theo, after a long day of job hunting, saw Death standing behind a woman on the train. Theodore could not see anything under that black hood but somehow he knew Death was smiling.

Jessica – Theo would find out her name later – had messy hair, brown with striking ginger streaks, and bore a vacant expression as she stared down at the floor. She wore an odd necklace, mismatched socks that she pulled up to her knees and a dress that drew distasteful expressions from the mother sitting opposite her.

Theodore had been watching her for the whole train ride, stricken with the most whimsical instinct to say hello, when Death had appeared.

Never before had such horror overcome Theo upon seeing Death's ethereal image emerge from the dark and crowd over a person as though he was actually making them smaller. The way Death seemingly grew, the way the woman shrank into his black design, injected such fear into Theodore that he froze as in slow motion. Death's misshapen hands glided towards the woman, skulking over each of her shoulders, as Theodore imagined all the possible ways she could die and what Death would do–

"Miss!" cried Theodore. Heads turned to him; not the one that mattered, not Death's, but Theo knew he was being listened to: Death's fluidity had shuddered to a stop, curious and amused. "Excuse me, Miss, there's a spider next to your head–"

"I'm sorry?" she said.

Death resumed consuming her, and Theodore lunged forward in such abhorrence that he could not stop himself from grabbing the woman's wrist, from snatching her away, from shrugging off the men that tried to pull him back. "I'm just protecting her, I swear, I'm not trying anything–"

"It's okay," the woman said. She was inspecting Theodore with gross interest. "It's okay. Thank you."

Her defenders backed down and Theodore relaxed, glancing at Death over the woman's shoulder. The woman followed his sight before turning back and frowning.

"Bit intense, don't you think?" she said, and smiled. "I didn't see whatever spider you were talking about but hey, I believe you. You've made my day a bit more interesting and I've got a new thing to check off my bucket list: 'random man swoops in and saves me a bad hair day.' Do you know how awful spiders are to get out of your hair?"

Theo was too stirred to be embarrassed. "I don't think they would stay in your hair for long."

"Well, yes, but they are a pain once they're in. 'Specially the rubber ones! My niece is obsessed with those at the moment, loves spiders so much her mother bought her a tarantula, and she put that on my head, too. Named him Sir Tronalon." She smiled daintily. "Don't ask me why. I'm Jessica. Jess, really, but either will do."

"Theodore Ivers," he replied. "Or Theo if you want. I have, er, never been acquainted with a tarantula myself."

"Oh, their webs are nasty, prey gets caught like that!" She snapped her fingers. "I've just got done buying her a new enclosure for him, you know–"

Death was still there, standing against that wall, his arms held disjointedly upwards. Theodore felt cold. For the first time since his first life, he found it hard to look at Death.

"Drinks," he said, interrupting Jessica, "With me. Interested?"

She was strange, this woman, being so open with a stranger (especially one that grabbed her on public transport). Theo had not been so open with anyone in many, many years. He didn't know how to take it but he did know one thing: for some inexplicable reason, he didn't want this woman to die.

"Actually," she said, and inspected him for a long while before smiling slowly, "I was just heading to my sister's house for tea, but the more the merrier. Want to come?"

"I'm not so sure–"

He looked back at Death's stark figure then to Jessica, who was saying something about him trying on Mr Tronalon like a hat, and conceded.

"Of course, I would be honoured to meet your sister."

"So long as you're not a killer," she jested.

Death dissipated into the background like ink fading into water.

❖

Sherry was the name of Jessica's sister. She was taller than Jessica and didn't seem to laugh much but she made a good roast dinner and stopped her daughter, Callie, from putting her tarantula on Theodore's head, so as far as Theodore could see there was nothing not to like. She seemed relatively unsurprised to see Theo arrive with her sister and Theo for one was thankful, although he wondered whether he should have been.

They had a bad relationship, he thought, the sisters. For a moment he questioned why he saved Jessica when he had not yet seen any reason to have done so – and then he saw Callie pulling on Jessica's necklace, laughing, asking whether she wore it all day.

"All day," assured Jessica. "This woman on the train even asked me where I bought it. She was so impressed when I said my little genius of a niece made it for me! Her own daughter had never made her something so pretty."

Woman on the train? With a daughter? Was she talking about the mother that was watching her with distaste? Theodore watched Jess get on the train, and off it, and had not seen her interact with anybody.

"I painted the macaroni and our teacher Miss Ivers gave us the chain!"

Theodore's current mother was a primary school teacher. And she was also particularly fond of a student named Callie.

Jessica grinned. "Aren't you so clever? I love the colour. You tell Mrs Ivers next time you see her that your best auntie really loves her present. Okay?"

"Okay!" chirped Callie.

So, there it was: the twisted connection all of Theo's actions seemed to end up having. His lives were always so convoluted and annoying. Just once he wanted to do something that didn't affect himself.

But there it was: his mother was Callie's beloved teacher, and his mother had a soft spot for Callie in turn. Connections like that were the reason Theodore tried to live as alone and as mundanely as possible. He had already 'done it all' anyway. Throwing one life away was like dropping one jelly bean and not bothering to pick it up.

"Children are so… capricious. Don't you think?"

The hollow voice came from behind Theo. He was standing in the backdoor, getting some air, and now Death had arrived to enhance his night. As if he needed it.

"I would call them ignorant," said Theo, "but I guess they can be both."

The night was warm, like a night abroad, lit with the yellow burn of streetlights. Theodore wiped sweat from his forehead and closed the door so no-one could overhear him talking, seemingly, to no-one.

"You would call everyone ignorant." Was that delight in Death's voice he could hear?

"No-one has lived as many lives as me, apart from you."

"Au contrare, I have lived many more times over than you ever will."

Theodore smiled bitterly. "Something to look forward to, then."

"Yes indeed. A shame your mother will not have the same assurance on her passing tomorrow."

In the middle of pulling out his handkerchief, Theodore stiffened. "I'm sorry, I'm afraid I didn't catch that."

Death gave a ragged laugh. "And I am afraid you did."

It wasn't possible. It wasn't possible, thought Theo, for his mother to die tomorrow. She had absolutely no reason to go. Maggie Ivers was in perfect health, only 45 years of age and with a husband to watch out for her. Surely she could not die.

But, Theodore had to remind himself, this was Death he was talking to.

"Is she sick?" he asked, and Death shook his head. "Has her time come? How is she to die?"

Death plucked a leaf from a tree, and it decayed in his hand. "I couldn't say. I haven't decided yet. Perhaps she will be hit by a car?"

Theodore's blood felt thick, like one large slug trying to push its way through a straw. Surely he misunderstood. Surely Death would not just take his mother from him without a reason.

"No, Theodore, you understand perfectly," Death assured. "Your mother is next on the list. You would do well not to interfere this time."

There was always a punishment for those who cheated Death but never had Theodore suffered the consequence himself. He had sniggered as other people's life strings were cut while they bungie jumped, or tugged while they ran – but he had never seen someone punished for keeping someone else from death.

Theodore took his phone from his pocket and tried to ring his father, but Death clicked his fingers and he had no reception. He tried texting but the message would not send, and with anger he threw his phone to the ground, and turned on Death.

"Take her, then!" cried Theo. "Take her! What do I care? Take them both if you have to! Hell, take me, too, why don't you! I'm more valuable a life than both of them put together. The Eternal Man," he spat, "a real reward, wouldn't you say? Leave Maggie out of this, she's not even my real mother, you can't take her to punish me."

"You would simply be reborn. That is no way to keep balance."

"Then take Jessica!"

"You have already saved her. There is nothing I can do. Maggie Ivers is to die within hours, and you will not stop it, not this time."

There was no sense to be had in Theodore's head. "She is my mother."

"And yet a few moments ago you were telling me otherwise," mocked Death. "You have always said your true mother died centuries ago in your first life on this earth, so surely Maggie Ivers' death will mean nothing to you." Death soundlessly walked to the door, and peered inside the house. "However, I do wonder what it will do to that little girl, losing her favourite teacher so suddenly. I suppose we will soon find out."

When Death turned and looked at Theodore, he could not look back.

"Children," said Death, "are so capricious. Don't you agree?"

It took only an hour after Death disappeared for Theodore to receive the phone call. His mother had died in a car accident, and his father was put in a medically induced coma.

"Figures," he said.

This was not the first time a father of his had suffered such a fate.

~o~

This piece is a chapter of a book Amber is in the middle of writing called 'The Eternal Man'. At first, Amber considered sending in the first chapter of this book as her entry but she has strained over it so much and feels it is not yet ready to be read. 'The Eternal Man' is currently a year in the making as Amber has had little time to write; however now she is out of college she has more free time and wishes to finish the first draft as soon as possible.

Amber is also writing a book about twins, namely what would happen in a universe where no such thing had occurred before, by drawing off her own experience. She also had an online presence as a writer a couple of years ago, hitting almost one million reads on her own piece, and was thinking of partaking in NaNoWriMo next year.

THOMAS PATEL
SEDNA

Born in 1995, Tom Patel is currently a student at Bangor University studying English with Creative Writing. Inheriting his love of reading from his mother and his grandma, Tom has been fascinated with books from a young age, devouring novels such as Harry Potter and Lord of the Rings. Since joining university, his tastes have widened, helped by an international year in New York. From Sappho and Homer, to Marie de France and Shakespeare, not forgetting Keats and the Brontës, his eclectic taste is reflected in his own work. Reading is not his only passion, he also enjoys travelling; learning as much as he can about the myriad cultures around him, including religions, mythology and the Ancient World. He enjoys keeping fit and active, through cycling, swimming and hiking, often listening to music and debating philosophy whilst doing so.

"And so, Aguta rained hellfire down onto those unbelievers. By his breath they perish, and by the blast of His anger they come to an end!" Spittle frothed from the Shaman's mouth and mixed with the soot seaweed dye on his lips. "Behold, the day of Aguta is coming! Cruel! With Fury and burning Anger, to make the land a desolation; and He will massacre its sinners!" Tiny tarlike bubbles speckled his beard as a result; Sedna felt the strangest urge to stroke one. She gagged; the thought of touching the Shaman at all was disgusting, with his rotten teeth and grubby skin.

"Remember, we are the righteous, and we have seven devils that torment us, tempting us astray. We must ignore these fiends, lest we sin!" Looking around, Sedna's eyes trailed over the whalebone racks pushed against the ice walls, covered in reindeer hides and mittens and boots and various other clothing, hung to dry. Everyone appeared enraptured by the sermon, besides Silla who was fidgeting in the male section. He caught her gaze and smirked. Sedna smiled back, turned and stared at the low entrance tunnel.

She wished that she and Silla could leave this place filled with hate and fear and return to their isle, never to leave. Yet people, neighbours she'd grown up with, murmured about Silla; outsiders were to be distrusted. If they distanced themselves too much, they'd risk becoming outcasts, or worse, scapegoats. Plus, the clan had never really forgiven that, with her dark narwhal eyes and curtains of black hair, she hadn't married within the clan. Sedna didn't care though, not about their bigoted opinions or whispering gossip, as long as she had Silla. However, if they even suspected what he was . . . she returned to the sermon.

"Remember," the Shaman said in a low voice, "those who stray from the virtuous path are cursed beings, trapped in the form of a monstrous bird. They appear as Inuit, but these degenerates are devious and duplicitous, bringing bad luck onto the clans." The entire congregation was silent as the Shaman lit the fish oil and watched the smoke dance through the spirit hole in the top of the shelter. Sedna wrinkled her nose at the smell whilst the elders, swathed in hide on their sleeping platform, started a cacophony of humming and drumming. Everyone else began ritualistically wailing; Silla and Sedna rolled their eyes at each other as they joined in. Her father, Anigut, enthusiastically led the song. The shaman danced around the seal oil lamp, working himself more and more into ecstasy. Scrawny limbs twisted this way and that, head rolling and lips foaming until he finally fainted in trance. The clan waited with bated breath, some squinting to see if they could notice his souls, climbing up the grooves on the walls, leap through the spirit hole and fly to Lord Aguta. Silence reigned, so quiet that Sedna could almost hear the sea ice groan with the ebb of the tide. She wondered whether this was how still it was when the hunting party, containing so many of her kin, was stalked and savaged by an ice bear. That was so long ago now, well before her father had fallen into this extremism.

The Shaman gasped awake, clutching his throat with his eyes still rolled back into his head.

"THERE IS ONE AMONG US!" The Shaman's voice soared over the crowd. "A BIRD DEMON WALKS AMONG US! WE'VE BEEN WICKED AND SINFUL AND NOW THE LORD, IN HIS VENGFUL PRIDE, HAS ALLOWED A DEVIL TO INFILTRATE OUR CAMP!" Among the uproar that ensued, Sedna ran to Silla and buried her head in his parka.

"Fa, I must leave. Me and Silla need to return to the isle"

"Return! Why?"

"To sprinkle the earthblood and speak the sacred rites. We don't want that *thing* living anywhere near camp."

"You should stay here –"

"But Fa –"

"- do not interrupt me. Silla can go by himself."

"Fa, what kind of wife would I be if -"

"What kind of daughter marries an outsider eh? I'm named after the Great Father himself, and my own child risked bringing shame onto the family, her own marrow! Consider yourself lucky Silla is the grateful man he should be. I don't tolerate dishonour." Sedna and her father were stood by the bay, where multiple skinboats bobbed in the black water. Silla was a way off, loading a boat with supplies. Sighing, Sedna looked out over the sea. The sky was overcast, the ocean wolf grey; its pelt fluffed up in places, the crashing waves downy white fur.

"Don't you look away from me you ungrateful little brat," he spat, his lips greased with saliva, like the Shaman. "Most fathers would have sacrificed their children if the mother had died, to spare the child a slow death from starvation. I found a way to keep you alive." He grabbed her arm and squeezed so tightly that Sedna was sure it'd bruise. "Aguta himself gave you beauty enough to win the hand of any eligible man in the clan. And you marry an interloper."

Sedna had vague memories of the love and kindness her father used to possess, but as she aged, those recollections had begun to fade, leaving her weary of the bitter rants said so many times before. Looking at Silla, she watched him sit in the boat and signal for her to depart.

"I must leave Fa," said Sedna, interrupting her father mid tirade, ripping her arm out of his grasp and running to the boat. Anigut screamed something at her back, but she couldn't bring herself to care. Looking back across the harbour as the boat skimmed over the waves, she noticed commotion around the shelter; a big dome of snow, connected to smaller ones with little corridors. People were coming in and out of the entrance tunnels; low to keep out the wind. Apparently, she thought to herself, the witch hunt had begun. What she didn't notice was the absence of her father, nor the missing skinboat.

They sped over the waves, powered by Silla's muscular arms. Sedna smiled, this is where he was happiest. Away from prejudice and persecution, he was in his element, at one with nature. Even feathery tattoos had begun to flow over his limbs. Sedna tried not to worry but even here, she felt bigots could be watching. Removing her bone visor and lowering her hood, she let the icy wind flow over her like oil and tried to banish apprehensions from her mind.

Before long, the isle came into view; a jumble of rock and ice spires, with baby waterfalls tumbling down the sides, sliding over the boulders like tears on cheeks. Myriad seabirds nested on the peaks but the black beach, where they unloaded their boat, was still. Silla climbed up to the cave where they made their camp, but Sedna stayed on the beach and watched. Something wasn't right, she felt as if they had been followed, but everyone had been caught up in the panic at camp. She'd fought with her father on multiple occasions, it seemed foolish to believe this time he'd have followed them home. Plus he was an old man, he couldn't have kept up the pace to follow them. Sedna repeated these assurances as she walked up to their cave.

Anigut paddled around an iceberg and into full view of the isle. Upon reaching the shore, he hid his skinboat behind some boulders. Muttering about honour, he began searching for his daughter.

The fire glowed into life, illuminating camp. Various tools for survival were hung about; parkas, boots, axes and knifes. Several bone harpoons lay in a corner, whilst fish hooks and sinew lines lay near the sleeping sacks, in need of detangling. Filled with seawater, a cooking skin hung above the fire, and Sedna added fish chunks to cook. Just buried in the ground was a slab of caribou meat, slowly roasting in the embers. While she prepared nightmeal, Silla stitched up some tears in her boots. A pile of salmon skin was next to him for the resoling. It was a comfortable quiet, both enjoying each other's company.

"Tell me a story," Silla suddenly asked.

"Which one?"

"You know which one." Silla grinned at Sedna as she rolled her eyes and began.

"You've heard it so many times before."

"What's not to enjoy? The Narwhal Queen, mother of the sea, who will be reincarnated as Inuit is a —"

A crack reverberated through the gloom. Sedna grabbed a knife, Silla a harpoon.

"I'm going to check outside," Silla said. Sedna nodded weakly. He grabbed a burning brand and left the cave. Silence. She gripped the handle so tightly that the slate blade cut into her skin, blood and sweat soaking the sinew binding. She crept closer to the opening. They'd tried to hide the meaty aroma, as not to lure ice bears, but sometimes the beasts were so hungry that they'd swim to the isle, searching for prey. Maybe the light from the fire had attracted it somehow. Quickly, she tipped the broth over the flames, snuffing it out. The knife quivered in her hand, so small and fragile. What could it achieve against the muscle of a beast? Wait. Was that thudding bear strides? It seemed to be getting faster, as if the creature was bounding towards the scent of sweet, succulent flesh.

"All clear," Silla called. Sedna breathed out and sank against a wall; the pounding was her heartbeat. Silla re-entered, and she started. He was in his bird form; black feathers covered his body, from the tiny ones that surrounded his face to the long luscious plumage that had replaced his hair. Instead of arms he had vast wings; powerful and alien. Yet his face remained the same; boyish and open, with curious eyes. Standing up, Sedna took his face in her hands.

"Have demons addled your mind? What if someone saw you? You saw what they were like today at that fanatic's sermon; they want someone to blame, to scapegoat and they'd come after you, a mob to rip you limb from limb if they knew . . ."

"Relax, Sedna. Breathe. In, and out. No one's here. We are alone." Hugging her, he affectionately nuzzled her nose and kissed her forehead. Sedna took a shuddering breath and sat back down.

"Do you want to hear the story?" she said after her heart had slowed back down.

"It's fine, I know what happens. Everyone is told it, that's why there's so few fish in the bay and no large prey like seals."

Sitting down, Sedna lay back as he started a new fire and snuggled into his sleeping sack. Soon, the meat was cooking away again, filling the cave with its aroma.

A stone sailed through the air and struck Silla, causing his arm to slip into the fire. He bellowed as the odour of singed feathers and burnt meat filled the air. Anigut ploughed through the entrance hole and threw Sedna against a wall. She screamed as pain lanced through her arm, but she forced herself to stand up. Her father was viciously attacking Silla, striking him with punches, kicks and whatever was lying around. Silla could barely defend himself, tangled in the sleeping sack and his arm gravely burnt. Yelling, she launched herself at her father. She bit, she tore, she scratched at whatever she could reach. Roaring, Anigut pinned her down. His eyes were red, his arms bleeding, his teeth bloody. Spit trickled off his chin and landed on her forehead, yet she didn't blink nor flinch.

"You tizheruk! You dirty, filthy little whore! You fucking slut!" Anigut's shout rose to a bellow. "You married that fucking piece of shit! That faggoty cunt! How dare you dishonour the family this way, how dare you dishonour the Great Aguta this way! You fucking bitch!" Anigut struck the ground next to Sedna's head. A strange light came into his eyes as Silla tackled him off her, finally untangled from the sleeping sack. Anigut dug his fingers into Silla's burnt flesh, causing him to scream. Standing up, he kicked Silla into a corner and picked up a harpoon. Looking at Sedna, he fired the weapon.

Sedna felt her whole world collapse. Silla lay there, his blood pooling around his body. His eyes were open, staring at Sedna, lifeless. She did not dare look away; she was frozen, too scared to break the stare that was the only connection she now had with Silla. Everything had changed. Nausea shocked her body as if she'd jumped into icy water, yet she didn't really feel it. She didn't really feel anything anymore, not the ground beneath her, not the pain of her arm, not her father grabbing her hair. Where he pulled her tresses, icy whiteness spread, replacing the inkiness all the way to the very tips, such was her grief. Sedna watched as her hair faded to silver, yet she didn't feel worried by this. All she felt was those dead stone eyes watching her.

Anigut began to drag her away, breaking that final connection. She started to scream and struggle yet he just threw her out of the cave and down onto the beach. She tried to run back to Silla but her father struck her in the stomach with such force she fell down. Physical pain was returning now, and Sedna embraced it, it was so much better than that nothingness before. She focused on the pain, tried to let it consume her, but the memory of those dead eyes, that broken body wouldn't dissipate. Pulling her hair, Anigut began cutting it off fiercely with a knife, ripping strands from her head, leaving her scalp bleeding. Sedna just lay there. She was so tired, and so lightheaded she seemed to be floating up, far away from here. He stripped her and threw an Ice Bear pelt on her, the garb of sinners. Just as the bear walked alone, so would she.

Her father walked off, and Sedna knew she should move, should run away, but she couldn't. Something weighed her down, her limbs felt as if the weight of the world was hanging from them. Blood trickled down her face and in her eye but wiping blood, or tears, away was just too much to ask. Her father walked back, carrying his boat and flung her into it. He then pushed off and began rowing away from that isle, from Silla. Sedna tried to call out, tried to move but grief pinned her down, such swirling despair.

The sky glowered with the storm. The clouds twisted into a serpentine mess, shifting and squirming with venomous lightning and thunderous hissing. As this great wyrm began to eat its own tail the clouds convalesced into something new. The sea grew choppier, frothing and foaming as Anigut struggled to stay afloat. He shouted prayers to up above, and Sedna's hatred grew as she beheld him, the man who had killed her husband.

The winds grew more powerful still, picking up the boat and sending it flying through the air. Anigut was flung overboard but managed to clutch the side, gripping with all his might. Maybe the ferocity of the storm had merged with her souls, but as Sedna looked at her father, vainly trying to climb back in, bloodlust took hold. This thing, this monster had murdered her husband, not in self defence or because he was protecting anyone. He had murdered Silla simply because he didn't like Silla's existence, his way of life. Grabbing an oar, she struck her father across the head. Dazed, he sunk in the churning sea. The storm still raged, but everything seemed to slow down for Sedna. The oar fell from her grasp as she looked over the side, trying to spot if he was coming back. Nothing but the frothing waves.

Anigut heaved himself up on the other side and threw his daughter overboard whilst she was reaching for a weapon. Desperately, Sedna clung onto the sides as her father had done. She couldn't, wouldn't die, for who would be left to mourn, or even remember Silla?

Anigut looked into his daughter's face, her dark eyes which hadn't changed one bit since she was a babe. Defiant, confident, strong. He knew what he had to do, but he didn't want to. She was his child, his baby. Screaming to the sky, he asked for her to be spared. Aguta gave his reply.

Sedna watched as her father yelled to the sky and then drew out a knife. This was his plan all along, she realised. There was no way he'd allow her to live, her existence was a stain on the family name. Sedna's fingers turned into fishhooks, digging in deep to the boat. She tried to climb back into the boat, but the cold had sapped away so much strength. She looked up as her father brought down the knife.

It didn't hurt as much as she thought it would, or even at all. Maybe it was the cold, or the pain was just too much for her to process, so she didn't feel anything. She sank beneath the waves, faster and faster. Her breath disappeared into pearly bubbles, and yet her ribs didn't feel constricted with the water that must be flowing into her lungs. Blue green curtains of light unfurled around her, hypnotically shifting, as if to a lullaby. She seemed to be floating in the night sky, with white light glowing from her body. Sedna's copper skin had faded to silver, and her lost fingers were remade out of sparkling water. Stars swam around her, oh what they must have seen, have touched! Shifting tides of effervescence gleamed from her feet as she inhaled cosmic dust and breathed out diamonds. These living, breathing, glittering diamonds, so shiny and new. She could see it, see it all; galaxies decaying into chaos and sweet starbursts erupting with beautiful baby stars. Those liquid diamonds in the night, that glowed and shined brighter, until ivory light filled her horizons.

That light was cold and chaste and remote; it showed Sedna visions of other bird creatures, like Silla, mutilated and tortured. She saw their flesh scored with knives and brands; some were crucified, blood dripping onto white snow whilst ice bears began gnawing at their bodies. She saw trees which well travelled traders would talk about, except these had hanging bodies, dangling like strange fruit. She saw these bird people burned at the stake, dunked in water, men, women, children slaughtered, maggots worming through innards and flies buzzing in and out of slack mouths, a cruel mockery of breath.

Sedna looked at where she stood, wearing nothing but that bear pelt, its head her hood and its skin rippling down her back. At her feet was a golden blue ocean, consisting of light or water, she didn't know. Above, great whales and seals and narwhals swam, made from constellations. They nuzzled her, grateful their queen had returned. Sedna smiled, but in that clear sea, she saw more pain, more suffering and death. And it made her angry.

~o~

I'd like to dedicate my first ever published story to my family; Mum, Dad and Zac. You've always taught me to pursue my ambitions, no matter how unattainable they seemed, so thank you for supporting my dreams.

The main inspiration behind this story was *Angela Carter's Book of Fairy Tales*. I admired how she rewrote various myths and legends from around the globe but disrupted the story somehow, making the tale seem fresh and new. Upon reading this, I knew I wanted to rewrite the myth of Sedna but was unsure how to accomplish this. I found my approach through my second influence; the *X Men*. The comic books use a fictional species, mutants, to explore discrimination in the modern world. Originally, I wanted to use Silla as a symbol for the struggles of the LBGT community, but I realised that prejudice has been experienced by myriad denominations throughout history, leading me to portray Silla as representing all those who have endured bigotry.

This is why, whilst the relationship between Sedna and Silla is loving, I don't portray them kissing nor saying "I love you" to each other because I don't want their relationship to be attributed to any one group, I want everyone to relate to the respect and affection Sedna displays to Silla.

As religion remains contentious for some, I used religious quotes in the Shaman's speech at the beginning, changing any mention of a specific deity to Aguta, who was the creator god in the Inuit tradition. This shows how the violent rhetoric is present in modern society, and how hate preachers use it to influence masses of followers into hating those who don't conform to their ideals.

Additionally, Anigut's murder of his daughter resembles the honour killings in Islamic families, which is another prevalent crime in society. It is mentioned a lot in the news, but I wanted to show how this type of murder wasn't unique to Muslim families which is why I included it in my story.

I kept the descriptions of characters' appearances minimal because I wanted to suggest that these characters could be anyone; they are not specific to a time or place. This is also why I wrote in third person and included modern swear words as I felt that this would better relay how the hatred Anigut exhibits towards Silla is reflected even in modern society. By ending the story so abruptly, I suggest that the story doesn't end with the last word, it continues past it which reflects Sedna's immortality and how the issues are still relevant today, but I also highlight the eternal nature of stories; how a myth of a goddess from eons ago can still adapt and change to modern society, mirroring the everlasting nature of tales themselves.

WILLOW TOPP
INK

Willow Topp is a new writer living in Tintern, Wales. Having just
completed a postgraduate course in Scriptwriting at the University of
South Wales, she is currently busy working on several projects ranging
from a podcast series to a YA novel she hopes to have published. When
she can't be found hunched over a desk writing or drawing, she enjoys
investigating the local coffee shops and making a fuss over her pets.

Routine was not something Emma ever deviated from. Ever since life's
responsibilities had flung themselves upon Emma, predictability had become
a comfort. It was a safety blanket in a world which was fast unraveling into
anarchy. If she kept her head down she could remain ignorant to everything
which threatened to fling her world into chaos. In such unpredictable times,
was she not fortunate to be able to live in such a settled manner?

Why, then, was she risking her stability on a flight of fancy? Even lying about
taking the day off from work had given Emma a guilty thrill, let alone her actual
plans.

Perched near the back of the bus, every tense exhale of hers fogged the icy
window she squinted through. It was a good thing that local public transport
was so reliable. The city had become too busy lately and she wasn't keen on
driving any more than necessary. Snow from last weekend had started to thaw,
leaving piles of grubby slush in every gutter corner. She knew her boots weren't

up for the walk ahead, but at least on foot the worst damage she could do was to her own pride.

The dismal, industrial landscape flickered past in a blur of drab colours. It took all of thirty seconds for her interest to waver and soon enough Emma's focus was drawn back to what she held. A business card for a tattoo studio rest between her fingers. Black and white, the simple, embossed card showed no examples of work, only several swirling designs in one corner. It provided no number or contact, only an address and the name of the studio. It was classy, classier than she recalled the studio itself being when she had visited as a child with her grandmother. Maybe that was the point: if the woman she had received the card from was telling the truth, nothing was as it seemed.

Her eyes darted to the glossy flyer behind the card. Pressed into her hands by a man at the bus stop, its obnoxious design couldn't help but draw her eye. Everyone else subjected to this blatant propaganda had already discarded theirs. The flyers sat stuffed in pockets to be long forgotten come the next wash, or found a new home wedged between seats.

Putanendtolivinginfear.

Buildastronger,saferfuture.

Erasetheillegaluseofmagicinoursocietytoday.

The strangers' persistence had been unnerving to say the least. Magic had been illegal for at least as long as she had been alive, and for her parents' lives too. This vehement hatred for something so long outlawed would once have been baffling if she wasn't carrying her own guilty secret now. Her heartbeat increased and her grip on the papers tightened as though she might at any moment be caught in possession of these items and hauled away. The reality was of course that nobody so much as noticed, let alone cared. From her research alone she knew the studio operated by legal means and her trip was a shot in the dark. Still, nostalgia and curiosity had finally overwhelmed a lifetime of complacency. She had to know about her history.

The shop itself, when she found it, sat beneath an inner-city bridge. It was an unsettling sight for Emma, who remembered shops beneath the arches best as simpler places. They had been family owned workshops or garages when she was a child, all wood and iron and vibrant paint. Music used to play in the now silent road. It was minimal and sleek now. Corporate. The ever-promised regeneration projects for the centre of the city had started to filter through. Emma chewed her lip. It was likely that things would have changed too much, even if the place was still here, to yield results for her search.

It occurred to her then that she needed to hurry up before her feet turned to blocks of ice. Under most circumstances she would have needed the time to steel herself for what was to come, perhaps taken a deep breath: this time she didn't wait. Still buzzing with excitement, Emma ducked into the tattoo studio and sighed in relief at the warm wall of air which enveloped her.

Within seconds it struck her just how silent the place was. No tinkling bell greeted her as she stepped in; no obnoxious music blasted over a sound system; no low hum came from the machines themselves at work. Emma had no tattoos herself, but instinctively she knew this wasn't the norm.

Spookier still was the absence of patrons, artists, or even a reception desk. The studio was an almost bare space, harshly lit and stark. Several posters and scribbled designs clung to the brick walls by frayed threads of tape, paper edges beginning to yellow with age. Two stations were set up at the back of the room, and a small table perched in the corner, all but collapsing beneath the weight of a hefty ring-binder. There was no phone, computer or desk. Although it contrasted the exterior, it was somehow exactly what she had expected. Minimalism at its finest.

Something urged Emma to stay, but with the place so bereft of life she began to wonder if she was welcome. Perhaps the small sign on the door was incorrect and the artists had disappeared for a late lunch? She fidgeted and huffed a breath. How dare they leave her disappointed like this? Build her up to finally take a risk and not even be polite enough to leave a notice if they were-

The door behind her slammed open with enough force to startle Emma from her indecisive state. A figure strode past without once seeming to acknowledge her presence, though the tang of stale cigarette smoke lingered long after their passing. He was a youthful man, boyish features dusted with a smattering of facial hair grown in an unconvincing attempt to add both age and respectability. There was nothing remarkable about his appearance, yet he seemed at once familiar to Emma in a way she could not quite describe. There was no greeting, not even the merest suggestion that the stranger had even noticed Emma as he focused on one of the ring-binders instead.

She watched for some time as he flipped through sheets of designs in silence, lips pursed in a thoughtful pout. Occasionally he traced a design with the tip of a finger and his expression softened, but no amount of soft coughing or shuffling of soggy feet would distract him. When at last he did register her, it was with a commendable level of indifference that he spoke. "You're early."

Emma stared. The bravery which had propelled her to this point was fast dissolving in the face of utter disinterest. "What?"

"Early. You're the three o'clock, aren't you?"

"Oh! No, sorry. I don't have an appointment. Uhm. Sorry. No. Yes, right, this is all new for me, I wasn't sure what to expect or I'd have tried to ring ahead, but you don't seem to have..." She could see what minimal flicker of patience he managed for her was on its way out; in a panic she blurted, "I came here about my grandmother."

That had his attention. Shrewd eyes narrowed and for the briefest instant flicked over Emma. She knew he was assessing her age based on the statement and hiding his amusement. Though he didn't seem in the least bothered to offend her, she was quick to clarify. "She passed away when I was young. Sorry. Should have been more clear."

"That's fine."

"Right. So, you see, I was out drinking with my, uhm, work colleagues and I got a bit brave at the bar. I started chatting to a lady who told me her grandmother used to get tattoos. Funny coincidence because so did mine - as I said - and she told me I should stop by. She gave me your card."

She offered the man the business card like a child might present a teacher with an absence note. He reached for it, paused, and Emma saw a shift in his expression she could only read as disgust. *Oh no.* Dreading to confirm what she already knew to have happened, her gaze followed his. In that split second she saw the flyer from the bus presented alongside the card.

"Oh goodness no, I'm not one of them! Sorry! Some man just gave it to me when I was on the bus. What an idiot. I forgot to...I never even thought-... Oh, you must think I'm an absolute... I'm so sorry!" She hastened to jam the flyer in a pocket. Five minutes and already this was getting far more ridiculous than Emma had expected it to be. In the protracted silence that followed, she could only stare until prompted again.

"You do understand that magic is strictly illegal, right?"

"Yes. Of course."

"But you know about the service we offer here?"

Another pause. "Yes...?"

"That's what your grandmother came here for, I presume. And why you're here."

Emma's voice took on a stiffer tone. "I'm not involved in magic," she replied, "but I don't condemn people who are. I don't even know if my grandmother was; I was tiny when I must have come here with her."

"And you felt compelled to come back now, why? You've had years to come here so why now?"

She knew this was another dig at her age. "Don't you have a manager or someone older I can talk to about this, perhaps? You don't look old enough to be running this shop yourself." No sooner had the words left her mouth it was all Emma could do not to cover her lips at her brazen attitude. The youthful man's eyes lit up at once to see a spark in her, though there was a deeper melancholy lurking in his reply. "Nah, it's just me now. Used to be a whole two of us working here but you know how businesses change. Come on - might as well sit down and dry off a bit before I get done for not having one of those wet floor signs."

"Okay. Uhm. My name's Emma, by the way."

"Right. Andy."

With a vague gesture towards the tattooing stations at the back of the room, Andy sauntered ahead for one of the chairs, leaving Emma to trail after. She took the opportunity whilst his back was to her to scrutinise him once again. There was an intriguing similarity between him and his shop. On first glance he had appeared average but logic began to spot the gaps after an extended time. Warm though it was indoors, he dressed more for summer than the freezing winter outside. Neither was he as tattooed as she had expected him to be. Through gaps in his baggy vest (which hung from him like wet rags on a figure made of sticks) she could make out several swirling patterns on his shoulders and a few more on his forearms. They were intriguing but few and far between: there were no recognisable designs and neither did he have so much as a half-sleeve worth of ink.

The workstation chairs were comfortable, but still Emma could not relax once she sat. The prospect of a new world opening up to her was an intoxicating rush but fear kept her grounded. It took considerable willpower not to blurt out several questions before Andy had sprawled himself into his own chair. Careful to keep herself still so as not to appear too impatient, Emma placed her hands in her lap and took a measured breath. When her gaze lifted again she was startled to find Andy already staring back. He was the first to break the silence.

"Where do you want to start first: your grandmother or how the system works?"

"You...seem to be trusting me a lot. Not - not that I can't be trusted, but if you're involved in illegal activities shouldn't you be worried about me telling the police about you?"

Andy snorted. He was beginning to come alive now that there was something interesting. A cheekiness came upon his face which Emma would have found appealing when she was a young woman. "And you'd show them what, exactly? This is a perfectly legal tattoo parlour, I just have a busy schedule and an unusual style."

"Then how do you-"

"-I'm telling you this because you mentioned your grandmother. Business cards like the one you have usually don't end up in the hands of the public. If someone else gave it to you then they must have wanted you to share that experience before we all end up disappearing. It's about time you learned about your heritage, don't you think?"

He was smiling but Emma's stomach had turned as cold as the slush she had trawled through. Dread was contending with excitement as reality began to creep upon her. Still, she was going to deny it just a little bit longer.

"I don't understand. If there isn't anything here, why is it so secretive?"

"I was wondering when we'd get to the interesting parts. See, this tattoo studio runs on two fronts. We do traditional tattoos for people who want to make a statement by getting one from a selective artist... And magical tattoos."

"Magical tattoos?"

"Yeah, magical tattoos."

"I'm sorry, I don't see how that even-"

"It's simple. See, when the government put anti-magic laws in place, the people who practiced it found more creative ways to weave their craft into everyday life. We found tattoos are a damn convenient method: you'd be surprised how many studios are undergound magic shops."

"I don't believe it. Isn't that... what if people find out?"

"Like I said: who would believe it? You'd need a working knowledge of magic to recognise any symbols, so any officials who understood them would implicate themselves. I've also got my materials covered; all that's here is ink, and you can't arrest me for being creative."

"How do the tattoos become magic, then?"

"When we have a design consultation we ask the clients to source and bring their own ingredients. We can help for a small charge but prefer to keep that to the clients' discretion."

Something clicked. The look on Andy's face earlier. "Aren't the ingredients illegal?"

"They say they are. They're all harmless, but people get arrested all the time for possession or dealing."

"Is that what happened to your colleague?"

For a brief moment it was the young man who was on the back foot, taken aback by the sudden turn in conversation. He hesitated, and Emma immediately regretted causing the sorrow to return to his eyes. "He made a different mistake. Nothing to do with the work we do here. We look out for our own in the community."

Silence sat heavy in the air as Emma digested what fragments of information she had received. She remembered the tattoo shop only as a dusty, vague memory, clutching tightly to the hand of her grandmother in the middle of a noisy room. The woman she admired most had been chatting with everyone inside, as vibrant as ever Emma had ever known her. She remembered having to wait to touch the small, simple symbol on the inside of her wrist, never thinking to ask what it meant. Grandmother said it was an impulsive decision, something to cross off of her list before she got any older. It must have been a lie.

Emma hadn't made the trip out of a curiosity about magic itself. She had wanted to try and understand why someone as conservative as her grandmother would have dabbled in the illegal. To think that she was more involved in the lifestyle made Emma light-headed, but she couldn't deny her own curiosity. Giddy with the myriad possibilities open to her, she glanced to her hands and, after seconds which passed like years, tried again.

"How long have you worked here?"

"A while. Why?"

"Do you keep your designs? I saw the book," she indicated the ring-binder again with a nod of the head, "and thought...if you kept archives. Or if your company does."

Andy cottoned on almost immediately. "Would you recognise it if you saw it?"

"I can see it in my mind now. Do you think you'd still have it?"

"I can't see a reason why not; the archives go back to the opening of this place. Let's go have a look, yeah?"

He was on his feet and heading for a small door in the back before Emma could process her own building excitement. Sliding back to her feet with an unpleasant squelch, she trotted after the young man in silence. At least, whom she now began to suspect as far more than a young man. His body language and speech patterns were normal enough, but there was something behind his words, his eyes. She was beginning, if slowly, to see that she was more perceptive than she realised.

In comfortable silence she followed him through the door to an area which proved to be even more underwhelming than the studio. Metal racks of storage crates lined the brick corridor, upon which sat plastic containers filled with a more fat black ring-binders. "You must have a lot of clients."

"It always surprises me when there's so much competition, but few magical tattoos are permanent so there's a big market."

"Sorry?"

"What year would you say your grandmother came here for a tattoo?"

"I'd have been around five, so early sixties-ish?"

"Say no more."

A few strides brought the tall fellow down towards older files. Emma hesitated at a gap in the racking, cautious not to interfere. She noticed several boxes contained paper folders instead of files; some of the crates weren't even plastic but metal.

"Did your mother not mention anything to do with magic in your family, though? Surely she would have been raised in a household where it would have been common when she was a child?"

"They never really saw eye to eye. I don't think she ever liked magic. After we went to the tattoo shop I saw less and less of my grandmother."

"No?"

"She passed away a few years later. She died in her sleep."

"You were, what, ten? If your mum didn't think much of the magic and the laws were set, it's not uncommon for families to sometimes-"

"Please. Don't."

Andy lapsed into silence as he began sorting through a crate, giving Emma the time to regain her composure. This was too much and she could only deal with one revelation at a time. The fact that magic - a dark underworld - lurked in her history was enough for her today. She didn't need to consider the possibility of what her mother could have done. After all, magic was dangerous, the government had been protecting them for years. Wouldn't it have been the right thing to do?

And what about this business? Andy, mysterious as he was, had been so open about such an illegal activity without even knowing who she was. Heritage - if she could even think of it like that - was hardly enough excuse. She had no explicit urge to get herself involved, she never had in anything. Regardless, wasn't it a moral obligation to look out for the safety of the wider world. He could be weaving any kind of magic, any influence into his body art, and even if he claimed to have nothing to hide in the shop the police were always keen to investigate. They always said to be safe rather than sorry.

She realised now that this was much bigger than just herself; than her own family; than the man crouched before her. This was a serious moral and social issue which could be the first step to saving thousands of lives. It was not a responsibility Emma wanted nor felt even remotely able to handle. She felt faint.

The next few moments were a blur as Andy sprang back to his feet and propelled Emma into the shop once again. Dropping one of the files into her lap, he perched himself on the tattooing bench behind her so that he could watch. As though in a dream she opened the file and began flipping through the pages. The designs, now that she was able to see them up close, were the same as the patterns pasted to the walls. "I always thought a magical tattoo would be more... intricate. Sorry, that's rude. I don't mean... They're very good."

"Nah I understand. The key with it is simplicity: you want as little as possible cluttering up the aim of the magic and getting confused for something else. It's why no two are the same - you can see there's a lot of repeating parts but there's little tweaks. You get to know your clients really well doing this work."

"I didn't realise there was so much of this about. Is it too nosey to ask you if you get requests for the same spells a lot?"

"You're new, ask what you want. Can't promise I'll give you every answer but curiosity's better'n making assumptions, right? Yeah we get a lot wanting the same basic things out of their spells. Luck; protection; health or increased longevity - not that we're doctors, mind - safe travel; spells for their babies if they're pregnant...Then you get more complex and interesting ones. Those are more like the stars and roses of the normal job."

He paused for a moment then, watching the pages of designs as they were slowly flipped and examined. Although his demeanour hadn't changed, it was clear that he had picked up on an unspoken, unconscious fear within Emma's question. "We don't make dangerous spells."

"Sorry?"

"That's what the entire campaign was always about, wasn't it? Dangerous magic." He gestured to Emma's pocket and with some reticence she dug out the flyer again, handing it over. "Yeah, see here, 'living in fear'. What's that mean to you, honestly?"

"Well...magic's not only a dangerous form in itself if things go wrong, but there's always the wrong sort of people with the wrong intentions. I mean - I'm not saying you'd ever go and cast a hex on someone or mean to hurt them but when people have that sort of power you just don't know what somebody with the wrong mindset could do."

"Right..."

He'd asked for honesty and Emma had complied without thinking. She paused mid-turn of the next sheet to consider her own words and cringed. An apology was in order, but the tattoo artist was speaking again. "Okay. I see. So it's not everyone who can use magic you think is a bad person, only the ones who use it destructively?"

"Exactly!"

"And when was the last time you heard a story about someone killed by magic?"

Again they lapsed into silence and Emma began to loathe how awkward this meeting was becoming. He was challenging her beliefs so quietly and politely that it was only now she realised. At her age, she didn't want to consider that her worldview had for so long been so mistaken. She hesitated. "There... There are always stories. In the news. You can see it all the time."

"And you trust the news these days, do you? Have you actually done your research into the stories they run?"

"I never-"

"Do you know anything about the community itself? The practices and beliefs?"

"Don't condescend to me-"

"If you did you'd know that violent magic isn't even a thing. The effect it would have on you... Everything works on balance, Emma: you can't curse someone without that bad luck coming back to you eventually. Even then you'd need to be ridiculously wealthy just to get the materials for something so risky - do you really think all those twenty-somethings or old wandering tramps are able to *afford* it?"

"Why would they even..."

"Because we're different. Simple as that. In the end it's about control. If they don't have the gift, they don't want anyone else to have it."

There were no words which came to mind, so instead Emma went back to looking at the designs without giving Andy an answer. Her mind was at an impasse between defensive anger and wanting to apologise for being so wrong, but how was she to know? There were no talks any more, nobody in her own limited social circle who had magical roots...

But she did now. She was implicated along with the others. No, not implicated. She couldn't keep looking at it like it was something so shameful.

Andy didn't seem to mind the silence; he was well aware that even this brief meeting had triggered something in Emma's mind which she could take forward. He stretched and glanced at his watch, letting his guest continue to search until-

"This. This was the one. Oh my god, it's actually here."

"Did you think it wouldn't be?"

"I don't know. Just seeing it here, it..." Fighting back a swell of emotions she couldn't yet make sense of, Emma traced the circular pattern on the page. The stark black lines proved to be another comforting simplicity in this complex society. "I didn't even know if the shop would have the same owners, let alone still have all the designs..."

"Let's take a proper look, then." Plucking the file out of her hands, Andy tugged the crinkled sheet of paper from its sleeve with a surprising lack of tender care. He flipped it over to observe the hastily scribbled pencil note on the back. "Irene?"

"That was her name, yes!"

The paper was returned to its pocket and with a tug the whole thing pulled loose from the binder. "Want to keep it, then?"

Emma blinked. "You've got years of archives for every tattoo for almost a hundred years and you want an annoying stranger to just take a design?"

"Not planning on running off with it to the station are you?"

"No!"

"Then we're fine."

"Are you sure?"

"'Course! No point keeping this history bottled up if it can be of use. You can always bring it back for safe keeping, of course."

She understood his coded invitation at once and offered an awkward grin. This level of casual hospitality was unlike anything she had expected when first she saw the young man. In honesty, it left her feeling more than a little uncomfortable. It did nothing to deter her, though: Andy had managed to uncover a wealth of her family's history she had only ever had vague inklings about. There was so much to learn about and still she didn't quite know if it was even a reputable world to venture into.

"Thank you. I don't want to be rude but...I should probably go. I've got a school run and if I don't get back now..."

"That's fine," again Andy looked to his watch, "I've got my three o'clock soon enough."

"What are they getting?"

"I don't discuss clients' work. You come back next week and maybe I'll give you a hint. Maybe I can explain what your grandmother's tattoo was as well."

"That would be wonderful."

There was no handshake or over-effusive well-wishing like Emma had feared; it was as though Andy could tell that she found such things uncomfortable. Still, he held the door open for her and, apparently unfazed by the cold on his bare arms, waited patiently until she had picked her way across the icy road before retreating inside.

The entirety of the bus journey home was spent staring at a single sheet of paper in a plastic wallet through glassy eyes. Her ancestry was intertwined with a community she had only ever been shielded from and taught to fear. Her own grandmother had led a life she'd never been able to know about; her mother possibly instrumental in something far worse. Late to these discoveries though she was, today's trip was an immediate catalyst for action. At once she began calculating how much holiday leave she had from work, and the best excuse she could conceive for taking it immediately.

~o~

Ink was one of those short stories which just grabbed me and ran without any consideration for planning - unusual because I adore all the groundwork that takes place before getting into the process of writing a piece. The story was conceived after a long trawl through my regular news sites, written raw and fresh over a weekend. Only after stopping to read the first draft did I realise that I had unconsciously produced a reaction to the litany of scaremongering appearing in the media I had just witnessed, and the impact it is having on our diverse societies.

With modern media making access to everything from news articles to individuals' points of view so easy (and it being inevitable that we can become manipulated by what we read or perceive to be an accurate source), I wanted to be able to explore the theme in a broad context. Using a fantasy genre, it's possible to delve into these real-world issues in a broad context whilst still communicating an issue applicable to our own lives.

The interweaving of fantastical elements with the everyday is something I have always been a fan of in literature. When we combine the two in the same text it enables us to draw a more stark comparison; to highlight a fault we might not originally have seen in our own society and make us reassess our own outlook on these issues.

The character of Emma developed from an urge to write not only a female character as a lead, but someone older. Considering the context of media bias, I wanted to work with writing a character who is old enough to have to really work to challenge her views, and to whom the impact of facing said change is going to be all the more difficult for. She isn't a lost cause by any means, but she has always actively avoided becoming involved in politics, allowing herself be steered along by others' opinions her entire life. Now, through Andy, she is being given the information to start making her own judgements and understand the cost of widespread complacency.

As I said earlier, there was very little groundwork laid down for the world before I started - in fact, the only remnant from an older piece of work which made it through was the essence of the tattoo artist Andy. Originally formed during a character creation exercise on my course, his personality has remained mostly in tact but his affinity with magic and role in the story developed as I was tossing around the concept of magical tattoos. Having now finally found him a home and a purpose playing off of Emma, it's sorely tempting to take *Ink* and look into expanding the world around it.

JAMIE L. HARDING
THE MUDLARKS

Jamie L. Harding is a twenty-four-year-old writer from South Wales, UK, with a First-Class Honours degree in English and the winner of several awards such as the Michael Parnell Prize for Creative Writing in Prose. He has an abiding passion for writing everything from war stories to feature articles. When not writing, he is to be found either in the corner of a café with a good book, or else strolling the streets of Cardiff looking for dogs to pet. Online, he lives at www.jamielharding.com

"Got another one, I think."

"You think?"

"Yeah, bit battered about. Bit pulpy, but looks like one. A kid, maybe. Hold on." There followed the gravelly crunch of concrete being pulled to one side. "Gah – Jesus. Yeah, I've got one."

"Alright, coming over to you now. Give me a second."

We scooped them up in buckets, what was left of them. Poured them out into wheelbarrows and carted them away to the awaiting graves. We dug them out of the ruins only to bury them again a few metres away. Pointless, really. Better to leave them where they were, in their homes, in the shelters that they chose that night, on the street they'd been running down, or the cars they'd been sitting in.

We found one chap with his skull fragmented, pushed down into the book he'd been reading just a few moments before his demise. The bits of bone sticking up out of the pages like little icebergs. In the leather fold of the spine we found a golden tooth too, which I think one of the others decided to keep. Something to pawn back at the camp, I suppose, in exchange for cigarettes, coffee, bread or a better bunk for the night.

Sometimes we'd come across a live one. They'd be buried under a mound of masonry, of dust and timber and powdered concrete, their faces white; or else they'd be slumped in a ditch, their hands drawn up over their heads like frightened children. Sometimes their clothes would be ripped off by the blast, and their skeletal frames would be lying there shivering in the shadows of their shattered homes. That's what they cared about too; their houses. They cared more about losing the house they'd grown up in than losing their own limbs. Broken bones meant nothing compared to broken homes.

Whenever we did find a survivor we were told to alert one of the guards. To call out. We were forbidden from speaking to the people we found – German citizens were above us, they said. The living ones were, at least.

The guard, usually a white-moustached, yellow-toothed *Volkssturm* chap with an old, single-shot hunting rifle, would then hobble his way over the rubble to us to 'carry out an inspection.' If the person was salvageable, then we'd all be ordered to carry them out, to place them in one of the wheelbarrows and return them to the camp's medical wing. Usually they wouldn't survive the trip, dozing off into the vacant-eyed emptiness of silence somewhere along the way, but we managed to save one or two. If the person was in too bad a condition to be moved at all, such as the ones pinned down under debris or already lying in pools of their own scarlet life, then it would be up to the guard to finish them off.

"An awful thing, war, isn't it?"

Those were the last whispered words of one man who that guard had to finish off. He, however, was one of us; a fellow prisoner, who'd had the unfortunate luck to tumble down a blown-out sewer and break his leg. In his efforts to claw his way back out he'd then only succeeded in bringing an avalanche of crumbled concrete pouring down on top of himself instead, lying there in the shit and the blood just waiting to be discovered. He couldn't call out very loudly, you see, for he had lost the use of his voice; a piece of shrapnel had slit his throat open as he flew over Dresden a few months prior, almost took his head off, and now all he could do was emit a faint mumble or two. An awful thing, war.

As for me, I wasn't a pilot, nor a soldier or sailor or airman. I was just a journalist, a foolhardy twenty-two-year-old, as all twenty-two-year-olds are. I had taken it upon myself to join a flight crew bound for enemy territory all because I wanted the best story, because I wanted to write from experience and bring in the most readers, the most money. I didn't care about the war because I didn't care about politics or fighting or earning any glory; all I wanted to earn was the money to write.

One minute I was sipping coffee in a London café in my father's old and only business suit, and the next I was hopping into the jeep of three airmen I had never even met. But it didn't stop there; inevitably my suit became a flight suit and the jeep became an airplane – an Avro Lancaster, they told me, though I cared very little for planes. The cobbled streets of London upon which my shoes had one minute been planted were now exchanged instead for the steel belly of the bomber bumbling its way down the runway.

Seven men accompanied me. The aircraft's crew, a family of men who allowed me to join them simply because they wanted their stories told. They treated me like royalty aboard that trip, offering me their rations, lighting my cigarettes, pushing me to 'check out their positions' in the cockpit, the guns, the bomb bay. They were excited to have a writer aboard, one who would potentially turn them into heroes for the whole country to read and dream about.

Instead, I only got to write about their deaths. All seven. I wrote about the moment our plane started 'taking flak' over a German pin-cushion of light far below. Of the way the fuselage suddenly shook and rattled around in the air like an old tin can filled with pellets. I wrote about the mangled twisting of metal, of the screeching tear of half the wing separating from the flame-licked fuselage. I wrote about the pilot screaming frantically at us to get out, about the flight-engineer stumbling out of his seat with two smoking, fist-sized holes in the leather of his jacket, about the rush of cold German air that flooded the world around us, dragging us out into the blackness like a creature ripping us into its icy jaws. I wrote too of the tail gunner getting trapped, half-crushed by crumpled metal, his fingers scraping for his revolver, his face a wall of passive, hardened resolve.

I didn't write about the three hours we spent together before take-off, where the pilot told me about his dreams of becoming a writer himself one day, and bought me drinks, or where the navigator showed me the pictures of his wife waiting back home in Coventry and made me swear I'd include her name – *Maria* – in whatever it was I wrote. I also didn't write of the picturesque way that the bombardier described first seeing the sunset from the air, or the moment he offered me his last cigar, to be smoked only 'when we all got back home.'

Whereas at six p.m. I had been dressed smartly and talking even smarter, contented and comfortable in *Café Canterbury* on Oxford Street, with a pen in my hand and excitement in my veins, at two a.m. the next night, on a freezing November's gale above a German town I had never even heard of, I then found myself tumbling down through the black nothingness towards it. Swallowed up in the rushing, roaring air I had nothing to do but wait. Wait to die, wait to live; but first, wait to land: somehow pulling the ripcord of the parachute – I've no idea how - which opened up above me in an explosion of white silk and strung-out nylon cable.

When the ground suddenly raced up to meet me, it hit hard, knocking my jellied legs up into my ribs and stealing the air from my lungs, leaving me a heaving, foetal heap on a soaking, muddy floor. *Escape and evasion* had meant, for me, crawling through the dirt like a wounded dog – no, not a dog, more like a beached whale, covered in blood and muck and aviation fuel, to the nearest road, where I lay for over an hour in an aching stupor of punch-drunken disbelief and denial. When I was finally found, almost squashed into the road by the wheels of a *Wehrmacht* patrol car, I lasted only thirty more seconds of consciousness. Perhaps that's when the reality of it all sank in, and overwhelmed me, I suppose. I told them my name, told them that I was hurt, and then told them nothing.

Three days later I awoke in the camp I would call home - that would become my whole life, for the next thirteen long, dreary fucking months, and much longer, really.

Our job was to pick away at the rubble like scavenging birds, to pull down the piles of bricks and then pile them elsewhere. Officially we were cleaning up the city that we had destroyed. Unofficially, we were simply being kept busy, kept occupied. Though our fingernails were scraped bare and bloody by the work, though our limbs ached and our eyes grew bloodshot and raw with the brick dust, we did not complain, for we were alive. They hadn't executed us or left us to starve; they had given us jobs, and pointless though they were, those jobs kept us alive.

They called us the Mudlarks, or perhaps it was we who called ourselves that. A name originally attributed to those who scavenged in the mud of the Thames for items of value, it was now almost comically appropriate for us. Ours was a river of ruin, a river which we, with our bombers and battleships and bombs and bullets had blown the dam of. Now it was we who would have to mop up the mess.

Among the mess, however, were indeed a few valuable items. At first we started collecting up the jewellery, the money, anything which sparkled or shone, anything with gold, silver, stainless steel; we collected it all, thinking, mistakenly, that they were actually worth something. It takes only a short amount of time, however, for a starving man to realise that bread is far more valuable than gold could ever be.

Soon we were smashing open silver-plated boxes just to get to the biscuits stored within, we were throwing aside the necklaces and the rings and instead checking only the tins of blown-apart pantries and the bundles of what we hoped would be stored meat. We'd scavenge like animals, because we were animals; hungry animals, starving animals. We'd lick at the wasted wrappers of food that wasn't even there, we'd bite into morsels of meat long-since decayed, we'd down whole bottles of liquid that could have been anything from wine to piss; it didn't matter. We were, in many ways, worse than animals, for we knew how repugnant our actions were but we just didn't care; survival was everything, and taste was nothing.

On one occasion, I came across a bar of chocolate, half-eaten, in the pocket of a corpse resting across another. The top one had been charred by the flames of the burning roof that had come down upon it, and the bottom one, a child sheltered in vain by its loving mother, had a chocolate bar in its trouser pocket, melted and distorted by the heat but still contained within the wrapper somehow, which had failed to ignite. Sitting there beside those two stolen souls, I devoured that chocolate bar as though it were the most delicious thing I had ever eaten; and it was, too. On that one occasion, just for a minute or so, survival became secondary; and taste, I believed, was everything.

On one rain-washed evening in February our boys bombed the town again, demolishing its only church in a barrage of high explosive and peppered shrapnel, a church which had stood there proudly for over a hundred years. As the foundations had weakened and cracked apart the whole building had pitched forward, its walls ripped up from the roots like a falling oak, and down it had all come; collapsing into its own graveyard as though offering out some last dramatic metaphor to the world.

Sixteen souls, all female but for one small boy, had been taking refuge inside, confident that the God above would protect them. By the time we got to them the following morning, it was difficult to distinguish whose bones we were digging up; those recently-perished, or those who had lain there in that graveyard for decades.

Better to just cover over the whole thing, I thought, to bury it all. What difference did it make anyway whether one was buried six feet under the ground or six feet above it?

Still, we dug for them. Sixteen souls inside, but our wheelbarrows collected up nineteen withered carcasses out of the graveyard that morning. Hard to tell the dead from the dead.

All of our group looked alike, us Mudlarks. Slight silhouettes and pale-white skin, moving in spasmodic leaps from one rubble piece to the other. Our eyes sat upon beds of dark grey, our lips as cracked as the walls we were clambering across. Only the guards showed any sign of nourishment; our own stomachs tending to slope inwards rather than away from us. All our hands were cut, all of our feet were stiff and calloused, and all of our faces wore the same blank, desolate stare.

We were a family of men - of creatures - united in our despondency, our waiting to one day be liberated.

In my thirteen months there, I only ever met one Mudlark who somehow remembered how to smile. We were not the sort to maintain 'life through laughter,' as a lot of captured troops apparently do. We did not focus on the positives. We didn't tell jokes or reminisce of home or even offer comfort to our fellow man. For us, we just had to be alive; being happy was not necessary - not with our job.

Harry Rawlins, however, was a man I did see smile. And on more than one occasion too, which made him different, and interesting.

The first time I saw Harry, he was nothing but a pair of skinny, torn-trousered legs sticking out of a hole in a wall of creaking timber and brittle brick. His jacket and shirt lay discarded at his feet, and when he finally emerged, squirming his way out like a triumphant terrier, his back and arms were scraped red-raw from the tiny gap's jagged edges. His body resembled that of a flogged sailor, his skin a crimson mosaic of snagged flesh and pink lines, but he was grinning.

He was grinning because, in his arms, dazed and whitened by brick dust but otherwise unharmed, he held a dog. An old Dachshund with a grey collar, which wriggled and licked at his fingers in heartfelt gratitude, whining in irrepressible glee at its newfound freedom.

"You silly fool," I had said to him, "You risk your life for a bloody dog?"

"A life is a life," Harry had responded, stroking his new pet softly behind the ears. "I could not ignore it."

"That building," I'd said, "is teetering on the edge of collapse. A single brick dislodged could have brought the whole damn thing down onto you. Better to leave the thing."

"A life is a life," Harry'd repeated, "and every life saved is a private war won."

These were the only wars Harry cared about by then. He cared not about borders or leaders or patriotism for patriotism's sake, as most soldiers do. Harry, I discovered, just wanted to save lives, be they British or German or American or other. For Harry, people were people, lives were lives, and every one was worth saving. Even a dog's.

At the time, I just thought him a fool, but a likeable fool at least.

Harry and I stuck together after that, when we could. We'd search as a pair, he starting on one side of a building and me the other, slowly picking our way through the rubble until we united in the centre. Whenever one of us found a body, we'd close in and work at getting it out together.

The worst sort of corpses to find were those that had been burned. One would smell them; a putrid, acrid smell of charred hair and skin, and the odour would cling to the air, to your fingers, inside your nostrils. And have you ever grabbed at burnt chicken before? The kind that peels away from the bone? Crispy skin sliding away from the cooked meat underneath; that's what it was like for us. And inevitably we'd end up vomiting too, adding to the stink.

It was a ghastly task.

There were other types of bodies too. There were the crushed ones, pummelled by falling masonry that left them blackened and bruised, their arms and legs facing in directions they shouldn't have been. Then there were the squashed ones, the ones truly squashed flat, sometimes their remains seeping out from underneath the debris as a dark, maroon mess. Also present were the impaled ones, often by timber, sometimes by poles or suspended on railings, blown into the air by the blasts like little ragdolls. We even found one up a tree, her back resting against the trunk, feet dangling casually, as though she'd simply climbed up there on a summer's afternoon to enjoy the breeze.

Harry, stood at the bottom of a fresh grave pit we'd just finished digging, once asked me if I was married. I told him that I was not, and returned the question, to which he chuckled and nodded his head.

"I have a girl waiting back home for me," he said. I asked her name, and he told me it was Lucy. Then, after a brief pause, he added, "There is one thing, though."

"What's that?"

"Well, I suppose there are two things really."

"Then what are they?"

"Well," Harry said, dusting off his hands, "the first is that she is all the way back home, whilst I'm stuck moving bricks about here. And the second," he smiled, "is that she's a dog."

I came to learn that Harry was a great lover of dogs. The incident with the Dachshund may have made that obvious, but I had dismissed it as just Harry playing the fool. Once mentioned, though, his beloved Lucy, an eleven-year-old Golden Retriever 'with eyes like little blue crystals,' soon came to be the thing he talked about most.

"She's getting on a bit now but she's still ever so playful, absolutely adores her walks. Let her find a river or a lake or a pond and she'll dive straight in and splash around like a pup. She's just the picture of happiness. Always smiling, y'know?"

I wasn't sure if I did know that a dog could smile, but I said that I did, just to please Harry. When he spoke of her he was filled with life, and I began to suspect that it was Lucy, this old dog thousands of miles away, that kept him so upbeat and positive and just *alive* compared to the rest of us.

At the time I didn't understand how anyone could feel so close a bond to something that couldn't even speak the same language as he did, but, of course, it was I who was a fool back then, not Harry.

He had worked in railway maintenance before the war. Sometimes as we worked he would tell me about it, and the way he spoke about a job most would find so mundane was quite beautiful. Harry had a poetic way of painting anything in a beautiful light.

"You should see it, old chap," he'd say, "the great big floodlights lighting up the tracks. We always work during the night, you see, when the trains aren't running as frequently. My office has a ceiling of stars and a carpet of moonlit stone; there's just nothing like it. People always think I'm exaggerating, compensating for a dull job, but I'm not. I'm really not. You'll have to come along one night, so you can see. You can write about it, maybe."

"I will do, one day," I'd say.

"What will you write about it?"

"Well, whatever comes to mind whilst I'm there, I suppose."

"I think you should write about the colours. There's some fantastic colours. Blue-green flames and white sparks against a background of blackness, and the little orange specks of the chaps' cigarettes hovering in the air."

"Very well," I'd say. "I shall write about the colours."

"And the sounds!" Harry would bounce in eagerly. "The clang of metal against metal echoing off into the night, or the songs the chaps whistle, and sometimes – if we're lucky –the birds come out early to sing to us as we work."

"Righto," I'd respond, "I'll include the sounds too."

"And the smells? The cold British night air – not like this German air with its thick stuffiness. No, sweet British air of farmlands and fresh manure and country lanes. Of daffodils and morning showers and wood smoke. Write about those too, won't you?"

"I'll write about it all, Harry," I'd assure him, and he'd grin that cheerful grin of his wider than ever at the idea.

Even with the negative aspects of life, Harry had a way of finding something – anything, worth appreciating. The way the wrecked hulks of the buildings sometimes resembled the trees of a windswept forest, or how the plane we once saw hurtling towards the distant ground in a fiery streak of carnage looked, to him, more like a shooting star against the evening skyline. Once, Harry even compared the way a corpse was angled, a young girl sandwiched between rubble into a kneeling position, to that of one comforted in the act of prayer.

He had a unique way of looking at the world, of seeing beauty in everything and recognising that even the most horrific of sights had their purpose: "One has to see the horrible, in order to fully appreciate the wonderful." Harry was a man who not only loved life but loved living, one who truly understood how lucky a person is to have ever lived at all. In a place where death surrounded us completely, he was a constant reminder of the luck we all shared simply in being alive.

"Even the worst of lives is better than no life at all," he once said to me. "Better to feel pain than to feel nothing at all. Better to be wishing one was dead than never to have lived."

When I thought of that chap who'd been pinned down in the sewer just a few weeks prior, I found it hard to agree. Still, I kept quiet about it, not wanting to spoil Harry's mood.

Occasionally, the old guard supervising us would fall asleep, allowing Harry and I time to wander, just for an hour or so, aimlessly meandering through the city like young boys out exploring. With our hands in our pockets we would roam the streets, nodding at passers-by as though we were meant to be there, as though we too were part of it all. The people didn't care; they were too preoccupied with feeling sorry for themselves to feel any anger towards us. They were the sort who just wanted to keep their heads down, to get the war over with rather than won.

On one particular Thursday we walked in a straight line along the road, glancing up every now and then at the buildings around us as though we were nothing more than fascinated tourists, and we were, I suppose. We walked all the way down to the river on the other side, then crossed and walked along it for a while, watching the water drifting and breaking against the banks, tempting us, taunting us. We couldn't drink from it because it was putrid; polluted with the years of death and bombed-out industry; factories that had leaked oil and waste and gunk, and a riverside cemetery some way further up that had collapsed its banks, sliding human remains into the current. Still, it tempted us.

Harry talked as we went of a river back in Coventry that was mostly covered over by the city itself, one which emerged in sporadic points along its route, "as though only to remind us that it's there."

When we finally made our way back towards our designated search zone, a horse-shoe shaped town square where the guard still lay dozing on a scrounged wooden deck chair in the centre, we came across a library to one side, its books strewn out all over the street like scattered confetti.

And as I scanned the tattered volumes for anything that happened to be written in English, Harry instead picked up the very first one he found; a copy of *Die Drei Musketiere,* which he leafed through reciting certain lines aloud to himself. I wasn't sure whether he spoke German or was simply sounding the words out, but he had seemed totally at ease, sincerely immersed.

"Odd," I had pointed out, "I'd have thought they would have burned that, it was written by a Frenchman."

"My father gave me a copy of this once, when I was a child. What are the odds that I'd find it here now?"

I didn't say anything at first, merely raised my eyebrow,intrigued, happy to see Harry happy. He had a look of comforted nostalgia upon his skinny face, like an old man showing a previously-forgotten photo album to curious grandchildren.

"You've read it?" I asked.

"Oh, no, no," Harry chuckled, "I was far too young, and never got 'round to it. I'll have to read it one day, when we get back."

It was like that there. Little snippets of assured optimism interspersed amidst the gloom. Little droplets of happiness in a puddle of despair. In a world where depression and evil was rife, we clung to these moments as tightly as we could, these glimpses of hope that allowed us to feel detached from it all, even if just for a second or two.

"A wonderful thing, literature, isn't it?" Harry said.

~o~

The Mudlarks was one of those stories that's half-written before you've even noticed you've begun; it poured out of me, and I was as much reading it as a spectator as I was the one writing it. By saying this I hope not to take anything away from the effort I put into the piece, but rather to capture the compulsion and enjoyment I felt whilst writing it – and that's an odd sentence to write, considering its content.

Yes, it's about death and destruction and waste, but it's also about camaraderie. It's about humanity; about the bonds formed between men united in suffering. It's about friendship and survival and relentless endurance. It is also, of course, a story which aims to capture the brutality of war – not to glorify it, but to shunt the reader into confronting the hellish reality that war is. I wanted the reader to be coughing on brick dust as they read it, to feel with their own fingers the flesh sliding away from the bones of rotten corpses. I wanted it to be as vivid as possible, so that those scenes would stick in the mind – this is a fictional piece, after all, but for those unlucky, heroic few who lived seven decades ago, scenes like this were anything but fiction.

Printed in Great Britain
by Amazon

28932521R00142